Also by Sue Latham

The Haunted House Symphony

The Science Professor's Ghost

by Sue Latham

Lonely Swan Books

The Science Professor's Ghost

ISBN 13: 978-0-9835843-3-9

Published by Lonely Swan Books

3883 Turtle Creek Boulevard

Dallas, TX 75219

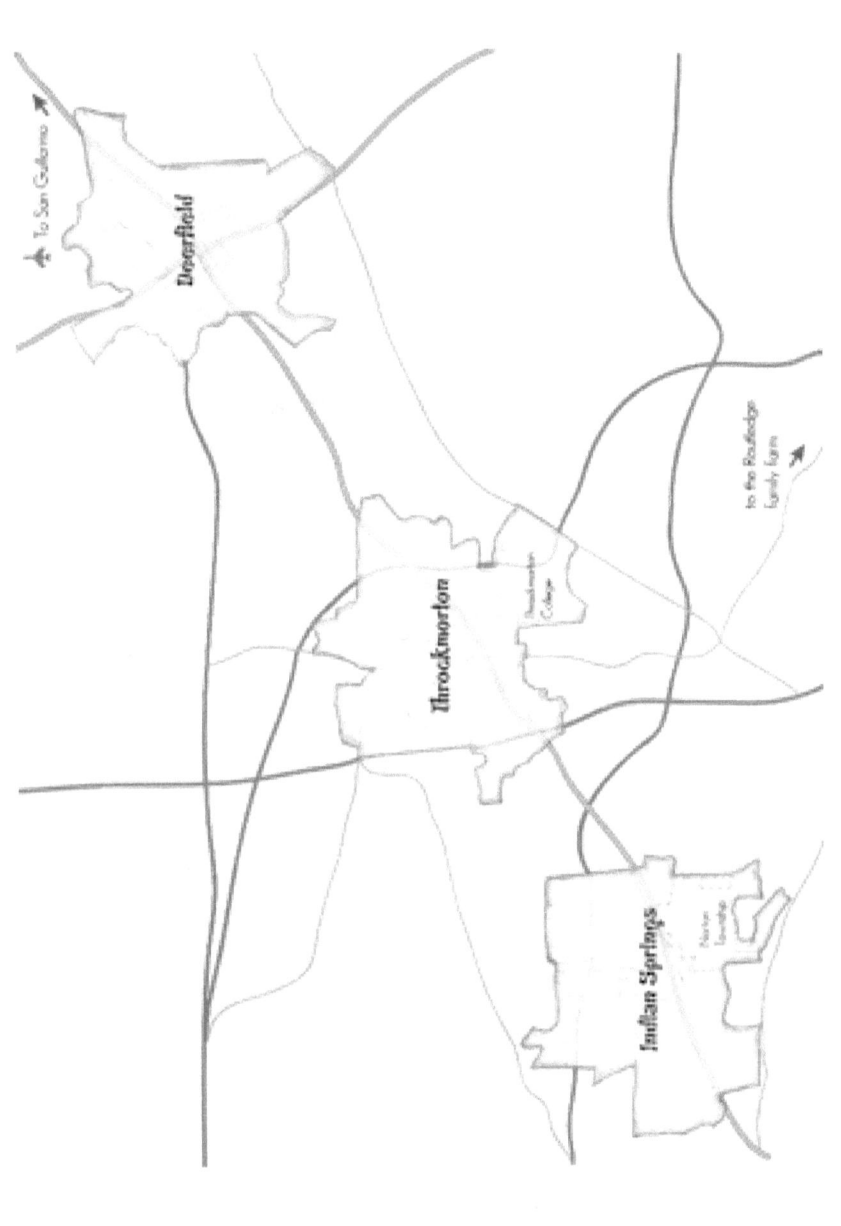

Special thanks to Kathy Klimpel and Dan Crider for your help.

Contents

Do Dead People Leave Voicemails? 5

The New Guy 20

A Post-Mortem Email? 40

The Things I Endure for My Job 54

The Date that Wasn't A Date 66

Uncomfortable Conversations 76

The Haunted School 95

Mr. Goodbody Makes a Move 113

A Close Call for Our Boss 127

The Writing on the Blackboard 148

So Much for a Romantic Evening with Tim 162

Homecoming 182

Security Breach 206

Haunted School, Round 2 225

Sandy Earns His Paycheck 243

The Storm 265

Enough Excitement for One Day 278

Another Message from Beyond the Grave?   307

Parents' Night   330

A Meeting with the Boss   347

A Moving Experience   365

The New Prof   380

Thanks From the Other Side   386

Epilogue   392

About the Author   396

Do Dead People Leave Voicemails?

I was sitting in my car, outside the old greenhouse at Throckmorton College, where I work, listening to a voicemail from someone who had been dead for a week. There was no mistaking that it was Professor Nigel Pritchett's voice, even though the speech was a little slurred and the voice was scratchy, like someone with a cold. But Professor Pritchett definitely had worse than a cold.

Communicating with dead people is not a big deal to me. Working with ghosts is what I do for a living. But it's usually me trying to contact them, not the other way around.

I studied the crowd of protesters lurking in the cordoned-off area and steeled myself for what had become a daily ordeal. The shouting started as soon as I opened my car door. A couple of the protesters who had been lounging on the steps sprang to life when they saw me. I have a hard time keeping a low profile these days, and they recognized my aging Subaru station wagon as soon as I drove up. I wondered yet again why these people didn't have anything better to do, such as going to work.

I'm Margo Monroe, and I hunt ghosts for a living. My team and I work out of a makeshift lab on the campus of the local college. The quaint old edifice, complete with a Victorian-era glass and ironwork greenhouse dome, sports a stone lintel engraved with "Horticulture Pavilion 1857" over the door. The greenhouse is tucked away in a quiet corner of the campus. Or at least it used to be a quiet corner. We had a high-profile investigation a few months ago, and our building has been besieged by every crackpot in the county ever since. When, with the help of a murdered girl named Louisa, we discovered a lost musical masterpiece, we suddenly became the darlings of the international music scene and instant local celebrities. We soon discovered, however, that fame has its downside, even in a little town like Throckmorton.

A bearded young man with a homemade sign rushed to the barricade. "Repent the work of the devil!" he yelled as I passed. His sign featured a crude drawing of a ghost, underneath which was scribbled "Margoe Munro WE demand that you STOP this Unholy Activity." Honestly, was I supposed to take these people seriously when they couldn't even spell my name correctly? A rotund middle-aged woman with frizzy hair ran toward me, waving a fist menacingly. She was wearing too-short shorts and a baggy, stained T-shirt that said "Jesus is my Home Boy." I wondered if the barricades would hold if she decided to throw her considerable weight against them. An off-duty policeman leaned against his car, examining his nails intently and smirking.

I went inside the greenhouse and the shouts faded as the doors closed behind me. I passed rows of shelves lined with plants, then turned down a nondescript, linoleum-tiled hall. People were milling about aimlessly whispering "Hey, there goes Margo!" and "Look, it's her!" I headed down the hall toward a janitor's closet. Amazingly, no one tried to follow me.

The closet is empty except for some rickety old shelves and a rusty utility sink. A naked bulb dangles from the ceiling. On the wall beside the old sink is another door with an electronic panel that always strikes me as being oddly out of place. I touched my fingertips to it and the panel glowed a phosphorescent green for a second or two. A green LED blinked, and the door to the lab popped open with a click. I stepped inside and glanced, out of habit, at the security monitor beside the door. The hall outside was still eerily empty.

Ernie, long-time friend and colleague, was perched on a tall stool and surrounded by bits of dismantled computers and miscellaneous electronics. Standing next to him was a chubby boy, about 10 years old, with thick round glasses and a cherubic, freckled face. His eyes widened when I walked in and he stared at me like I was his favorite rock star.

"What have we here?" I asked, hanging up my jacket.

"Margo Monroe, allow me to present Chester. Chester, this is Margo," said Ernie.

"Nice to meet you, Chester. I'm guessing you're not here on a social call."

"No," he replied earnestly. "I came to ask if you would investigate my school. It's haunted."

Ernie was doing his best not to smile.

"And which school might that be?" I asked.

Chester's round face broke into an angelic smile. "Rhonda Q. Mills," he said proudly. He pushed his glasses up on his nose with a pudgy hand and beamed up at me. He reminded me of a cartoon character.

Ah, yes. Rhonda Q. Mills Magnet School for the Gifted and Talented. I guess I shouldn't be surprised. He looked every inch the budding mad scientist.

"Well, have a seat over here, Chester, and tell us what's been happening."

It was a good thing that Ernie recorded the conversation as Chester described the happenings at his school because I was having a little trouble staying focused. My mind kept drifting back to the creepy phone call and I was desperate to tell Ernie about it.

"...so anyway, Mrs. Cartwright believes us now, and...well, my class has to do a semester project."

Did we really want to help with a school science project? Call me a skeptic, but I'm inclined to think chalkboard erasers going missing and books mysteriously finding their way into the supply closet has more to do with mischievous fifth graders than anything paranormal.

"I don't know..."

Ernie interrupted. "Let's not be so quick to dismiss it, Margo." As if he'd read my thoughts, he said, "I know what you're thinking. But the school's security cameras have never picked up a thing."

I considered it for a minute and conceded it would probably end up being the most interesting thing on our upcoming schedule. "Oh well, why not?" Chester clapped his hands in delight, his face lighting up.

I checked our schedule on my iPad. "Who do we need to talk to?"

Chester pulled a grubby business card that read "Emily Golding, Principal" out of his back pocket. The school logo was embossed in dark blue in one corner. "My phone number's on the back of it," said Chester. I flipped the card over. His phone number was carefully printed in a round, looping hand. In pencil.

"Okay, Chester. We'll get to work on it right away. Um, how'd you get here?"

"The bus." He shrugged into a backpack. "It goes right by my house."

I didn't even know Throckmorton had a bus. I live in Indian Springs, which is just a couple of miles down the road, and we don't have public transportation. "Someone from the team will be in touch." Shaking hands didn't seem to be quite the right thing to do and I had to restrain myself from patting him on the head. "I'm not sure we should let you go out there alone. The natives are restless today."

Ernie said, "I'll make sure he gets to the bus stop." Chester stared over his shoulder at me and waved goodbye as Ernie propelled him out the door.

I took advantage of the quiet time to look through back issues of the campus newspaper. I tapped in a few search words on my trusty iPad and scrolled through the results.

> Nigel Pritchett, 57, was found dead Saturday night at his home in Indian Springs. Few details are available but sources close to the Indian Springs Police Department report that homicide is suspected...

This was nothing I didn't already know. The *Indian Springs Herald* from the next day shed only slightly more light on the subject.

> Pritchett, a professor of science at Throckmorton College, was asphyxiated. A plastic bag believed to be the murder weapon was found near the scene. Police believe the perpetrator entered Pritchett's bedroom shortly after midnight and left through a ground floor window, but no details have been released regarding how the assailant was able to gain entrance to the professor's home.

I flipped back to the search results, but found only more of the same. The Throckmorton *Tribune* carried the announcement of the funeral. But of course, I knew the details already.

The door opened and our research assistant Sandy strolled in. He was still wearing the black T-shirt and jacket that he'd worn to the funeral, and he looked uncharacteristically gloomy. He was tugging on a leash at the end of which was the ugliest dog I've ever seen. The hideous animal sauntered over to the chair where I'd tossed my purse and sniffed at it disinterestedly, then flopped down on the floor and gazed at me mournfully.

"Oh, my. Where'd you find him?"

"Well, he sort of found me. My roommate found him hanging around in the back yard. I was going to take him to the shelter, but I just didn't have the heart."

"Does he have a name?"

"Not yet." Sandy is our go-to guy for all kinds of things. He's tall, good-looking and blond with broad, athletic shoulders. If he were but a few years older, I would probably be pursuing him wantonly. His only shortcoming, if you want to call it that, is that he's terrified of ghosts. But he's an all-around good egg with a contagious, high-voltage smile. We couldn't function without him. "Who's the kid I saw Ernie with?" he asked.

"New client. He wants us to do an investigation at his school."

He stared at me and shook his head. "Super. Now we're moonlighting as babysitters."

"My thoughts exactly. However, Ernie thinks it has potential."

Watching Sandy putter about the office, I had an inspiration. "Sandy, weren't you in Professor Pritchett's class?"

"Yeah, nice guy. One of the best instructors I've ever had. Hard to believe anybody would want to kill him."

"Have you been to the science building in the past few days?"

"What? You mean since he was murdered? No, classes were cancelled this week."

"Let's go for a walk. Bring your buddy," I said, motioning to the pathetic creature, who was now licking his own nether regions.

"Where are we going?" asked Sandy, suspiciously.

"To the science lab."

"Margo, I really don't think...."

"I just want to have a look around. Come on, where's your sense of adventure?"

Both Sandy and the dog eyed me warily, but followed without further protest as I started toward the main door. Sandy glanced at the video screen above the door. A few people were still lurking in the hall. I suspect some of them, the girls anyway, were just there hoping to get a glimpse of him.

"On second thought, maybe we should go out the back way," I said.

The service door slammed shut with a bang behind us, and we scurried quickly across the expanse of grass and a parking lot that separated the horticulture pavilion from the rest of the campus. The sun shone brightly but didn't provide much warmth, and I shivered and zipped up my jacket.

Our destination was Braxton Hall, the science building and one of the original buildings on campus. Built in an era when buildings were designed with style as well as function in mind, it still has wood floors and marble columns. It always smells faintly of a mix of lemony furniture polish and formaldehyde. Like the horticulture pavilion, it had somehow managed to escape a well-meaning but misguided modernization campaign that ravaged most of the older campus buildings. Today the halls were deserted, even though it was the middle of the week. Our footsteps echoed loudly around us. We passed a cluster of professorial-looking types, dressed in somber dark clothes and chatting quietly.

"Margo," Sandy whispered, "I really don't think this is such a good idea. For once you need to leave the detective work to the police."

"I just want to have a look. Call it morbid curiosity. Which way?"

He scowled at me. "Down this hall."

We paused in front of a door with a frosted glass pane. "It's here," said Sandy. I tried the door, not expecting it to be unlocked. But to my surprise, it opened easily.

At the same time, the dog began to growl angrily. He leaped toward the door, straining against his leash, and began barking hysterically. Then he turned around and looked imploringly at Sandy.

"This is as far as I go," said Sandy, regarding his scruffy new companion with concern.

"Well, then, wait for me right there."

"Nope. No way. We'll meet you outside."

"Suit yourself. I'm just going to have a look around."

They hurried away down the hall. I'm not sure who was leading.

I flipped the light switch and fluorescent lights flickered uncertainly for a few seconds before filling the room with a harsh, slightly greenish light. Several tall tables, each cluttered with glass containers and trays, took up most of the room. Wooden cabinets lined the perimeter walls, their Formica countertops covered with glass beakers and odd-looking contraptions. I tried to open one of the cabinets, but it was locked. A large metal office desk stood against one wall, and a clunky old computer sat on the corner of the desk.

I spied a heavy-looking wood door across the room from where I'd come in. I deduced it must lead to a closet. I tried it and found it locked. But in the opposite corner was another door, of the same dark wood as the lab door and also sporting a square of

15

frosted glass. It had an ancient glass doorknob and no keyhole. Some dark smears around the door jamb might have been grime, but were more likely where detectives had dusted for fingerprints. An engraved plaque on the door jamb said "Dr Nigel Pritchett."

I started to question my wisdom in coming here. My fingerprints were now on the hall door outside, and I wasn't sure if I wanted to leave any more on an interior door—they would be difficult to explain. But when classes started again on Monday, any fingerprints I left behind would be obliterated. I reasoned that the Throckmorton Police Department had finished in here. Deciding nevertheless that discretion was the better part of valor, I used a tissue from my jacket pocket to grasp the knob. The knob turned smoothly, but the door didn't budge. I had to tug firmly to make the door creak open.

I entered a room that was dominated by an old wooden desk. A suspiciously dust-free square on its surface indicated that a computer had been here but was recently removed, no doubt, by the Throckmorton PD as evidence. Apparently the PD had also removed any personal effects—the room was now barren except for several full bookcases lining the walls. I ran my fingers over the ponderous-sounding titles and wondered what I was looking for.

I glimpsed something just beyond my peripheral vision. I looked around, but nothing looked out of place except what appeared to be a piece of melted plastic on the floor a few feet from where I was standing. I examined the dust on the shelves to see if I could tell where it had fallen from, but the books were neatly organized and I didn't see any suspiciously dust-free spots. I started to toss the plastic in the trash basket, but decided to pocket it.

Disappointed, I concluded that coming here might not have been the brilliant idea I thought it would be. The dog's reaction, however, had been quite interesting. Animals can be great paranormal investigators because they can detect things that we can't, and it looked like Sandy's homely new friend might have potential. I figured, however, that our chances of convincing Sandy to let us take the dog on an investigation were somewhere in the neighborhood of slim and none.

I decided it wouldn't be in my best interests to be caught snooping around the office of the only homicide victim in Throckmorton in more than 50 years. I gave the room a last glance before turning out the lights and closing the office door as quietly as I could. I peeked out into the hall but didn't see a soul.

Before closing the science lab door, I examined the latch. It was an antique deadbolt with a fancy knob that could be turned only from the inside, or locked on the outside with a key. It seemed odd to leave the lab unlocked, but that was how I'd found it. I shut the door quietly behind me and went to look for Sandy.

I found him on the lawn with a cluster of guys who were taking turns throwing a ball for the dog. The mutt ran after it with boundless canine enthusiasm. Sandy waved when he saw me. "I'll be along in a little while."

I trudged back to the horticulture pavilion, trying to stay out of the wind, with the gears spinning in my head.

I wasn't prepared to simply let this go. Tempting though it was to simply chalk it up to crappy phone service, I knew perfectly well that the late Dr. Pritchett had tried to contact me, and I very much wanted to know why. Although it wasn't an official case, by the time I got back to the lab I was itching to get started. Something told me this could be a blockbuster case if we handled it correctly. As for Chester and his haunted school, I wasn't so certain. I was wrong on this point, of course. But regarding the

Pritchett case, it turned out that I was—if you'll pardon the pun—dead on.

The New Guy

I was very much hoping Ernie would be in the lab to let me in the back door, but to my extreme annoyance he didn't answer the phone when I called. Nor did he respond to my text, which meant I was forced to go around to the front and past the unruly mob again.

The cop I'd seen earlier was nowhere to be found. The protestors were chanting in unison now, and as soon as they saw me, they started really going for it. By the time I reached the sidewalk, their voices had merged into so much garbled, incoherent white noise. It was like being chased by a small jet plane.

A neatly dressed young man quietly held up a sign that said "No School Funds for Pseudo-Science." Although more literate than some of the others, he was woefully misinformed. The college doesn't foot the bill for us; we rely on the generosity of a reclusive philanthropist for most of our cash flow. At first, the school was understandably reluctant to publicize our existence for fear it would lead to just the sort of situation we were dealing with now, so when we started out we operated in secrecy. Ernie and I enrolled in classes and masqueraded as horticulture students, although—I'm a little ashamed to say—I seldom went to class. (Ernie, on the other hand, discovered he has quite a green thumb. He provides me with hothouse tomatoes and a never-ending supply of exotic house plants that usually don't live very long.) This arrangement worked well enough until we landed ourselves in the international spotlight. Our cover was blown, and the next thing I knew people were shouting and waving signs in my face.

I ignored the protesters as best I could and dashed inside. No one was hanging around in the hall outside the janitor's closet. Somewhere down the hall a door slammed shut with a loud bang. Then I heard a woman's strident, screeching voice and it became crystal clear why our usual contingent of fans and assorted horticulture students had taken cover. It was Irmalene Gibson, a person to be avoided under the best of circumstances. I ducked hastily into the janitor's closet and went into the lab.

I had just logged onto my email when I heard several deep, insistent thumps. It was Ernie, pounding on the back door. "It's about time you got back. What took you so long?" I asked, thoroughly irritated.

"Oh, I, um...waited with Chester until the bus came. I didn't want to leave him there by himself." He went back to the pile of electronic entrails he'd been tinkering with. It was Ernie who got me this job. I'd been doing some amateur ghost-hunting with my friend Elaine when Ernie asked me to meet him here at the college. I didn't know it then, but the school had recently received an endowment to fund a position for a paranormal researcher and Ernie recommended me for the job.

He's a top-notch ghost hunter and master inventor of gadgets and tools, a true geek savant with electronics. He single handedly developed most of the tools we use in our work. We've known each other since high school—he was one of my best friends then, and remains one of my best friends all these years later. He's a thin man—some might even say skinny—with longish brown hair and oversized dark-framed glasses. There's nothing wrong with his eyesight. But he has big brown eyes and long, silky lashes that many a woman would kill for, and he's under the mistaken impression that the glasses hide them. In reality, the glasses only focus attention on his eyes. I've tried to convince him that his puppy-dog eyes are an asset, but he doesn't listen to me.

"Have you seen Holmes today?" I asked.

"He was in his office earlier," he said, nodding toward the door.

"That would explain it, then. Irmalene's on the war path."

"Irmalene? What does she want?" he asked.

"What does she usually want?   To pick a fight with somebody is my guess."

Occasional snippets of their conversation were loud enough for us to hear. I could hear Irmalene scold shrilly "I didn't ask to have..." and bits of Holmes' conciliatory answer, "...be patient while we work to resolve...". I heard something that sounded like "... freaks and ghouls..." and "superstitious nonsense..."

Irmalene is the horticulture instructor. She's a grandmotherly-looking lady with halo of wiry silver curls that contrast strikingly with her chocolate brown complexion. She comes up to about my shoulder. Appearances are deceiving, however, and she is anything but the angelic character she appears to be. Plenty of people have found this out the hard way. Irmalene is resentful of us, to put it mildly. I can't say I blame her; we take up half the building and she desperately needs more space for her overcrowded classes. It doesn't help matters that she thinks what we're doing is a bunch of hooey. To say she despises the very air I breathe is something of an understatement.

Down the hall a door slammed and a few minutes later, Professor Holmes, my boss, wandered in. Instead of his usual threadbare tweed jacket, he was wearing an even more threadbare dark suit that was at least fifteen years out of style and shiny at the elbows. His hair was in an advanced state of entropy, and he looked as if he hadn't slept in a week.

"How are you holding up?" Ernie asked him.

"About as well as can be expected under the circumstances." He sighed wearily. "I'm going home now. I'd take pains to avoid Irmalene for a while."

"That's my usual strategy," I replied.

He managed a wan smile. My heart ached as Ernie and I watched him leave.

Ernie shook his head sadly. "He's taking it pretty hard."

"Wouldn't you? Dr. Pritchett was one of his oldest and dearest friends. They went to school together."

"I so hope they catch the bastard that killed Dr. Pritchett. He was a nice man."

"Me, too, Ernie...me too." We were quiet for a few minutes, then I remembered what I had been dying to show him all morning. "Ernie, I have something I need you to listen to."

I dug my phone out of my purse and played the voicemail for him. He listened to it several times, his face grave.

"It sounds like him all right," he said finally.

"Practical joke?"

"Maybe. But it's in awfully poor taste. Mind if I copy it? I want to run it through some filters, see if I can clean it up a little."

"My thoughts exactly."

He poked around on the phone, then handed it back to me. "You look beat."

"Yeah, I think it's starting to get to me. I'll be at home. Call if you need anything." I dropped the phone in my purse. "You going to hang around?"

"Hmm? Oh, yeah. I'll stay here for a little while."

When I left, he was frowning at the computer screen and rubbing his chin.

§

When I got to work the next morning, the closest parking spot I could find was two blocks away. I was fuming by the time I got inside. Ernie was sitting in the exact same spot where I'd last seen him. For a minute I thought he'd been there all night, until I realized he was wearing different clothes.

"Those ignoramuses out front are about to get on my last nerve. It took me fifteen minutes to find a place to park," I growled.

"Really? I got my usual place right in front."

"I noticed. What makes you so special?"

"Couldn't sleep. I figured there was no point in lying in bed staring at the ceiling, so I got up and came in."

"How long have you been here?" I asked, throwing my purse on a table with perhaps more force than I intended.

"I don't know. I guess I got here around six."

"Six? In the morning? You've been here three hours already? This has to be a first for you." He did look a little bleary-eyed.

"Time flies. Hey, remember that prototype 3-D mapping program I've been working on? I think I've made a breakthrough. Come look."

I peeked over his shoulder at the computer. "All I see is a bunch of numbers."

"I'm measuring temperature and the electromagnetic fields, so those numbers are the data that's been streaming from the EMF meters and temperature gauges I set up at various spots around the room. They send a constant stream of data into this database. These are the physical coordinates of the room. Now all I have to do is translate it into a visual model…"

The door opened and Professor Holmes strolled in, looking more like his usual old self than he had in a while. With him was a staggeringly good-looking man I'd never seen before. He towered over Holmes. His sun-bleached, sandy brown hair was fashionably shaggy, and the way his faded jeans clung to his contours hinted at many long hours in the gym. Muscles rippled under a crisp white shirt, the sleeves of which were rolled up just enough to show off an elaborate tattoo on each arm.

"Ah, here she is," said Holmes. "Seth, I'd like you to meet the famous Margo Monroe. Margo, Dr. Seth Carling." The newcomer gave me the once-over. Then, flashing a toothpaste-commercial smile, he gripped my hands with both of his as though I were a long-lost relative. His aqua eyes twinkled as he looked deep into mine. "At last! I was wondering when I would have the pleasure."

I was at a total loss for words. "Pleased to meet you," I said lamely.

"The pleasure is all mine," he said, with a faint, unidentifiable accent; Aussie, perhaps, or a Brit who'd lived in the States for a long time?

Ernie, who had been watching with great interest, slumped behind the computer screen to hide a smirk. I flashed him an evil look. Oblivious, Holmes continued, "Dr. Carling will be filling in at the science department. Until a replacement can be found for Nigel," he added sadly.

"I'm on loan from the Sheldrick Institute," Carling said cheerfully. "They were kind enough to allow me a short sabbatical."

"Wow," I said. "The Sheldrick Institute! This must seem like quite a come-down to you."

"Not at all. Sheldrick is very...impersonal. Enough to make a man feel positively lost. A small school in a charming little town will be a welcome change."

"Are you staying here in Throckmorton?" asked Holmes.

"For the moment, yes. But I thought I might look around Indian Springs for something more permanent."

Indian Springs, a pokey little town straight out a 1950s sitcom, is about ten minutes down the main road from here. I've lived there most of my life, and while it is less trendy than Throckmorton, it has a certain organic charm.

"It's pretty quiet in Indian Springs," I said. "Most of the night life is here in Throckmorton."

"Oh, a little peace and quiet won't hurt me. In fact, might do me some good." He flashed me another blinding smile.

"Well," I said, "I'll probably see you around, then."

He took the hand I offered and just held it for a few seconds instead. "I'm certain of it," he said.

Behind his monitor, Ernie coughed to camouflage a snicker. Holmes and Carling left and I shuffled to the kitchenette in a daze.

The coffee maker was half empty, and the countertop was sprinkled with sugar. Luckily the coffee in the pot was ice cold, so I had an excuse to pour it out. Ernie is a paranormal researcher of the highest caliber, but his attempts at making coffee invariably result in an undrinkable substance that looks and smells remarkably like used motor oil. We normally entrust this most important of responsibilities to Sandy, but since there was as of yet no sign of him, the job of making coffee fell to me.

I scooped the grounds into the little paper filter, wondering—in spite of my best efforts to stop—what the rest of Seth's tattoos looked like. The last time I saw a physique like that was in an advertisement for men's underwear. They certainly didn't make college professors like that when I was in school. Unable to stop myself, I imagined how he would look without a shirt on, and the image that formed in my head met with my approval. Suddenly, another image replaced it. Tim—my much loved and very far away boyfriend.

I poured a cup of coffee and added copious amounts of cream as I chastised myself.

Ernie was watching me.

"Shall I pour you a cup?" I asked.

"Thanks, I'll get it myself." He strolled over and retrieved his cup from the drying rack next to the sink. "So," he said, as he prepared a mixture of approximately one part coffee to two parts sugar, "I see the new guy made quite an impression on you."

"Who? Dr. Carling? Hey, I'm just trying to be friendly."

"You were practically drooling."

I gave him a dark look. "He seems like a nice guy."

"Excuse me while I go throw up. Quite a contrast to his predecessor, wouldn't you say?" Very true. The late Dr. Pritchett was short, portly, and utterly bald. In fact, his was a baldness the likes of which could just about blind you on a sunny day. I once heard some students call him "The Eggman." At the time I found it hilarious, but the joke didn't seem so funny now.

It seemed like a good time to change the subject. "How's Elaine? I haven't talked to her at all this week."

"Neither have I," he snapped.

"Oh? Trouble in paradise?"

Ernie's body language changed immediately. He glared at me and went back to the computer. "If you don't mind, I'd rather not talk about it."

Elaine is my friend and Ernie's off-and-on girlfriend. "Hey, it's none of my business. But we're going to need a team to investigate this school haunting. I can't have the two of you on an investigation if you're not speaking. By the way, have you met Sandy's new dog?"

"Oh, so that's what it is. I thought maybe he'd discovered a new species."

"He's not much to look at, but he might have a useful talent." I told him about my clandestine visit to the chemistry lab.

"Wait—you went into the chemistry lab yesterday?" He looked thoroughly alarmed.

"Don't worry, Ernie. Nobody saw me and I didn't touch anything."

"But how did you get in?"

"The door was unlocked."

"That's *so* weird. I started thinking about that voicemail you got, and I had the same idea. I went by there on the way home. But I couldn't get in because the place was locked up tight."

"There's a logical explanation for it. I must have accidentally locked the door when I closed it." Except I knew perfectly well I hadn't, for the simple reason that the door could only be locked and unlocked with a key.

He looked as unconvinced as I'm sure I sounded. I remembered the piece of plastic in my jacket pocket. "What do you make of this?"

He examined the fragment. "Piece of plastic, that's all. It doesn't look like much of anything," he said.

"I agree. What's interesting about it is that it fell off a shelf in Dr. Pritchett's office. I wasn't anywhere near it."

He shook his head. "Coincidence."

"You're probably right, but I'm going to hang on to it just in case."

The door opened and Sandy and the dog came in. The dog wagged its tail twice, then flopped into a furry heap on the floor.

"You're eventually going to have to give him a name, you know," I said. "Hey, does this look like anything to you?" I leaned over the table to show Sandy the odd plastic thing. Suddenly the dog began to growl.

"That's strange," said Sandy. "That's the second time he's growled at something."

On a hunch, I put the whatever-it-was on the floor. The dog scrambled frantically to his feet, his toenails clicking as he struggled to get a purchase on the hard floor. He barked at the plastic thing, then backed away whining.

"I'm guessing I don't want to know," said Sandy.

"Probably not," I responded. "It came from Dr. Pritchett's office."

"You stole something from Pritchett's office? Margo, has it ever occurred to you..."

I held up a hand to stop him. "I didn't steal it. I was looking at the books on the shelves and it fell off onto the floor."

"I've heard enough. It's possessed or something— who knows? I don't even know what it is, but keep it away from my dog."

"Don't worry about the mutt." I retrieved the plastic thing and put it in a drawer. The dog eyed me warily. "By the way, here's the contact info for our new case. Try to set something up in the next day or so." I gave Chester's card with Principal Golding's phone number on it to Sandy.

"Your wish is my command, " he said with a bow.

§

I spent the afternoon trying to catch up on paperwork, but my mind insisted on drifting back to Seth Carling. Every time I thought about how he had held my hand and looked into my eyes, a little shiver went up my spine. Get a grip on yourself, I chastised myself. I went back to my computer and tried to banish the image from my head, but emails and reports were having a hard time competing with Seth's tattoos.

I finally gave up and decided to see what Elaine was up to. I opened my video chat program and saw that she was online, so I called her from my computer.

"Hey, Margo," she said, adjusting her computer's camera. "I was just about to call you." Behind her I could see her office window with its spectacular view of beautiful downtown San Guillermo, the closest city around here big enough to have an airport.

"Are you doing anything later?" I asked.

"I was about to ask you the same thing. I was hoping I could talk you into a drink at the Pig and Whistle."

"That would be just what I need long about now. I haven't been there in ages."

Soon I was at a table in a dark corner of the Pig and Whistle, with a Belligerent Bastard Irish Cream Ale—my all-time favorite beer—in hand. Elaine sipped a gimlet and nibbled daintily on a wedge of lime.

I met Elaine when I was still in the corporate world and we worked at the same company. She usually accompanies us on investigations, albeit in an unofficial capacity. Elaine was the one who introduced me to ghost hunting in the first place. She's an enthusiastic and competent ghost hunter, but it's just a hobby to her—she would never consider leaving her well-paying, high-profile job.

As always, Elaine looked dazzlingly elegant, in a form-fitting pencil skirt and cropped sweater. On anyone else, they would look outlandish, but they looked stunning on her. Elaine has a trim, athletic frame and long black hair with a natural white streak in it, of which I am eternally envious.

Some businessmen were seated at the table next to us. One of them wasn't bad-looking and I caught him staring at Elaine a couple of times. That she didn't pay him the slightest notice indicated that something important was bothering her. But whatever it was, she didn't bring it up. "Do you remember the investigation we did in here?" she asked between sips of gimlet.

That was strictly a rhetorical question. The case stood out in my memory clearly. We came to the Pig and Whistle last year to investigate claims of poltergeist activity.

"Ugh, do I ever!"

"I remember you got hit on the head by a flying beer bottle. You had a bruise that practically glowed in the dark for a while."

In poltergeist manifestations, objects move of their own accord, sometimes quite violently. It's tempting to dismiss poltergeists as the brats of the paranormal world, except that as far as I've been able to determine they're not hauntings at all, but psychokinetic disturbances. Usually a teenager is involved. In this case it was the owner's stepson, a rebel without a cause if ever there was one. "Yeah. No concealer in the world could cover up something like that. I still had it when I went on my first date with Tim."

That was, in fact, our last attempt at a poltergeist investigation. These days, we try to steer clear. Our formal mission is really quite simple: to make contact with the dead. When we get an occasional request to investigate a poltergeist, I refer them politely to somebody who specializes in that sort of thing.

"Hey, you'll never guess who I met today." I said. "Holmes brought around Dr. Pritchett's replacement. You should see him—he's stunning. He looks more like a model than a college professor." As I described Seth, Elaine seemed to perk up a bit.

"He sounds yummy. I can't wait till I get a look at him for myself," she said, and I immediately regretted bringing it up. She took a sip of her drink and said suddenly "You know, you're really lucky."

"Lucky? How so?" I asked, surprised.

"Well, you have someone who genuinely loves you."

"That's true. But he lives half a continent away."

"But you talk to him almost every day, don't you?"

"Yes, but it's a poor substitute for actually being together."

"Then aren't you about due for a trip to San Francisco?"

The businessmen at the next table got up to leave. Elaine watched them walk out. The good-looking guy caught her staring, and she smiled at him disarmingly.

"Well, I haven't thought about it," I admitted, "but yes, probably."

Suddenly she looked at me and blurted out, "I'm probably not going to be able to help you investigate anymore."

I feigned ignorance. "Oh? Are they giving you trouble at work about it?"

"Oh, no. It's not that." Elaine and I were good friends when we worked together, and she knew about the circumstances under which I got fired. My boss, a darkly comical character named Noel, demanded I give up my extra-curricular paranormal activities. I told him what I thought of that idea, and before I knew it I was packing my personal belongings. "It's just that, well, I'm not seeing Ernie anymore. He hasn't told you?"

"Well, he did say he hadn't talked to you in a while..."

"I think it's over between us."

This really wasn't what I wanted to hear. "But why? What happened?"

"I don't know, really. I just don't think I'm ready for the kind of relationship Ernie wants."

"I don't mean to pry," I said (not entirely truthfully), "but what brought this on?"

"Look, you might not know this, but I've always liked Ernie." I was a little bit shocked—it was common knowledge that Ernie had carried a torch for Elaine for years. But that she had ever been the least bit attracted to him was a revelation.

"I'm stunned. You never showed him the slightest sign of encouragement. Frankly, I would have guessed you barely knew he existed."

She sighed wearily. "Ernie was—is—always so kind to me, and I'm grateful to him for being there for me when my marriage ended. But, Margo, I've had two bad marriages. I'm just not ready for a serious relationship yet."

"Have you told him this?"

"Certainly. We've discussed it—several times— but he just doesn't want to hear it."

The waitress came by and we ordered another round of drinks. It looked like we were going to be here for a while.

A Post-Mortem Email?

While I could do a lot of what I need to do for my job from home, it suddenly seemed really important to spend more time at the lab. So the next morning I got up at a decent hour—in spite of the late evening the night before—and went to the lab.

Sometimes my job bears more than a passing resemblance to an ordinary office job. We aren't always out chasing specters. The task we've been charged with—to find proof of life after death—requires us to conduct our research in a professional manner. Which unfortunately means reports, spreadsheets, and other paperwork that were the bane of my existence when I was a software engineer. Yet, I'd much rather be doing what I'm doing now, even if it means I have to spend time writing reports. Those reports go a long way toward justifying our jobs to the reclusive millionaire who pays our salaries.

We had received several emails over the last couple of days from clients purporting to need our help. Some of them were probably genuine. The volume of requests we'd been getting had increased dramatically over the last few months, and it wasn't always easy to tell which of them were from people who truly needed our help. I plowed through the dozen or so potential prospects, trying to intuit which were genuine and which were from people who just wanted to meet us, now that we were semi-celebrities.

One email was from a woman whose situation sounded dire. If the events she described were genuine, this might be a great case. But alas, she was in England and I had to write back and explain to her politely that for the moment we had to limit our activities to Throckmorton County.

I keep an eye on other ghost hunting teams' investigations. An investigator in a neighboring state posted on her team's blog about an eight-year-old girl who began having unexplained behavioral problems. Until recently a bright child with a sunny disposition, she suddenly started getting in trouble in school. Her grades had plummeted, and she was getting into fights with the other kids almost daily. The child insisted that she was being kept awake nights by people coming into her room. The child's parents, members of an obscure religious order, punished her harshly, which naturally only made things worse. Fortunately, a family friend with connections in the paranormal research world recognized the signs and was able to intervene on the child's behalf.

My heart went out to the little girl. I bookmarked the blog page and was about to send them an email asking them to keep me up to date on the investigation's progress, when a friendly chime sounded to let me know I had a new message in my inbox. I tapped over to the email program and my knees turned to jelly—it was from Seth.

Hello, there! Now that we've been formally introduced, I hope we can be friends. Looking forward to learning more about the ghost hunting business. Yours, Seth.

Luckily I was alone in the lab because I could feel myself blushing. "This is stupid," I said out loud. "You're too old to be acting like a school girl." But still, I couldn't help but smile.

§

That evening I decided on a whim to stop by Indian Springs' lone Thai restaurant. I was overjoyed when the enticingly named Empress of Siam opened last year in a strip mall not far from my house. The shopping center, a relic of the 1960s, had been a decaying eyesore for as long as I could remember. But then an organic grocery opened. A few weeks later the Thai restaurant followed, and suddenly the area was showing signs of transforming into a hot spot. In the space next to the restaurant, a sign caught my eye. It said "Coming Soon! Green Lotus Booksellers - New and Used Books."

The Empress of Siam was already doing a brisk business. I didn't realize how hungry I was until I walked in and the exotic, mouth-watering smells made my stomach growl. I ordered some *yam woon sen* to go and sipped a glass of ice water while I waited. When I heard a chime from the depths of my purse, I didn't need to look to know it was a text from Tim. I've always looked forward to his texts, but I didn't look at this one right away. I'll save it for after dinner, I promised myself as I drove home.

Normally I'm happy to go home to my mid-century ranch-style for a little peace and quiet, but tonight, eating my dinner alone in my humble abode seemed unusually dismal. As I chased noodles around the plate with my chopsticks, I kept seeing Seth's twinkling aqua eyes boring into mine. Just as I finished the last bite of tofu, the phone chimed again.

I chastised myself for not looking at it earlier as I intended. "Hey, havent heard from U everything OK?" Then the one from earlier: "Hi hows your day going? Love you XX".

Sighing and suppressing an uncharacteristic spark of irritation, I picked up my iPad and called

Tim. He answered immediately, his semi-exotic face filling the small screen. I detected a look of concern in his eyes.

"Sorry," I said. "I got your text, but I was at Empress of Siam."

"Oh, really? With who?" he asked with exaggerated casualness.

"Nobody. I just brought something home."

His expression changed to relief. "I love that place. Much as I hate to admit it, their yellow curry is as good as anything I can get around here," he said. "How's work?"

"Well, we're all a little concerned about Dr. Holmes. Things got a bit crazy yesterday." I told him about the latest encounter with Irmalene.

"How is Holmes holding up?"

"Oh, it's been pretty rough on him. But I'm sure he'll be back to his old self in no time." Tim knew about Professor Pritchett's murder, of course, but I'd been oddly reluctant to tell him about the strange voicemail. If he suspected I was keeping something from him, he didn't say so.

"When are you supposed to check out Chester's school?"

I sighed. "Next week, but I don't know what kind of team we're going to be able to put together. There's been some drama between Ernie and Elaine—he won't tell me what—but they're barely speaking to each other. I think I'm going to be short an investigator."

Tim chuckled. "Poor Ernie. When has there not been drama with him and Elaine? Hey, I have a idea I want to run by you. Our alma mater's homecoming game is in a couple of weeks."

"Is it?" I shouldn't have been surprised. Tim sometimes knows more about what's going on in Indian Springs than I do.

"Yes. What would you think about going to it?"

"Me? No, the idea hadn't crossed my mind..."

"Not just you—us. I want to fly out and go to the game."

For a moment I just stared at his image on the screen, speechless, a reaction that was not what he was expecting, I'm sure. His smile faltered.

"Am I to take it you're not particularly thrilled with the idea?" He sounded hurt.

"Sorry, it's not that. It's just that I haven't been to an Indian Springs High School game since we were students there. Of course, I think it's a fabulous idea. It will be fun. But you don't need a football game as an excuse to come out." The truth is, I hate football. My best friend Roxy and I went to every game when we were in school, but they were social occasions. We

Sue Latham

couldn't have cared less about what was happening on the field. "You know, Timmy, I doubt if anybody we know ever goes to homecoming."

"I know, Margo," he said with exasperation. "But that's beside the point. Okay, confession time. When we were in high school, my dream was to take you to homecoming. Every year I imagined buying you the biggest mum at the florist and taking you to some fancy place for dinner afterwards."

I had an instant flashback. Suddenly I was a teenager again and sitting in the school stadium bleachers with Roxy, proudly wearing the flamboyant chrysanthemum and ribbon concoctions popular in this part of the country, while our boyfriends *du jour* were battling for the honor of Indian Springs High on the gridiron. That the teenage Timmy might have wanted to ask me to homecoming would never have crossed my mind. I was deeply touched. "Well, then," I said when I'd gathered my composure. "It's about time you finally asked me, isn't it?"

§

As is my habit, I checked my email before going to bed. I've been getting more and more emails these days, a *lot* of it junk mail. I clicked the Delete button without reading most of them, but a few were from real people, some personal, some work-related. Then suddenly I froze. I blinked, but it was still there. An email, dated today. From the late Dr. Nigel Pritchett.

My hands had gone clammy. I cautiously opened the email. There was nothing in the body of the email, only an attachment. My heart pounding, I reached for the phone and called Ernie, but all I got was voicemail. I called Elaine, but there was no answer on her phone, either.

I couldn't decide whether I should open the attachment or not. Surely this was a practical joke, and the attachment most likely contained some kind of virus. But curiosity got the better of me.

The attachment was a lengthy document, and I waited impatiently for it to download. As far as I could tell, it was some kind of scientific paper, filled with formulas and equations. I couldn't make heads or tails of it.

I decided that it was a not very funny practical joke. Ernie had to be behind it, or maybe one of the protesters. I clicked Reply. "SO not funny. Surely you can do better than that," I fired back. Almost immediately a new message appeared in my inbox. I stared at it in disbelief: "Message delivery failure. Server doesn't exist."

I tossed the iPad aside and turned out the light. I kept telling myself that it was just somebody's idea of a joke—a really stupid joke—but sleep eluded me until the wee hours of the morning.

§

"It wasn't me, I swear!" Ernie exclaimed, with the desperate sincerity of someone telling the truth, and I was inclined to believe him. "Where would I get a document like that? I can't even read it. I passed chemistry by the skin of my teeth!"

"Okay, okay. I had to ask."

Ernie's expressive brown eyes reflect his every emotion, and he looked genuinely wounded. "I can't believe you'd even suspect me. I'll bet you any amount of money your new pal had something to do with it."

"My new pal? Who....are you crazy? Surely you don't mean Seth?"

"Why not? You don't know the guy. Look, let's not argue over a stupid practical joke ...or...whatever this is. I don't know who it was, but it wasn't me." My expression evidently conveyed my belief and he continued, less exasperated. "Which reminds me— what would you think about a little trip to the science lab? We'd have to keep it under wraps, but I think we can get in without much trouble."

"Great minds think alike. When?"

"The sooner the better," he replied.

"I'm not doing anything tonight..."

Our conversation was interrupted by a loud knock at the janitor's closet door.

"I'll get it," said Ernie and fairly bounded toward the door. He glanced up at the surveillance screen and stopped short. "Were you expecting Seth?" I've known Ernie long enough to be able to interpret his body language. I suspect he had been hoping it was someone else.

"No, but let him in."

"Do I have to?" He made a face, but opened the door for our visitor.

"Hello, all," said Seth cheerily. "I trust I'm not interrupting anything important."

"Not at all. We were just discussing, um, a new case," I said.

"Well, forgive the intrusion. Margo, could I have a word with you? In private?" He looked pointedly at Ernie.

Ernie straightened up and squared his shoulders. I jumped in quickly before he could say anything. "We can go out back," and motioned him to follow.

I propped the door open with a brick that we keep around for just such an occasion and waited for him to speak. Seth was standing so close to me that I could smell his cologne.

"So. What's up?" I asked, hoping I sounded nonchalant.

"I was just wondering if I could convince you to have dinner with me tonight. I thought we might pop into Café Toulouse." Café Toulouse is Throckmorton's trendiest new restaurant, the best place to see and be seen. Actually, it's the only place to see and be seen. I wasn't sure whether I was disappointed or flattered. Maybe both. And you don't just pop in. Without a reservation, you don't have a prayer and they're usually booked solid weeks in advance.

"We have an investigation tonight." There's that, and the fact that you have a boyfriend with whom you are madly in love, said my conscience.

"Well, how about tomorrow night, then?"

The correct response here would have been something like "Thanks, but I can't. I'm seeing someone." So naturally I said, "Tomorrow night would work."

"Great, see you then." He turned and strolled away for a good five seconds before raising his hand and wiggling his fingers.

When I went back inside, Ernie was clattering away on one of the computers. The instant the door closed behind me, the typing stopped.

"Are you crazy?" shrieked Ernie.

"Mind your own business. It's just dinner."

"And were you planning on telling Tim about your dinner?"

"Oh, for heaven's sake, Ernie. I'm having dinner with a colleague. What do you think's gonna happen?"

"So if it's just dinner with a colleague, why aren't you going to tell Tim?"

"Because it's not important, that's why. Subject closed."

He sighed and rolled his eyes. "Fine. We need to round up a team if we're going to try and do this investigation tonight. Who's it going to be?"

"I figured you and I could handle it by ourselves."

"Oh...okay." He sounded disappointed.

"I could always call Elaine."

"I'd rather you didn't," he reply huffily.

"Suit yourself. I guess it'll just be me and you, then."

There was a long, awkward silence. I was working on a long-overdue report when suddenly Ernie said, "When we were in school, did you ever consider Tim as anything but a friend? Would you ever have considered dating him, I mean?"

"You must be joking. Back then that would have seemed like...like incest or something. He was the little brother I never had."

"But he didn't look at it the same way."

"Apparently not. Look, he was always a really special person in my life, but if you'd asked me then if we'd ever be together, I would have said no, of course not. He was still a kid—I guess you could say he was something of a late bloomer." Tim was one year behind me in high school. I regarded him as something of a surrogate kid brother, nothing more. After I left for college, we lost touch. That was almost twenty years ago. Then last year, when Tim was in town on a business trip, he asked to see me. Imagine my surprise when I discovered that the pudgy brainiac with big round glasses had evolved into a mouth-wateringly gorgeous man.

"Maybe it was always meant to be and you both just needed to grow up first," posited Ernie.

"You're waxing unusually philosophical today," I pointed out. "Did you know back then how he felt about me?"

"Guys don't really talk about that stuff the way girls do. But yeah, I sort of knew. I remember once after a football game we were hanging around at the Pizza Palace. Tim was there, and Roxy. Since he was younger than us Tim didn't get to go out with us very often, so he was in hog heaven. But then some guy you had a crush on showed up. You ended up leaving with him, and I ended up giving Tim a ride home."

I hadn't thought about that incident in years—a night out after a football game, one of many such nights. Memories flooded back, but they were all jumbled. "I didn't even remember that Tim was there that night. I never had any idea I hurt his feelings."

"No reason why you should," said Ernie. "I think I was the only one that noticed it, but he was crushed."

"I feel awful."

"It was a long time ago."

"You're right," I said, hoping I sounded more lighthearted than I felt. "Let's hope he's forgiven me."

"Oh, I'm sure he has. Hey, he's probably forgotten all about it."

But I was sure he probably hadn't, and my jubilant mood was dissipating. I deemed it a good time to change the subject. "About investigating the science lab..."

"I'll take care of everything," he said. His phone chimed and he lunged for it. But when he looked at the display, he tossed the phone down in irritation.

The Things I Endure for My Job

Ernie yanked on the handbrake of his battered 1967 Austin Mini and tilted the rearview mirror so he could watch out the back window.

"What are we waiting for? I asked.

"Security guard. He usually finishes up here right about now. And...there he goes." He checked the time on his phone. "Right on time."

I craned my neck to peer out the back window in time to see the brake lights of a campus security car.

"We have about three hours before he makes it back around. We should be finished long before then," he added.

"I still think we should have cleared this with somebody."

"We've discussed this. If they said no, we'd just have to sneak in anyway, but they would know we were coming. This is better."

We got out, gathering up backpacks and cases, each of which weighed approximately one ton. He closed the car door softly. As we staggered toward the science lab, looking like commandos about to storm a beach, a thought struck me.

"What if we can't get in the building?"

He stuck a hand in his pocket produced an access card.

"Where'd you get that?"

"I have my sources," he said. He slid the card through the reader and the door opened with a click.

Inside, the only light came from a distant streetlamp filtering in weakly through the windows. When we turned down the hall to the lab, we lost even that. It was nearly pitch black; the exit signs at either end of the hall provided the only illumination.

"Shouldn't we be worried about security cameras or something?" I whispered.

"Nah—there aren't any. This building is so old they decided it would cost too much. We just have to be sure we're out of here by the time the security guard comes around again."

We paused in front of the lab door and listened. The only sound was the hum of a generator somewhere in the bowels of the building.

"What if it's locked?" I asked.

Without a word, he produced something from his pocket.

"What's that?"

"Lock pick."

"Do you know how to use it?"

"No, not really," he admitted.

But we didn't need the lock pick. As soon as I touched the knob, the door creaked open. "Super," said Ernie. "We haven't even started and I'm already getting creeped out."

I shone my flashlight around the room. It looked just as it had when I'd paid my previous visit, but in the darkness the weird shapes on the tables took on a sinister air.

Because it was just the two of us in a very small space, setup didn't take long. Ernie hooked an infrared camera up to the digital video recorder while I did a sweep with my EMF meter. This took all of five minutes. The baseline readings of the electromagnetic fields—EMFs—were discouragingly normal, with nary an EMF spike in sight. Lots of things give off electromagnetic radiation—wall sockets, stereo speakers, old wiring. A high EMF reading usually indicates something mundane, like an electronic device or old and badly shielded wires. But it can also indicate paranormal activity. Likewise anomalous temperature fluctuations. In my experience, an unexplained cold spot is a fairly reliable indicator of paranormal activity. The digital temperature gauge indicated a constant ambient temperature of a comfy 72 degrees. So far, nothing particularly interesting was going on here.

I set my EMF meter on the corner of a table and slung my super new digital recorder over my shoulder. Until now my iPod has done double-duty as a digital voice recorder. Small, portable digital recording devices are standard equipment for paranormal researchers. My iPod does a great job and I've recorded some truly amazing electronic voice phenomena with it. But in the spirit of professionalism I invested in a fancy high-end recorder, a book-sized gadget sporting an intimidating array of buttons and switches.

I took my recorder and an EMF meter into Dr. Pritchett's office and tried again. Nothing happened that would give me any reason to think there was anything of interest here.

Ernie took a few photos with an ancient Polaroid camera. He swears by instant photography, claiming that it's especially well suited for paranormal work. "What are you going to do when they quit making the film?" I asked.

"Actually, they already have—several years ago. But a company in the Netherlands makes the film for vintage Polaroid cameras. It's great for art projects, but you have to be careful with it. I thought I'd test out their black and white film tonight."

"Well, good luck."

We spent an hour alternately listening quietly and imploring any entities that might be present to speak with us. Everything remained quiet on our various gadgets; no temperature fluctuations, no EMF hits, nothing.

Lest you think that ghost hunting is non-stop excitement, let me take this opportunity to enlighten you. You spend hours sitting around in a dark room, asking questions and fiddling with gadgets. Most of the time, absolutely nothing happens. Typically, you have to wait until you go over your videos and voice recordings before you know if you've made contact, and even then it's not always easy to determine if something you have captured is a genuine paranormal event. Very often what looks convincingly like a ghost is just a trick of the light or a digital artifact—garbled digital data caused by hardware malfunctions or software quirks, such as when the picture on your satellite TV freezes during a storm. Getting any kind of solid physical evidence is rare. But it's the cases where you do get proof that make it all worth it. I've been doing this long enough to recognize when a room has a different energy. This one, I was fairly sure, had something out of the ordinary in it. Still, I knew it might be a long, quiet evening.

After about 45 minutes that seemed like hours, Ernie said, "I think we've about covered this room....any idea what's in here?"

"Probably just a closet—Ernie, what are you doing?" He was on his knees in front of the closet door I'd found locked earlier, his lock pick in one hand and a flashlight in another. I heard a click and Ernie pumped a fist in the air triumphantly.

It wasn't a closet but a tiny office, with a desk and computer, a couple of chairs, and a few bookshelves. A brand-new top-of-the-line computer sat on the desk; its box was still on the floor. One shelf held a few books and some haphazardly stacked binders; the other shelves were bare. "This must be Seth's office," remarked Ernie. "Nice computer. I didn't know professors got such snazzy stuff."

"Well, don't touch it."

"Why?" he asked.

"Fingerprints."

"You're just being paranoid. Relax!"

"No, Ernie, come on. Let's get out of here. There's something about this I don't like. I don't want to hang around any longer than we have to."

We spent the next few minutes packing up our stuff. Maybe it was just my conscience prickling me, but I was feeling uncharacteristically nervous and couldn't wait to get out.

As I was tossing some gadgets into a backpack, I heard a noise in the hall. Ernie heard it too, and we both froze. With growing unease, I realized that the noise was footsteps, and they were getting closer.

"Somebody's coming," he whispered. "Grab the stuff and let's get into Pritchett's office."

"What if they go in there?"

"Shhh! We don't have time to discuss it. Get under the desk. Quick!" He pushed me through the door to Pritchett's office and we wedged ourselves and our equipment under the desk with seconds to spare. We heard a clink of keys and the hall door opening, followed by footsteps. The intruder was wearing hard-soled shoes; we could hear every step he took as he walked around the lab. A few seconds later, a faint blue glow lit up the frosted glass pane in the office door. I heard a friendly chime from the lab.

"They've turned on the computer!" Ernie whispered.

"Great—we're going to be here for a while."

The minutes we were crammed under the desk felt like hours. We could hear the person in the lab on the other side of the door typing away on the clunky old computer on the desk.

"What time is it?" I asked, in what I hope was the softest of whispers

"How'm I supposed to know?"

"Don't you have a phone or something?"

"Are you crazy? The glow from the screen might give us away."

After what seemed like light-years, Ernie began to squirm.

"Be still!" I hissed.

Instead of replying, he buried his face in his gadget bag and sneezed. He emerged from the bag with a horrified expression on his face. It was not the kind of sneeze you could muffle, and when he glanced into the bag his expression changed to disgust.

The typing stopped. We froze, still as statues. Neither of us dared breathe. I could hear my heartbeat, and I think I might have heard Ernie's too. Footsteps came toward us and paused outside the door. We heard the doorknob being jiggled, first gently, then harder. The glass pane rattled, but the door didn't budge.

The footsteps retreated and the sounds of typing resumed. We listened for another eternity until finally we heard another chime and the lab went dark. The intruder paused again at Pritchett's office door on the way out, trying the doorknob one more time.

At long last, we heard the outer door close, followed by the sounds of keys in a lock. I waited a few moments, then extricated myself carefully from under the desk. "What a relief. I need to go to the bathroom...bad."

Ernie crawled out from under the desk on all fours."Why didn't you go before?"

"I did! I didn't know we were going to be here for hours."

"It's 2:00 a.m. We only got here three hours ago."

"Only? It seems like years," I said, flexing my foot, which had fallen asleep.

"Let's get out of here," he said, gingerly getting to his feet. "The security guard is due back any time now."

I tried to stand up, but my foot was completely numb. It began to tingle as the circulation started back.

"Ouch, ouch!" I rubbed it, which only made it worse.

"Shhh! I heard something." Reluctantly I ducked under the desk again.

Somebody was at the outer door. I held my breath. Horrorstruck, we heard the hall door open. After a second, the frosted pane was brightly lit as the lights went on in the lab. Much to my relief, they went out again after a few seconds. We heard the door shut and the jingle of keys. We waited for a few seconds, straining our ears for any sounds, but the lab was silent.

"Jeez Louise, this place is like Grand Central Station," remarked Ernie.

Carefully, I opened Pritchett's office door an inch and peeked through the crack into the lab with one eye. "It's safe. Let's go before I explode," I said.

"Wait a minute," said Ernie. "Did you notice anything weird?" He was on his knees, examining the doorknob using the light from his phone as a flashlight.

"Weird? Uh, no, Ernie. What's weird about spending two hours in the middle of the night wedged under a desk? I do it all the time."

He fixed me with a baleful stare. "Think of it as a hazard of the job. No, I mean whoever it was out there tried hard to open this door. I thought he was going to shatter the glass. But there's no lock on it. It opened right up for us."

"It's just an old door that sticks sometimes. Come on. This is an emergency—I'm not kidding."

"We still need to be careful. That security guard can't be far." Ernie opened the door into the hall and peered through the crack. "Coast is clear."

I gathered up as much stuff as I could carry and was halfway down the hall when I realized Ernie wasn't behind me. "What are you doing now?" I hissed in my best stage whisper.

"Trying to lock this door."

It was certainly the first time I've ever heard of anyone trying to use a lock pick to *lock* a door. "Oh for —look, you're just going to have to leave it unlocked. Probably no one will notice, and if they do they'll think the security guard just forgot to lock it back. Let's *go*."

We crept down the hall, cradling our equipment to prevent any clanks and jingles. The relief I felt as we slipped out the door was indescribable. I was urgently in need of another kind of relief. But to my extreme annoyance, Ernie was staring at his car, scratching his head.

"Come on, Ernie. Open the door. I need to go."

"No. We'd better walk back."

"What? Have you totally lost it? It's halfway across campus!"

"Yeah, but I don't want to take the chance on firing up the engine. Or turning on the headlights."

I considered mugging him for the keys, but conceded that he did have a point.

"Then I suggest we stop farting around," I said, zipping up my jacket. The nip in the air wasn't helping matters. We stashed the heaviest gear in the car, quietly closed the doors, and began our trek.

The walk across campus (more like a jog, if you must know) seemed to take eons. At least there weren't any protesters to dodge at this hour of the morning. My dash to the ladies' room may have set a new record.

When I went back into the lab—feeling considerably better—Ernie was plugging a flash drive into his computer.

"What on earth are you doing?"

"I just wanted to check something."

"It's 2:30 in the morning! We can look over the evidence later."

"We will, but I want to check something before I go home. Don't worry about me. You go on; we'll talk tomorrow."

I was in no mood to argue with him. "Whatever floats your boat," I said.

The Date that Wasn't A Date

The next day the lab was deserted when I got in, although it was early afternoon. I took the opportunity to flip through my emails while I sipped a cup of tea. With no one in the lab it was eerily quiet. Suddenly my phone chimed, startling me. It was a message from Tim: "Really need to talk ASAP."

I launched the video chat program and clicked on Tim's thumbnail likeness. He answered almost immediately.

"Hey, babe," he said. "How's my girl?"

"I'm fine, Timmy. What's up? Is everything okay?"

"Everything's more than okay," he said, grinning broadly.

"You're up to something, I can tell."

"I bought my ticket."

"Ticket? For….?"

"My plane ticket. For homecoming. It's less than two weeks away."

I stared—rather stupidly, I fear—at his image on the little screen.

"Did I catch you at a bad time?" he asked.

"Sorry…sorry, Tim. That's wonderful."

"That's all you can say? 'That's wonderful'?"

I managed what I hoped was a convincing smile. "I guess I'm not quite awake yet. Really late night last night—I'll explain later. When are you getting here? I can't wait." I wrote down his flight information and tried to focus while he chattered away enthusiastically.

It got quiet suddenly, and I realized he'd asked me a question and was waiting for an answer.

"I'm sorry, Timmy. I heard a strange noise. It was probably just the protesters out front. They make such a racket."

He frowned. "Hmm. I didn't hear it. I just wondered what time you're getting home tonight. I want to hear about your investigation."

My stomach had suddenly turned into a block of ice. "Oh, well, I might be a little late. I'm ...um... having dinner with a friend."

"Oh. Well, that sounds like fun. Where're you going?"

"Um, I don't know," I lied. "I guess we'll just play it by ear—you know, see what we're in the mood for."

I spent the rest of the day trying to convince myself that I hadn't really lied to Tim. After all, he never asked who I was having dinner with.

§

An hour before I was supposed to meet Seth, I was still digging frantically through my closet. I'd tried on at least half a dozen different skirt and blouse combinations and rejected them all, before finally deciding on an aqua dress that hadn't seen the light of day in a while.

I studied my reflection in the full-length mirror. The dress was a little on the short side. Maybe that's the reason I don't wear it very often. But the color compliments my auburn hair, and I told myself that it wasn't really *that* short.

I tried to drag a comb through my hair, but it refused to cooperate. I decided to let my hair do as it pleased, usually the wisest action. I slapped on some extra makeup, and after a protracted search through the bathroom vanity, found my contacts.

The final result was sophisticated without being overtly sexy. Or at least I hoped.

I was now running late. As I dashed out the door I blew a kiss at the picture of Tim I keep tacked to my refrigerator door. "This is *not* a date," I said out loud.

§

Café Toulouse is one of those places where everything is over-the-top trendy. The sleek, hypermodern decor, the unobtrusive techno music, the ridiculously expensive, miniature servings—everything is carefully calculated to create an ambience of urban elegance. I didn't ask Seth how he managed to get a reservation on such short notice, but from the way the maitre d' fawned all over him, I suspected some money had changed hands.

Seth looked fabulous in an exquisitely cut black suit *sans* tie. Several women—and a few men—stared at him as we walked past.

Seth glanced quickly at the wine list and asked the self-consciously hip waiter for a Bordeaux of a specific vintage. The waiter disappeared and reappeared in a few minutes with a dusty bottle. After the usual tasting ritual, the waiter filled our glasses, took our orders, and retreated.

"Cheers," said Seth, clinking my glass with his. He swirled his wine in his glass and studied it before taking a sip. "A passable vintage."

"It's very nice." Actually, I couldn't tell that it was any better than what I usually get at the grocery store, but what do I know?

Seth was studying me closely. "You seem preoccupied."

"Sorry, I'm just a little tired."

"Out late last night?"

"Well past my usual bedtime." No point in trying to be coy about it—no concealer in the world would hide the dark circles under my eyes.

"Oh?" Was it just my imagination, or did I detect a sudden surge of interest? "Out on the town, were you? So was I. I'm surprised we didn't run into each other."

I wondered who he'd been out with and felt a small twinge of jealousy, which I quickly squelched. "It was just an investigation. Late nights are part of the job."

"Sounds interesting. Where was this latest adventure—a haunted mansion, maybe? Or the library? I hear it has a ghost or two." He smiled casually, but his eyes were fixed intently on mine.

"It was nothing interesting," I said. "Just a small case. It probably won't amount to anything, but we'll know more after we've had a chance to go over everything."

"Was it someplace here in town?"

He certainly was asking a lot of questions, and they were starting to make me uncomfortable. "Well, yes," I said, "but I wouldn't think it's the kind of thing you'd be interested in, you being a man of science and all."

"Who me? Why, I find it all very fascinating," he said jovially. "Although I'm not a believer, myself."

"I used to not be. But I've seen and heard too much."

"So you think they're out there?"

I thought I detected a slight note of condescension in his voice. "Trust me," I said, "they're out there. Ghosts are everywhere, and they really don't care whether you believe in them or not."

The waiter appeared and placed oversized plates in front of us with a flourish. In the center of mine was a dainty mound of artfully arranged pasta, garnished with sprigs of fresh herbs.

"*Bon appétit*," said Seth. "What do you think they are, these ghosts?"

"My personal opinion is that there are anomalies in the space-time continuum, and that there are many more than the four physical dimensions that we learn about in school. I believe that what we consider paranormal phenomena are just beings trapped in these extra-dimensional anomalies, for whatever reason, and it's my job to help them any way I can."

"Oh my," he said, putting his elbows on the table with a dramatic gesture, "I didn't know you were rocket scientist. And here I was thinking you were about to tell me a good ghost story." He leaned toward me eagerly.

"Sorry, but we try not to discuss active cases. I hope you don't think I'm being rude," I said, trying to ignore his condescending comment and hoping I sounded suitably casual.

"Of course not," he said, smiling again. I had a feeling that maybe I'd just told him too much. A change in the topic of conversation seemed in order. "So, where did you learn so much about wines?"

"Well, when you've spent as much time in France as I have, you can't help but pick up a tip or two."

"So you've traveled a lot then?"

"You might say that," he chuckled. "I guess you could say I've seen more of the world than most people even dream about. And you, Margo? How much of the world have you seen?"

What was it about his tone that was making me feel defensive? "It's not as if I've spent my entire life in Indian Springs. After college I lived in Boston for a while and then…"

"No, I mean how much of the *world*. Europe, Asia, the Middle East."

"Europe a couple of times. To Austria on a high school trip. Then, after college some friends and I bought Eurail passes and spent a month traveling around Italy. But I haven't been there in years." I shrugged. "At some point you have to settle down and start earning a living."

"Indeed," he said dreamily. Looking into the depths of his glass, he said, "I could show you places you've only dreamed of, you know. And it wouldn't be on a Eurail pass."

I laughed, but this whole conversation was making me nervous. "I'm sure you could. I guess that's one of the advantages of teaching. It must be lovely having the whole summer off."

He didn't respond. I concentrated on trying to twirl some linguine onto my fork. It kept sliding off, and I wondered whatever had possessed me to order pasta. One of my tried and true rules is never order noodles on a date. But then, it wasn't really a date, I reminded myself. I looked up to find that Seth was watching me intently. "What do you suppose the likelihood is, Margo," he purred, "that Braxton Hall has a ghost?"

What little appetite I had left vanished. "Why Braxton Hall in particular?" I finally managed to ask.

"Oh, you know," he said softly, "it's such an old building and all. Surely it has a ghost or two?"

"Well, a building doesn't have to be old to have a presence, you know." My stomach was now churning, which made it difficult to sound convincingly nonchalant. "We did an investigation once in an office complex in a new subdivision on the edge of town. We didn't have any theories as to why there might be activity there until somebody pointed out that the area was once known as Getty Falls. It took a little digging, but Sandy found out that it was named that because a man named Getty was killed by Indians and buried there."

"Indeed?"

"Yes, and in fact the word 'falls' in the name indicates that water is present nearby. Flowing water has been known to enhance paranormal activity, you know." Suddenly, I was acutely aware that it must have seemed to Seth that I was babbling nervously. "Sorry. I'll stop talking shop now."

§

I convinced myself that it wouldn't be a real date if I paid my own way. But when the waiter arrived with the bill, Seth snatched it up quickly, refusing to let me even see it. I made a valiant effort to wrest it from him.

"Nonsense," he said. "I invited you."

At the door we paused to retrieve my jacket. He gallantly helped me on with it, his hand brushing my shoulder in the lightest of gestures that gave me goosebumps.

He walked me to my car. He had offered to come to my house and pick me up, but I had insisted that we meet at the restaurant, reasoning that it didn't make sense for him to drive the five miles to Indian Springs, just to drive back to Throckmorton. This also made it less like an official date...at least in my mind.

"Thank you for a lovely dinner, Seth."

"The pleasure was all mine."

It was one of those awkward moments when I didn't know what to do. Would it be rude, I wondered, to offer to shake hands? He resolved the issue by lifting my hand to his lips and kissing it. "Drive safely," he said.

He was certainly the most debonair man I'd ever been out with. And more than a little bit mysterious. I glanced in the rearview mirror as I drove away. He was watching me intently, hands in his jacket pockets. I waved into the mirror, but he didn't wave back.

Uncomfortable Conversations

With all that had been going on, I'd almost—but not quite—managed to forget about the creepy email from the mystery jokester. The more I thought about it, the more I felt it was something my boss should know about. It was weighing on me and I decided there was no sense putting it off any longer.

Dr. Holmes seldom closed his office door, and I caught a glimpse of him before I knocked. He was at his desk, elbows propped on the desk, cradling his head in his hands and it seemed to me that he'd aged ten years in the past few days. He looked worse than tired—haggard. I tapped on the door. When he saw me, he straightened up and managed a feeble smile.

"Margo, do come in. Please, sit down." I sat in the chair he motioned to. "What can I do for you today?"

"Is this a good time? I mean, you looked like you were deep into something. I don't want to disturb you."

"Think nothing of it, my dear. I'm just feeling my age today. The recent...events...have left me somewhat more aware than usual of my mortality."

This was an unusually frank admission. He's the best boss anybody could hope for, but we'd never ventured into personal territory before. I decided to be bold—perhaps even a little nosy. "How are you holding up?"

He shook his head. "As well as can be expected. At my age, you understand on an intellectual level that sooner or later you're going to lose people near and dear to you. But no matter how often it happens, you're never really prepared for it. You never, ever get used to it."

"I heard you and Dr. Pritchett grew up together."

"Yes, yes, we did. Nigel's family moved here when he was only eight. They came from England, you know. Manchester."

"I didn't know that."

"Yes, his father also taught science. He found life here to be quite a culture shock, I'm afraid. I'm not sure they ever really adjusted."

"He was one of Sandy's favorite professors."

"I'm not surprised. Nigel was a born scientist. Even when we were young he was forever concocting formulas. We used to do experiments in his basement. One time there was an explosion and we almost burned the house down. Nigel got into rather a lot of trouble, I'm afraid." Holmes chuckled. "Nigel and I had dinner just a couple of days before he died. I guess

I'm still coming to terms with the knowledge that I won't see him again in this lifetime."

"I'm really sorry." I wish I could have thought of something more profound to say. "Have there been any leads in the case?"

"If there are, the powers that be haven't seen fit to share them with me." He was trying to sound light-hearted, but I noticed that his hands were trembling. "But here I am, prattling on. You came to discuss something with me."

I took a deep breath. "I don't quite know where to begin." I told him about the voicemail message and the weird email, leaving out the part about our late-night foray into the chemistry lab. "This is the attachment that came in the email that said it was from Dr. Pritchett."

His face, which had already been looking rather gray, turned deathly pale as soon as he started reading the document I handed him. He read a couple of pages closely, then flipped rapidly through the remaining pages. Suddenly he slapped the papers down on his desk and looked at me, staring at me for a few seconds without speaking. "Margo, I need your solemn promise…" He paused and regained control of his wavering voice. "Promise me that you won't show this to anyone, or mention anything about it ... to anyone. Ever."

"Of course, but I—I mean, what is it?"

"It's better—and safer—for you to not know anything." He stood up abruptly and walked over to his paper shredder. Seconds later, the document was confetti. "Delete every copy of this email and empty your trash folder. It's better that we not discuss this again." He had regained his composure and was starting to sound more like his old self, but I noticed his hands were still shaking. "I hope you haven't mentioned this to Ernie."

"Well, I, um, that is..."

He shook his head and pinched the bridge his nose. "I'll speak to him. Now, not another word about it—to anybody."

I took this as a dismissal and beat a hasty retreat.

§

The look I got from Ernie when I got back from lunch would have been comical in any other circumstances.

"Fer cryin' out loud, Margo! What did you say to him? I thought he was going to cry!"

"All I did was show him that document. The one that came in the weird email I told you about. He glanced at the first few pages and ran it through the shredder. Told me to trash every copy."

"Well?"

"That's where I was just now—at home, cleaning off my computer."

"I have a bad feeling about this."

"You're not the only one."

The door opened and in sauntered Sandy and the world's ugliest dog. The dog wagged a mangy tail, sniffed hopefully at Ernie's backpack, and flopped down, crossing one paw daintily over the other.

"I've decided on a name for him," announced Sandy triumphantly.

"Oh? I can hardly wait for this one," said Ernie.

"Willis."

"Willis? What the hell kind of a name is that for a dog? A really ugly dog at that. I think you should call him Spuds."

"Huh?"

"Haven't you noticed that he sort of flops to the ground like a sack of potatoes?"

Sandy clutched his chest dramatically. "Stop! You're crackin' me up!"

"No, really. He doesn't lie down so much as...fall a short distance," Ernie chuckled.

"His name is Willis, and he is a most noble beast," sniffed Sandy indignantly. "He's a regular chick magnet."

"A flea magnet, more like," Ernie retorted.

Before they could get into an argument, I intervened. "You know, Sandy, Spuds...I mean Willis —shows signs of sensitivity. I think he would make a great paranormal investigator—"

Sandy cut me off before I could even launch into my spiel. "Not in a million years!"

"But Sandy, he's a natural."

"'Natural' is not the first word that springs to mind. Speaking of which, you know you have an investigation tomorrow night."

"So can we borrow Willis ?" asked Ernie.

"No, you most assuredly may not."

"So who's it going to be, then? Is Elaine available to help?" I asked.

"I have absolutely no idea," said Ernie snippily.

"The two of you *still* aren't speaking?"

"I haven't talked to her in over a week."

"Well, do you have any objections if I call her?"

"Yes, as a matter of fact, I do."

"Oh, honestly!" I said.

"If I may," said Sandy, who'd been listening to this exchange in silent amusement. "I may have the answer to your problems—Seamus."

Seamus is the librarian at the Indian Springs Public Library. We met him when he helped us with some research on our last case. He has long, curly red hair and looks more like a rock star than a librarian. As it turns out, he's a music student at the college. His pride and joy is a band called the Oxymorons, in which he plays bass.

"Fine," I said. "Call him."

"I'll be right back," said Sandy as he dashed out the door, cell phone to his ear, leaving Willis in our care.

I turned to Ernie."Did we get any evidence from our little adventure at the science lab?"

He looked distinctly uncomfortable. "We did, as a matter of fact."

He motioned me over to a large, clunky computer we affectionately call "The Monster." It doesn't look like much, but it has enough computing power to run a mission to Mars. Opening a spreadsheet filled with rows and columns of numbers, Ernie explained, "This is just a record of the temperature and EMF readings. Nothing unusual except a small uptick in the electromagnetic readings, right here."

"What about the Polaroids you took?"

He shook his head. "Didn't get anything there. And there's nothing interesting on the video footage, either." He played an almost comically sped-up video, in which the entire escapade was compressed into only those frames where there was no motion from one frame to the next. "However," he paused for dramatic effect, "I did catch something on the audio."

He launched another program and loaded a file. Every sound recorded by my device that evening was reduced to a series of zigzag waveforms in a scrolling box. "I stripped out the silence, and ran it through the voice recognition program, which was easy, since it was just the two of us that night. And what we're left with is this."

He clicked Play and a vertical line scrolled merrily across the waveforms. What I heard turned my blood to ice. A voice that I didn't recognize said, very clearly, *"Look out...Ben."* Ben being the first name of our boss, Dr. Ben Holmes.

"Ernie, you don't think..."

"I don't know what to think. I mean, he's been acting so weird lately."

"You'd act weird, too if your best friend had been savagely murdered."

"And how do you explain his reaction when you showed him that document? What if there was something incriminating in it? Why else would he react like that? You should have seen him—his face was completely white..."

"Like he'd seen a ghost?"

"Har har, very funny," he snickered.

"You know as well as I do Dr. Holmes would never..."

He held up a hand to silence me. "There's more. And you aren't going to like this."

He played some video footage. In the grainy image, I could see most of the science lab, from somewhere near the entry door. I could see clearly the high definition camera I'd set up in one corner, the only camera we'd set up that night. I watched myself taking it down and packing it up.

"What's this? I didn't set up any cameras from this angle."

"I know. While you were packing up, I installed this wireless web cam."

"Oh Ernie! Why?"

"Call it a premonition, I guess. It was taping the whole time we were trapped in Pritchett's office." He fast-forwarded and I watched the two of us make our mad dash to the office. Seconds later, a man walked in and looked around. I got a clear view of his face and my heart fell into my sneakers. It was Seth.

"We have almost two hours of him working on the computer in the lab," Ernie added.

"And so what? Maybe he's a night owl and decided to work a little late." I didn't like where this was going.

"Maybe. But why use the lab's computer? Why not use the one in his own office? There's a top-of-the-line beauty sitting on his desk, fresh out of the box. Why come to the lab in the middle of the night to use that old clunker?" he asked.

My head was starting to pound. "I admit it doesn't make sense. But I'm sure there's a perfectly logical explanation for it all."

He raised an eyebrow. "No doubt."

"You can't leave the camera there, you know."

"Why not?" he asked.

"Because if somebody finds it we're screwed, that's why not."

"You worry too much. It's well hidden. In the meantime, we can see what's going on in the science lab any time we want." To illustrate his point, he showed me the live feed. There was no sound, but we could see students at several tables, working diligently on various projects. Someone must have made a joke, because the room suddenly erupted in laughter that we saw, rather than heard. Seth was nowhere around. "By the way," asked Ernie with careful nonchalance, "how was your dinner with Seth?"

"Well, if you must know—"

"I must! I must!"

"We had a lovely dinner."

"At...?"

"Café Toulouse."

"Café Toulouse!" He whistled softly. "I'm impressed. Not bad for a first date."

"I keep telling you, it wasn't a date!" I said, exasperated.

"Oh? So you split the check? Isn't that going to cut into your spending money for a while?"

"Seth paid."

"Did he? Man, they must pay the teachers at the Sheldrick Institute a lot more than they pay them here."

I glared at him. "Mind your own business."

Sandy fortuitously chose that moment to return with Seamus in tow, cutting short the argument that was brewing. We spent the rest of the afternoon explaining the basics of paranormal investigation to Seamus. When we were about to leave, I got a sudden urge to check my email. Among the usual junk mails and newsletters I spotted a message from Seth.

Margo, thanks for a wonderful evening and delightful company. I hope this will be the first of many enchanting evenings.

I must have had a stupid grin on my face because when Ernie saw me he rolled his eyes. "Looks like somebody got a message from Seth!" he said in a mocking voice.

"And so what?" I closed the mail window quickly.

He smirked, but didn't respond.

If you must know the truth, Ernie had a point. Seth had tossed money around last night like a trust fund baby. It bothered me more than I cared to admit. To distract myself, I opened the file from a case we'd worked on in Deerfield just before Professor Pritchett's murder. The recently appointed executive director of the Deerfield Chamber of Commerce, Beatrice Foster, called us shortly after the C of C moved from a soulless downtown office building to a new location. The activity she claimed to be having in the converted gas station, that according to legend was once robbed by Bonnie and Clyde, sounded tantalizing. Unfortunately, we didn't find a shred of evidence. I'd been putting off contacting her. I didn't relish having to tell her we had nothing to show her.

My contact with her had been limited, but she seemed to be the kind of person who thrived on drama. When I called her, she seemed eager to talk to me, so I arranged to meet with her that afternoon.

§

"Nothing? As in...*nothing*? I just really find that hard to believe." My meeting with Beatrice Foster had started out convivially enough. As I'd predicted, however, she didn't take kindly to being told we hadn't tracked down her supposed ghost. She glared at me from behind a pair of huge gold-framed glasses.

I took a deep breath and continued. "We went over the evidence carefully. We have several hours of audio and video..."

"Well, then, there must be something wrong with your equipment."

"We've used the same devices since then and have gotten plenty of good, solid evidence, and on multiple occasions. Of course, just because we didn't get anything doesn't mean there's no paranormal activity here," I added diplomatically. "It just means that we didn't record any physical evidence this time."

But Beatrice was having none of it. "I thought you people were supposed to be professionals."

Mentally, I counted to ten. "Beatrice, we're researchers. We can't conjure up an entity at will. If whatever's here doesn't want to come out to play, there's not much we can do about it."

I'd like to be able to report that I was able to convince her that absence of evidence was the rule rather than the exception, but by the time I left her office, Beatrice was fuming. I was a more than a little rattled myself. Her reaction puzzled me. When I tell people we didn't find anything, they're sometimes disappointed, but this was the first time anyone had gotten downright belligerent. It gnawed at me all the way home.

I was driving past the shopping center near my house when I noticed a portable marquee sign in front of the new bookstore. It said "Grand Opening Today!" On impulse, I whipped into the parking lot.

Inside, I found an eclectic mixture of new and used books and a coffee bar offering the usual espresso drinks and an assortment of baked goodies. A sign proudly proclaimed that they offered free wireless internet. The smell of books mingled with coffee enticed me to hang around, and I did a quick reconnaissance of their offerings, starting, naturally, with the paranormal section. I was flipping through *Haunted Pubs of England* and had just come to a story about a particularly juicy-sounding haunting, when I felt a tap on my shoulder.

Nearly jumping out of my skin, I whirled around.

"Sorry. Didn't mean to startle you."

"Seth! What are you...sorry," I stammered. My heart was hammering...and not one hundred percent from fright.

"I saw your car out front and thought I'd find you here. I've been looking at apartments in your neck of the woods." He held up a section from the newspaper with several items circled conspicuously. "What's so engrossing?"

I held up the book for him to see. "*Haunted Pubs of England*. Sounds fascinating." He was smiling, but my bullshit meter detected condescension again. "Fancy a cappuccino?" he asked.

"Oh, I...well, why not?"

He went to the coffee bar to order while I paid for the book. When I joined him at a cozy table in a dark corner, our drinks were waiting.

"Well," he asked. "How is it?"

"It's delightful," I replied, truthfully. "How's yours?"

"Passable. I've had better."

"Really?" I was a little surprised. "Well, maybe I've been in Indian Springs too long." It was meant to be a joke, but I regretted it as soon as I said it.

"I know little place in Paris that serves the best coffee in the world. It's right across from the Bois de Boulogne. One of my favorite haunts, if you'll excuse the expression. Have you ever been to Paris, Margo?"

"No. I was a recent graduate and my funds were limited. I had to choose between France and Italy, and Italy won. Do you go there often?" Of course Seth had been to Paris. Why should I have been surprised?

"Oh, a few times. Perhaps some day I'll have the pleasure of taking you there. It would be great fun to show you around."

I should have been flattered, I suppose, but the implications made me uncomfortable. "Well, I'm sure Paris is teeming with paranormal activity. I certainly wouldn't mind investigating there." I tried to steer the conversation back into more comfortable waters without sounding like a hayseed. "But I suppose you've been to a good many interesting places."

He chuckled. "Yes, you might say that. I was once surfing off the coast of Western Australia when I tried to rescue a tourist—Australia is really a very dangerous place, you know—who'd run into a swarm of jellyfish. Box jellyfish. Some of the most venomous creatures in the world. They can sting you even when they're dead. The locals wouldn't dream of getting into the water without a stinger suit on—"

"'Stinger suit'?"

"I believe you say 'wet suit.' Anyway this poor old rube, being a tourist he didn't know any better, you see. Now, the sting of the box jellyfish is excruciating. Some say it's not so much the venom from the animal that does it, but the pain that kills people. It's said to be one of the most agonizing ways imaginable to die."

Suddenly my cappuccino tasted like cardboard. "But what about the tourist? Did you save him?"

"Oh no, poor bugger. Nothing to be done for him. All I could do was watch him die. When the end came, it was a blessing, let me tell you. Nothing worse than a box jellyfish. Perfectly dreadful, the agony he went through. I can still hear his screams." Seth paused to take a drink. Then our eyes met, and he looked deep into mine. "Have you ever watched a man die, Margo?" A kind of strange fire in his eyes gave me a chill.

I suddenly wanted nothing more than to be somewhere else. "No, can't say that I have. I live a pretty quiet life."

"Except for the ghosts," he said, with a little smile.

"You get used to them after a while."

"Do you suppose my predecessor's ghost haunts Braxton Hall?"

Now what the hell kind of question was that? I thought he was joking, but his expression assured me he was not. "I'm sure Professor Pritchett's ghost has better things to do than hang around Braxton Hall." I tried to laugh it off, but I was seriously creeped out now.

"Do you?" He was quiet for a moment. I used the opportunity to slurp down my drink. "Finished so soon?" he asked. "But we're just getting started. How about we continue this conversation? Over dinner tonight?"

"Oh, thanks, that's very kind of you, but I'll have to take a rain check. We have an investigation tonight. I have to go home and gather up a few things. In fact, I really need to run. I'm supposed to meet Ernie at the Taco Loco in less than an hour."

I couldn't get out of there fast enough. I considered for a moment taking a circuitous route home, but decided that if Seth wanted to find out where I live he could do so easily enough without following me home. Still, I checked my rearview mirror approximately every three seconds. I started punching the button on the garage door remote halfway down the block and sat in my driveway mumbling "Come on, hurry up," as I waited for the door to roll open. I pulled in and hopped out. As the door lowered with glacial slowness I peeked out underneath it, searching up and down the block. No cars turned down my street. Nevertheless, when I went inside I ran through the house, opening closets and checking locks on doors and windows.

The Haunted School

Seamus dipped the last remaining chip in some fiery hot salsa and munched it happily as we ate at the Taco Loco. "I can't believe I'm finally going ghost hunting with you guys."

"Well, I hope you won't be disappointed," said Ernie. "A lot of times an investigation is nothing but sheer, unmitigated boredom."

"And then you have to look at all the evidence afterwards," I added. "Boredom doesn't begin to describe it." Seamus remained unconvinced that ghost hunting was anything but non-stop, spine-tingling excitement.

"Hey, feel free to send it all my way."

Ernie clapped him on the back. "You're going to be a valuable member of the team." He was unusually jovial this evening. He wasn't giving the impression that he felt any resentment toward Seamus for being there in Elaine's stead.

The waitress returned with my credit card in a little black folder. I signed it and left a generous tip. "OK, boys. I guess it's time. We're supposed to meet Principal Golding in twenty minutes."

Seamus opened the door for me and we walked toward the parking lot where my car and Ernie's were parked side by side, both loaded with equipment.

"Dude, somebody's checking out your car," said Seamus.

"Yeah, it happens all the time," answered Ernie proudly. "You don't see many of them around...is that Seth?"

It was indeed Seth. He was standing at the curb, staring intently at Ernie's car. Then he saw us, and his expression changed fleetingly to something... anger, possibly, or recognition. Ernie, flattered at the attention to his beloved 1967 Mini, was oblivious.

Seth was suddenly all smiles. "It must be yours, then," he said to Ernie.

"Restored it myself," answered Ernie proudly.

I listened politely to the ensuing man-talk with a growing feeling of unease. I was one hundred percent certain Seth couldn't care less about Ernie's car. Alarm bells were going off in my head, but I couldn't quite put my finger on it. Something tickled the edges of my subconscious like a not-quite-forgotten dream. Then Seth turned his attention to me with a nod of his head and I promptly forgot all about it. "Margo, always a pleasure."

"Nice seeing you again, Seth. Well, guys, we need to be on our way."

§

Principal Emily Golding didn't look at all like the plump, grey-haired, grandmotherly sort of person I had pictured. Instead, she was insect-thin, about 35, and wearing a designer suit. Her glossy black hair was so dark it gleamed purple under the light. She greeted us calmly, as though having a team of ghost hunters in your school was an everyday occurrence.

"I appreciate you coming out. Normally I don't put much stock in stories about this kind of thing. But when a dedicated teacher like Lucy Cartwright threatens to quit, I simply have to do something."

Ernie and I left Seamus to keep an eye on the equipment and went on a tour of the school with Principal Golding. The Rhonda Q. Mills Magnet for Gifted and Talented Children was a marvel of modern architecture, with sunny classrooms and spacious hallways.

"How many students do you have?" I asked, scurrying to keep up as Principal Golding ushered us briskly down first one hallway then another. She stopped to let us look into a couple of classrooms. They were open and modern—almost clinical—with whiteboards, computers, and sturdy plastic furniture.

"The school opened its doors eight years ago with 127 students. We now have almost 300." We turned a corner and the open, glass-enclosed hallways abruptly gave way to a dark, narrow corridor with dingy linoleum floors flanked with rows of dark wood doors. It was a jarring contrast to all the sleek modernity we'd just come from.

"As you can see, a much older building on this site was incorporated into the new building's design. It wasn't in the original plan, but it turned out that these buildings were designated historical landmarks —this was once the Norton Township School. It housed grades 1 through 12 until Norton Township was surrounded by Indian Springs."

"When was that, do you know?" asked Ernie.

"Sometime in the 1960s. The buildings had been sitting vacant for decades." She unlocked a set of double doors and opened them to reveal a school auditorium. "This auditorium was restored at great cost. When it was built, it served as the performance hall for the entire town. The music and drama departments use it as a rehearsal hall now." We stuck our heads in and looked around. It could have been any school auditorium anywhere, with a stage, curtains and seating for maybe 200. It still had most of its Victorian ornamentation and a stately, dignified air.

We stopped at a classroom, and Principal Golding unlocked the door. "Supposedly, strange things have happened all throughout the school, but most of the reports seem to be centered in this wing, and in this classroom in particular." She turned on the lights and we went in. No whiteboards here—the walls were lined with good old-fashioned blackboards. This room probably still looked much as it always had. Where there once might have been orderly rows of wooden desks, however, were groups of sturdy chrome and plastic tables and chairs. They looked oddly out of place. I deduced from the wall decorations and mélange of musical instruments scattered about that this was the music room.

"If the reports were coming just from students, I would be inclined to dismiss them. These are fifth graders, after all, and these old building seem to fire their imaginations. But now I've got teachers complaining to me. I hope you can help."

"Tell us again what's been happening," said Ernie.

"This is the music room, as you probably guessed. Lucy Cartwright teaches fourth and fifth graders here.

On some days, she finds things out of place. She normally keeps the furniture arranged pretty much as it is now, but some mornings she finds the desks and chairs lined up in precise rows. I've seen this with my own eyes. She comes in sometimes to find the chalkboard erased, books and instruments in disarray..."

"Aren't there security cameras?" I asked.

"That's just the thing." She looked decidedly uncomfortable. "We've gone over and over the security footage, but nothing has ever turned up."

"What about the cleaning staff?" I asked.

"Yes, that's exactly what we thought at first. But they don't come in every day, and most of the incidents happened on nights when the cleaning people weren't working in this wing. We even switched companies, but the incidents continued. The cleaning people have all passed lie-detector tests." She turned to me and fixed me with the practiced stare that had no doubt struck fear into the heart of many a small child. "Ms. Monroe, you must understand, I am an educated woman. I simply don't believe in this foolishness. I called you hoping you'll be able to get to the bottom of this."

"And what are you going to do if we find solid evidence of paranormal activity?" I asked.

Her shoulders sagged and for a moment she looked very tired. "I don't know."

Mrs. Cartwright's music room seemed like the obvious place to set up. We went back to retrieve Seamus and gather the equipment, stacking our cases of equipment onto dollies. I had to admit that Seamus was turning out to be a welcome addition to the team so far. He worked tirelessly to unpack cases and unroll what always seems like miles of extension cords.

Ernie extracted a gadget from one of the cases. "I hope you're not planning on using that tonight. You know I put absolutely zero stock in those things."

"This? Why, I'll have you know, this is no ordinary speech synthesizer," he replied. "Well, it was at one time. But I've been tinkering around with it."

"What's a speech synthesizer?" asked Seamus.

"Something gullible people waste their money on," I replied.

Ernie ignored me. "A speech synthesizer, my dear boy, is a nifty little tool for those of us in the know. This small box contains recordings of several hundred words and individual phonetic sounds. It has environmental sensors in it that translate fluctuations in the electromagnetic field into sounds. Some of us believe an entity can use it to voice the recorded words. Or even articulate words by assembling the phonetic sounds."

I shook my head. "Ernie, I've used these before and the noises they make are random gibberish."

"Ah, but this is no off-the-shelf Ovilus. My version records all the environmental data it picks up for later analysis. Plus, I've personally gone through the recorded words and sounds and added a few of my own. I know exactly what's in it and what's not.

"Look," he continued, "we won't know until we try it out, right? We should still be able to catch sounds in the subsonic range, and I've personally seen to it that the level of electromagnetic energy required to set it off is significantly higher than normal."

"I don't understand how that helps. Doesn't that just mean that you're making the entity work harder?"

"Possibly, but it also reduces the chance of ordinary background radiation accidentally generating synthesized speech."

It was a losing battle. "Fine," I said. "Use it if it rattles your cage, but I'll take anything you get from it with a huge grain of salt." I left him with his playthings and went out into the hall to set up a video camera. I positioned it with a view of the doors to the music room and auditorium. After a quick inventory of extension cords, I decided to put another camera inside the music room as well, while Ernie installed wireless webcams at all the entrances to this wing of the building. Next, I dug through the bags of miscellaneous goodies looking for something I'd bought earlier that day, just for this particular investigation.

"What have you got there?" asked Ernie.

"This is a highly specialized paranormal research tool otherwise known as a toy car. Observe."

I placed the plastic car in the middle of the hall where it would be in clear view of the digital video camera, and marked the position of its wheels with some chalk from the classroom.

"A stroke of genius," he muttered reverently.

"Well, it's not as glamorous as your gadgets, but I thought it would be appropriate, considering where we are," I said. And, frankly, ghost hunting doesn't always have to involve a lot of high-tech equipment. In fact, sometimes low-tech is best. Unexplained battery drain, for example, is a real and very pesky problem. It's not uncommon for battery powered devices to go abruptly dead, even when they were fully charged going in. It happens more often than not, and we always keep a stash of extra batteries on hand. One possible explanation is that entities use the power from the devices when trying to manifest. Whatever the case, I was rather proud of my toy car idea. No batteries here to go flat.

I went back into the music room to help Ernie finish with the rest of the equipment. Possibly my favorite of Ernie's inventions is a listening device with a parabolic microphone, which we've affectionately nicknamed the sonic ear. It's an odd-looking device that looks like a cross between a toy rifle and a tiny satellite dish. Off-the-shelf, it's used with headphones to amplify very faint sounds. Ernie's modified version has been rigged with a transmitter that sends a feed wirelessly to a computer.

It's capable of capturing the faintest of sounds, and allows us to listen in real-time as well as record. This we set up on a table near the front of the room. Several similarly altered temperature gauges located at strategic points send a constant stream of data back to the computer, where we would be able to detect at a glance any anomalous changes in temperature.

The last thing we did before turning out the lights was to register our voices on the recognition program Ernie had created, which helps us quickly identify any disembodied voices we might have recorded. It saves us hours of tedium later when we examine the evidence.

After assigning Seamus the thankless task of monitoring the computers, we turned the lights out, turned on various meters, and officially started our investigation. I spent some time in the old school auditorium with an infrared camera and EMF meter, where I got absolutely nothing.

I found Ernie in a classroom with a digital voice recorder and a Polaroid camera. "Any luck?" he asked.

"Nope. Nothing so far."

He handed me a stack of instant photos. "There's a small anomaly on this photo, but it might just be a speck of dust."

I studied it for a minute and shook my head. "Moth."

He scowled at me. "Maybe—we'll see."

"Let's go back in the music room and try for some EVPs." EVPs—electronic voice phenomena—are sounds we capture on our electronic devices that we don't immediately hear; we only find them later when we listen to our recordings after the investigation. EVPs are not at all uncommon, but they vary widely in quality and can be categorized according to distinctness and intelligibility. Most of them are very hard to hear and virtually impossible to understand— Class C EVPs in ghost-hunting parlance. At the opposite end of the spectrum is Class A-EVPs that are clearly understandable. We've had a few that were chillingly distinct. In fact, it was an EVP that led us to the astounding discovery we made in our biggest case to date.

I turned my recorder on and crouched as comfortably as I could in a child-sized chair. "Is there anybody here with us tonight?" I asked. "Please don't be afraid of us. You're not in trouble—we just want to talk to you."

Next to me Ernie was fiddling with a K2 meter, an EMF meter that uses colored LEDs that light up in response to electromagnetic radiation. Suddenly all five lights lit up for just an instant, then went dark. "Can you do that again?" he asked, placing the device gently on the edge of the table. As if in response to his questions, the device lit up brightly again. "I think we have a live one here," he said softly to me. Then out loud, "Let's play a little game. We're going to use this machine to find out a little bit about you. We're going to ask you some questions. To tell us yes, just make these lights light up again."

In response to "Are you an adult?" the gadget remained dark. But when he asked "Are you a child?" all the lights flashed and remained lit.

"Are you a girl?" asked Ernie.

The meter remained dark. But when he said "So you're a boy?" all five lights lit up.

"Are you younger than ten?" Nothing.

"Older than ten?" All lights flashed. "Are you eleven?" All the lights lit up and twinkled vigorously.

"That's so cool!" exclaimed Seamus, who had been watching, fascinated.

We continued in this manner for several minutes. If the responses on the meter are trustworthy, our visitor was a little boy about eleven years old, who seemed like a typical kid. This was his school. He liked to play games, seemed to have a particular passion for baseball, and apparently thoroughly enjoyed school. But unfortunately, as often happens when we do this, the answers didn't always make sense.

I asked, "Can you tell us what year it is? Is it before 1900?"

The lights remained dark.

"Is it between 1900 and 1910?" I asked. We waited. Apparently not. There was a positive response for between 1910 and 1920 and 1920 and 1930, then nothing.

"Doesn't really narrow it down, does it?" said Ernie.

I said. "Let's try something else. Is the United States at war?" The lights flickered hesitantly. "Is the year 1918?" There was a feeble flicker that I didn't know how to interpret. "Nineteen forty-two? Forty-three? I don't think this is working, Ernie. We're not getting anything."

"Let's back up. Is it before 1920?" No response. But there was no response for after 1920 either.

"I think I'll try a different line of questioning," said Ernie. We got a few more responses when we tried to find out where our entity lived, but they were confusing. "Do you live here?" got a positive response. But "Do you live in Norton Township?" got no response, no matter how we phrased the question. When I asked "What's your name?" the device went dark and didn't light up again.

We waited patiently, asking questions, in hopes that our new unseen friend would return, to no avail.

"I think it's time to try something else," I said finally. Pointing to my high-tech voice recorder, I said "Can you try speaking into this? It might be able to help us hear you so you can tell us about yourself. Can you tell us your name?"

We waited dutifully, but a shake of his shaggy head told us Seamus wasn't getting anything.

We tried for a little while longer, but got no indications on any of the equipment. "I guess we've lost him," Ernie said finally.

I sighed, frustrated. "We were doing so well. I'm knackered. I think it's time to pack up." They agreed reluctantly and we turned the lights on and started to pack up our stuff.

I was tucking a monitor into its padded case when I heard a shout of excitement from Ernie out in the hall. Seamus and I exchanged glances and went to investigate.

Ernie pointed excitedly to the toy car. It didn't take a particularly close examination of the chalk marks to see that it had rolled several inches from whence it started.

"That's so cool!" muttered Seamus.

"It is pretty exciting," said Ernie, now on his knees measuring the distance the car had traveled. "I just want to check something." He went back into the music room and came back toting an old-fashioned carpenter's level, the kind with the little bubbles trapped in a cylinder of liquid.

"Do you always bring one of those on an investigation?" asked Seamus.

"Well, of course," replied Ernie. "Doesn't everybody?" On his knees again, he crouched next to the toy, shining a flashlight on the level, which he placed carefully. He examined it, then pulled a device out of his pocket.

"What's that?" asked Seamus.

"The electronic version. According to both of these, this floor is about as close to perfectly level as it's possible to get." He picked up the plastic car and examined it closely. "I wish we could leave it here for him to play with. He must get bored and lonely."

"What? With all these kids around in the daytime?" I asked.

"Yeah, but what good does it do when they can't see you or hear you?"

I felt a sudden pang of sympathy for our ghostly little friend. "If you leave it here, some kid'll just take it. Come on, let's go. We can come back."

"You're right." He smiled. "I'm worn out."

§

Exhausted though I was, I couldn't sleep when I got home. I was happy with the way the investigation had gone, and felt it had the potential to be a good case. The meeting earlier at the Deerfield Chamber of Commerce was also on my mind. I couldn't help puzzling over Beatrice Foster's attitude, so I decided to do a little sleuthing. It took me a grand total of five minutes to find the answer. A quick search of the Internet revealed that Beatrice had been the director of marketing for a small non-profit before being offered the job at the Deerfield Chamber of Commerce. A few more clicks and I had what I was looking for. Prominently displayed on the welcome page of the Deerfield *Daily Gazette* was a teaser for an article titled "Haunted Happenings in Deerfield."

I clicked on it, and underneath a color image of the Chamber of Commerce was the subtitle: "Do the ghosts of Bonnie and Clyde still haunt the old Sinclair station?" The author of the jaunty little piece was, unsurprisingly, Beatrice Foster. In the sidebar, ads invited me to check availability at some local B and Bs. The article was basically a marketing campaign, thinly disguised as a travel essay. I was not altogether surprised when I scrolled down and found my name. Between a pitch for the Chamber of Commerce and a recounting of the Bonnie and Clyde gas station robbery legend was a paragraph proudly proclaiming that Margo Monroe and company conducted an investigation there. The Deerfield Chamber of Commerce had not asked my permission to use my name, and there was no mention of the results of the investigation. Although I am slowly getting used to the idea of being a walking tourist attraction—I don't have much of a choice with the way things are around campus these days—I was thoroughly annoyed. Although misleading, nothing in the article was actually false. I fumed over it for a while, then decided that there was nothing to be gained from confronting Beatrice with it.

Smugly satisfied at having gotten to the bottom of at least one mystery, I put my computer away and turned out the light. I was on the verge of finally falling asleep when I remembered something else that had been rattling around in my head. I sat up in bed, my heart pounding. I reran the conversation with Seth at the bookstore coffee shop in my head. Running into him at the Taco Loco was no coincidence—I had told him exactly where to find me and when.

Mr. Goodbody Makes a Move

When I woke up the next day, it was well after 10:00 a.m. I stumbled groggily into my kitchen and was waiting patiently for my fancy new espresso maker to rumble to life when I heard a chime from my purse. I knew before I picked up the phone that it was a text from Tim. In fact, it was the third he'd sent since the previous evening, and I hadn't even noticed. Oops. We talk every evening, or at least exchange texts unless one of us can't for whatever reason. It dawned on me that I hadn't even told him about the investigation at the school. The first message, "Have a good evening Love U," was typical Tim.

The second message, sent quite late the night before said "Hey, where are you? Tried to call but your phone is off." A quick check revealed that I'd missed two phone calls from him as well. The latest message: "Starting to get worried. Is everything OK?"

I texted back "Had an investigation. Sorry I missed you, will explain later." Nothing quite like an attack of guilt so early in the morning. Okay, so it wasn't so early, but still.

After my economy-sized, industrial-strength espresso, I was wide awake but still feeling out of sorts. I slapped on some makeup on and got dressed. Before I left for the lab, I checked the phone again. Tim's reply to my text was a terse "k." I sensed his hurt feelings in that single letter, so I sent another one: "Checking evidence today. Let's talk tonight."

The day was gray and chilly. A light but relentless drizzle had taken the enthusiasm out of the few bedraggled protesters, who were stamping their feet and fidgeting, trying to stay warm. They barely paid any attention to me as I climbed the steps of the horticulture pavilion.

No one was in yet and more coffee was the last thing I needed, so I tried calling Tim. But it rolled to voicemail, so I busied myself with paperwork. I was slogging through the daily barrage of emails, clicking Delete without reading most of them, when I came to one from Seth.

My stomach lurched when I read it.

Some strange things have been happening around the chemistry lab. Can I interest you in having a look?

It sounded intriguing, given the current circumstances, and this seemed as good a time as any to go over there. If I hurried, I'd be able to catch him between classes.

My timing was perfect. I got there just as the last of the students from the morning lab session were leaving. It took every ounce of willpower I had to keep my eyes from straying to the top of the cabinet in the corner where Ernie's webcam was. At least I hoped it was still there.

"Margo, how good of you to stop by. I'm delighted you could come 'round so soon."

"I needed a break," I replied."What's been going on?"

He didn't reply, but instead motioned me into his office.

"Nice computer." I was pretending to admire the impressive chunk of hardware on his desk when I heard the door behind me close quietly. "So," I said, "your email…"

"Yes, Margo, what about it?" I realized he was standing right behind me, a little *too* close behind me. He put his hands on my shoulders and I sidestepped him. This was the wrong thing to do. In the tiny office there was no place to go. He had me wedged against the desk and, before I could get my wits about me, whirled me around and wrapped me in a bear hug, with my arms pinned in front of me. He kissed me hard—so hard that it hurt. I managed to get enough leverage to squirm out of his grip just as he was trying to get his tongue into my mouth. I pushed him away. "Seth! What the hell are you doing?"

He looked stunned for an instant, then recovered smoothly. "You didn't really think I wanted to talk about all that ghost nonsense, did you?"

"Uh, well, yes. As a matter of fact I did."

"Look at me, Margo." He put a finger under my chin and tilted my face up gently. His eyes bore into mine. I didn't have the willpower to look away. This time his kiss was much more gentle. I shivered as a thrill went through me—then I came to my senses and pushed him away.

"Seth, stop. We can't do this."

"Why ever not?" he purred. "You want it as much as I do. Do you deny it?"

"No. No, Seth. You're an attractive and interesting man and I enjoy your company. But that's all. I'm in a relationship, and I don't intend to do anything to jeopardize it."

"What he doesn't know won't hurt him," he murmured, moving toward me again, but I dodged his grasp and was to the door before he could react. An ugly expression crept over his face. "Or maybe it's a 'she.' Perhaps men don't turn you on…"

"Oh, for crying out loud, Seth. What's so hard to understand? I have a boyfriend. I love him. Don't take it personally." I opened the door and was out into the hall before he could respond.

A few students watched me with interest as I practically ran past them into the hall.

When I got back to the lab, Ernie was parked in front of a computer with a huge pair of headphones clamped to his head. When I tapped him on the shoulder, he practically jumped out of his skin.

"You just about gave me a heart attack!"

"Sorry, thought you heard me come in."

"Well, wait till you see what I found…what happened to you?"

"Huh?"

"Your mouth's all swollen. Aren't you a little old to be getting into fights?"

"Oh, that. Yeah, well. There was a little…incident." I told him about the encounter in Seth's office.

"Now do you believe me?" he asked, sounding somewhat self-righteous.

"Honestly, Ernie, I don't know what to believe. By the way, it was all I could do not to look for that camera you left in there. Don't you think you we ought to get it out of there?"

"In due time, my dear, in due time. I'm still keeping an eye on your pal Mr. Goodbody."

I almost broke down and told him about the conversation in the bookstore coffee shop. But I talked myself out of it, rationalizing that it was just a sad story about an unlucky traveler's fatal encounter with a particularly lethal species of jellyfish. "What is it about him that irritates you so?"

"Well, maybe it's the fact that we caught him lurking in the chemistry lab in the middle of the night."

"Yeah, or that he almost caught us doing the same exact thing. Anyway, I thought you and Seth were buds now. He likes your car."

"Everyone likes my car. It's a man thing. You wouldn't understand. You planning on talking to Tim later?"

"Yes. Why?"

"Because you'd better find some excuse to make sure it's by phone and not video."

"Is it that bad?" I dug a mirror out of my purse. It *was* that bad—a bruise was already starting around my mouth. I snapped the compact shut with a sigh. "I'm willing to concede that Seth might be a jerk. Something just conveniently went wrong with my computer's camera."

"Here's something I want you to look at." He tossed a couple of Polaroids in front of me. "Use the magnifying glass."

The images were mostly black, with a couple of fuzzy places here and there. They didn't look like anything to get excited about. "Where were these taken?"

"In the hall. Here's the same view taken with the full-spectrum camera. This bit of red here is the exit sign. But there's something right here." He pointed to a faint glow near one edge.

"Honestly, I think it's just a light artifact. Perhaps a glow from the monitors? You said yourself that Polaroids are good at picking up things conventional photography misses. Doesn't necessarily mean it's an entity."

"Maybe. But I think I see the outline of a human form."

I squinted and stared hard at the image. "I don't see it. What've you got there?" Ernie was clicking through some video footage frame-by-frame.

"Video from the night-vision camera we set up in the hall. Look at this."

He pulled a chair next to him and turned the screen so I could see better. In the night-vision camera, everything has an eerie greenish glow. The plastic car was clearly visible in the center of the floor. He zoomed in on it. "Watch!"

So slowly that at first I wasn't sure it wasn't just my eyes playing tricks, the car moved. The tiny movement was visible only in the tread on the miniature plastic wheel. Then it moved again, a small jerky movement, clearly visible to the naked eye. It rolled another inch or so, then stopped.

"Is that cool or what?" He held up his hand for a high-five, which I returned enthusiastically.

"How about the audio?" I asked.

"Nothing so far. I've run everything through the filter. That's what I was listening to when you came in."

"Can I help?" I asked.

He shrugged. "Be my guest."

I found a pair of headphones and made myself comfortable. Sifting through hours of evidence can be a long, tedious task, even with Ernie's many handy inventions.

One of Ernie's creations was an application that flagged any sound that wasn't a voice of one of investigating team members. I clicked through the file, listening carefully to our conversations. I heard myself say *"Is there anybody here with us tonight? Please don't be afraid of us. You're not in trouble—we just want to talk to you."* Then Ernie's voice: *"Can you do that again?"* as we were getting the hits on the

EMF meter. I was hopeful that our entity, having seemed so eager to communicate through the lights on the meter, might also have managed to make audio contact in response to our questions. But after playing back the recording several times, I came to the conclusion that I was wasting my time.

I glanced at Ernie's monitor. He was watching the video of the same incident. I poked him in the ribs.

"Are you getting anything?"

"No," he said, holding up one earphone. "Nothing but you and me."

"That's disappointing. I was hoping we'd get a name or something."

At that moment the door burst open and Sandy rushed in, out of breath and looking very pleased with himself.

"Where's uh...Willis?" I asked.

"I took him to the groomer's. He's getting all spiffed up."

Ernie rolled his eyes. "It's gonna take more than a trip to the groomer's to help that miserable creature. Is there such a thing as a plastic surgeon for dogs?"

Sandy just smiled at Ernie's jab. "You'll see. When they get finished with him, you won't recognize him. You'll wish Fang looked half as good."

Ernie snorted. "Fang has chew toys that look better than your mangy beast, mate." Fang is Ernie's dog—a minuscule bundle of white fur with enough energy to power a small city, an ear-splittingly shrill bark, and a wardrobe of rhinestone collars. In Ernie's defense, most of the collars had been gifts from fans. Fang had his own following—such was the notoriety we'd gained from our last case.

Sandy ignored him and turned to me, tossing a folder on the table in front of me. "I had some spare time and decided I'd like nothing more than to spend it digging through old property records. You might be surprised to find out that the Rhonda Q. Mills Magnet for Gifted and Talented Children was built on the site of an abandoned orphanage."

A chill ran up my spine. "What about the Norton Township School?"

"Backed right up to the orphanage grounds. All the kids in town, including the children from the orphanage, went to school there. The orphanage was home to indigent kids from all over Throckmorton County. At one time there were as many as a thousand, in a facility designed to house about half that. Interestingly, only a few of the kids were technically orphans—most had been left there by parents that could no longer take care of them. The orphanage was shut down in the 1950s because of allegations of abuse. The buildings fell into decay, and the school district finally bought the land. They got permission to tear the old dormitories down, but the old school building is designated a landmark."

"That explains a lot. I'd be surprised if they didn't have any activity," I said. "Once again I find myself wondering what we would do without you, Sandy."

He flashed a sunny smile. "Hey, it's my job. I thought you might like to see these pics I scanned." He opened the folder and we leafed through copies of some grainy photographs of austere brick buildings. People appeared in a few of the photos. Many of the children were barefoot, and few were smiling. I studied the thin faces and wondered how many of them made it to adulthood. No wonder the school was haunted. A lonely, abandoned child who might not realize they'd passed over would naturally be attracted to a school and the children in it. I thought about the toy car, and sadness suddenly threatened to engulf me.

Ernie took the photo from me. "Life must have been pretty rough for most of these kids," he said thoughtfully. "Good work, Sandy. Are you leaving already?"

Sandy shouldered his backpack and was zipping up his jacket. "Gotta go. Class in five minutes and it's all the way across campus. I just wanted to drop this off first. Cheerio!"

The minute Sandy was out the door, Ernie turned to me. "I want to know what Seth was up to that night we had to hide in the chem lab."

"Oh, come on, Ernie. It's none of your business."

"I'm making it my business."

"Look, I admit you were probably right about Seth. But just because he's a little on the smarmy side..."

"A lot on the smarmy side."

"Okay, just because he's a sleazy, lecherous creep doesn't mean he's up to anything sinister. I think we have other concerns," I said.

"Such as?"

"Such as, that EVP we got from the lab investigation. Think about it—what do we really know about Holmes? Maybe the mild-mannered professor bit is just an act. Just because he's our boss doesn't mean we really know him that well."

"What are you implying? You can't be serious!" he exclaimed, genuinely irritated now.

"No! No, Ernie....I didn't say I suspected him of anything. The whole thing is just starting to make me a little...nervous. If you could have seen his reaction when I showed him that document...."

"I did see his reaction, remember? Look, Margo, something's going on here, and I think Seth is somehow involved. I intend to get to the bottom of it."

I rubbed my forehead; a nasty headache was threatening to erupt. "Why are we discussing this?"

"Because I have a friend with certain...skills."

"Skills? What kind of 'skills'? I'm not sure this is anything I want to know about."

"Get your mind out of the gutter. I know someone who's an ace hacker."

"A hacker? Oh, Ernie, sometimes I think you're starting to lose it."

"Maybe I am. But something about the guy isn't right."

"Well, you're on your own with this one. If you get caught, I will deny everything." I turned to my computer and tried to concentrate on work, but the encounter with Seth had left me in a sour mood. I pushed it out of my mind then, against my will, found myself ruminating over our conversation in the coffee shop. The more I thought about it, the more it struck me as being utterly sinister. I poked around on the internet until I was convinced that his harrowing story about the jellyfish might actually be true. It wasn't until I needed an infusion of caffeine and got a cup of coffee that I remembered what else we'd talked about.

"Hey, Ernie. Have you ever been to Paris?"

"Yeah. Why?"

"What do you know about the Bois de Boulogne?"

"The Bois de...isn't that the red-light district? If you're asking if I've been there—no, I haven't. Why do you ask?"

"Oh, nothing. Just something Seth said that made me wonder."

He arched an eyebrow but said nothing.

A Close Call for Our Boss

Ernie's phone rang. He seemed relieved. Maybe the conversation about the Bois de Boulogne was making him uncomfortable, or maybe it was just his general disdain for all things Seth. "Yes, speaking," he said. I could tell by the tone of his voice and the way he wrinkled his brow that something was wrong. Our eyes met and he shrugged. "Well, yes, of course, sir. We'll be there right away. Of course, no problem." Pause. "Okay, bye."

He disconnected the call and gave me a sideways glance. "Dean Cresswell wants to see us. Right away."

Oh dear. This was rather like getting a summons from the Pope. "Did he say what it was about?"

"Nope, but it was the man himself, not his secretary."

A thought too horrible to contemplate crept into my brain. "Oh hell! You don't think they found out about....?"

He slapped his forehead. "Let's hope not. Anyway, how would they know it's us?"

"Possibly because the school bought us fifteen cameras just like that one last year." My legs suddenly felt all wobbly. "Well, no use putting it off," I said, trying to sound more confident than I felt.

We slunk out the back door and trudged across campus. I felt like a naughty child being summoned to the principal's office.

The administration office was in a sleek, modern building on the other side of the campus. A hundred scenarios, each more horrible than the last, went through my head on our walk over. By the time we got there, I was certain we were both about to be fired. I'd have to find a normal job. What if I couldn't? I might have to sell my house and move in with Tim. Come to think of it, maybe getting fired wouldn't be so bad after all.

Ernie opened the glass door for me and I approached the receptionist, a heavyset, middle-aged black woman whose hair was pulled into a sleek bun so severe it made my eyebrows hurt to look at her. We introduced ourselves and she smiled at us perfunctorily. "Dr. Cresswell is expecting you. Right this way, please." We had to scramble to keep up with her as she led us down a carpeted hallway and knocked on a door.

"Yes, yes. Come!" said the muffled voice behind the door.

As we entered the office, she closed the door and retreated soundlessly.

"Mr. Stapleton, Ms. Monroe, come in please." Dr. Cresswell was a stiff, rather formal-looking man with a neatly trimmed white mustache and a fringe of wispy white hair. Judging from the cut of his suit, I figured he must have been going to the same tailor since before I was born. "I'm afraid I have something rather unpleasant to discuss with you." He motioned to a couple of chairs. "Won't you have a seat?"

I took this as a good sign—surely if you were planning on firing somebody you wouldn't invite them to sit down.

We settled meekly, into the chairs. Neither of us could have predicted what came next.

"I called you both here because I'm afraid I have some very bad news. Ben—Dr. Holmes—was in an accident this morning. He was badly injured and is in ICU at Sisters of Mercy. I wanted to tell you before you heard about it from someone else. " He paused as if expecting me to say something, but words utterly failed me. "The officer on the scene reported that the car's brakes appear to have been sabotaged."

It didn't take long before the implications of what the dean had just said hit me. I stole a glance at

Ernie. He was gripping the arms of his chair so hard his knuckles were white.

"What happened? Does anybody know?" I managed to ask.

"His brakes failed and he plowed into the back of a delivery van. He's exceedingly lucky to be alive."

"Is he conscious? Can he have visitors?" asked Ernie.

Cresswell shook his head. "Unfortunately the answer is 'no' to both of your questions. I'm afraid that's not the worst of it, however. His house was also burglarized. The police would like to speak with both of you. As a matter of routine, of course. Unless, perhaps, either of you knows anything that might shed some light on this?"

"We—that is, I don't think so, Dr. Cresswell," I said.

"Mr. Stapleton?"

Ernie shook his head and swallowed hard. He looked like he was fighting back tears.

"Then here's a number for you to call. Please contact them as soon as possible." Dean Cresswell handed me a card embossed with a number and the logo of the Indian Springs Police Department.

Meekly we mumbled our assurances that we would, and the receptionist materialized to show us out.

§

An hour later Ernie and I were at the police station in downtown Indian Springs. We were shown to a bleak, windowless room with the kind of overhead florescent lighting that makes everyone look slightly ill. The only furniture was wooden conference table with a scarred linoleum top and some ancient armless metal chairs.

We'd been sitting in the overheated room for perhaps twenty minutes when the door flew open and two cops sauntered in. Much to my dismay, one of them was Officer Kruszinsky, my nemesis on the Indian Springs police force. Ernie's face turned the color of oatmeal. We'd had a minor run-in with Kruszinsky the previous summer. One of Ernie's hunches had turned out to be spectacularly wrong when were snooping around in an abandoned church that he was convinced would yield clues in a case. Kruszinsky discovered us and hauled us down to the police station. Rollie, the church's custodian, came to our rescue before we could be booked for trespassing, but not before I'd been spotted by my ex, Roger, and his nubile, surgically enhanced new girlfriend. Kruszinsky seems to have since taken an irrational dislike to us. The feeling was quite mutual.

"Can I get you a coffee or something, ma'am?" asked Kruszinsky. He said 'ma'am' as though it left a nasty taste in his mouth. To Ernie he just pointed and raised an eyebrow.

"No, thanks," we said in unison.

The other policeman was a painfully thin young man wearing glasses with thick black frames. He introduced himself as Officer Toby Garcia of the Throckmorton PD. It took me a minute to figure out what the Throckmorton PD was doing here. Although the accident was in Throckmorton, Dr. Holmes lives in Indian Springs.

We were joined shortly by a balding man with a large nose. He was wearing a tacky polyester tie and a short-sleeve shirt and introduced himself to us simply as Sullivan. His name was on the card the dean had given me.

Officer Garcia sat across from us watching my every move. Detective Sullivan stood behind them, hovering like some kind of very large bird of prey.

"You understand that this is strictly routine," said Sullivan.

"Excuse me," I asked, "but are we under suspicion for something?"

Kruszinsky paced around the room like a caged animal. "No," replied Kruszinsky smoothly, in a tone that suggested we were very much under suspicion for pretty much everything. "But we do need to ask you a few questions."

"This won't take long," added Sullivan.

Officer Garcia started off. "Any idea if Professor Holmes might have been involved in anything outside of work? Something that might have been in some way dangerous?"

In retrospect, I probably should have told them right then and there about the weird email attachment, but I pegged this motley assortment of small town cops to be the absolute *least* likely people in the world to take seriously a story that starts with a voicemail from a dead man. I decided to keep my mouth shut and hoped I didn't seem nervous. Luckily, no one seemed to notice that Ernie looked like he was about to woof up his lunch.

"Do you know if Dr. Holmes has any enemies?"

"No, no, of course not. Dr. Holmes is very well respected," I said.

"Was he acquainted with Nigel Pritchett?" asked Sullivan.

The question hit me like a thunderbolt. Of course there had to be a connection. Why hadn't it occurred to me? They were waiting patiently for an answer.

"They were good friends," said Ernie.

"When you say 'good friends' do you mean *really* good friends?" sneered Kruszinsky.

"What are you implying?" Ernie snapped indignantly.

"Well, two single men…"

"Dr. Holmes is a widower. His wife died a few years ago after almost 30 years of marriage. Pritchett, from what I read in the papers, was divorced. Of course they were friends—why wouldn't they be? They've known each all their lives. They went to school together. Anything other than that I have no idea," replied Ernie hotly.

Detective Sullivan stepped between Ernie and Kruszinsky with a disgusted look at Kruszinsky. "Do you recall Dr. Holmes ever seeming particularly nervous or anxious about anything?"

Unbidden, the EVP we picked up on our investigation popped into my head. "Not that I know of." I forced myself not to look at Ernie and hoped my body language wasn't giving anything away.

On it went in a similar fashion for a few more minutes, the cops posturing and strutting. It dawned on me that they were grasping at straws.

"Look," I said finally. "I know you have to cover all your bases, but we don't know any more than you do. We work for him, that's all. In fact, I was hoping you could tell us something."

There was an awkward silence. Finally Sullivan spoke. "All right then, we'll level with you. We don't have much in way of any leads on this case. All we know at this point is that it was no accident and no amateur job. Whoever cut your boss' brake lines knew exactly what he was doing. It's clearly attempted murder, but we have no motive, no suspect. No one seems to have any ideas why someone would try to murder Dr. Holmes. Two professors from the same college, one dead, one almost. There hasn't been a murder in Throckmorton County since 1934. The chiefs of police and mayors of both Indian Springs and Throckmorton are on my ass, and I don't have a single thing to go on."

"So you think there's a connection between Dr. Pritchett's murder and Dr. Holmes' accident?" asked Ernie.

"That's what we're trying to find out here, Mr. Stapleton," said Kruszinsky.

"Dean Cresswell said Holmes' house had been broken into," I said. "Do you know what was stolen?"

Kruszinsky paced the floor for a moment, then shook his head. "We're not sure if anything was actually stolen. Nothing that usually makes an attractive target for thieves was touched. But the house was ransacked from attic to basement. The contents of every drawer, cabinet, and closet were emptied onto the floor. Even the mattresses and pillows had been slashed open."

"I'd appreciate it if you'd think about it carefully. Try to remember anything that you think might help," said Sullivan. "You have my card. If you can think of anything—anything at all, no matter how trivial it might seem, you call me. Any time."

As we were walking to my car, I heard someone call my name.

We turned to see who it was. "Oh, great," mumbled Ernie. "I wonder if this is some kind of interrogation ploy. Let them think they're free to go, catch them off their guard."

"Excuse me!" The skinny cop with black glasses that had been staring at me was trotting toward us. "Ms. Monroe?"

"Um, yes..."

He caught up with us.

"Sorry, officer," said Ernie. "But is something wrong?"

"Oh, no. Not at all. I just wanted to tell you that I think what you're doing is really great," said the cop, his face coloring. "With the ghost research and all, I mean. Toby Garcia." He offered his hand, still staring at me.

"What a nice surprise," I said. "It's nice to know I —we have a fan."

"Yeah, that thing with the symphony—man, that was really cool."

"Thanks." I replied. "It's nice to know our work is appreciated. Speaking of which, we ought to be getting back to the lab."

He narrowly missed running into a lamp post. "Oh, right."

"Well, Officer Garcia. It was a pleasure meeting you...um, this is my car."

"Okay Marg—Ms. Monroe. Maybe I'll see you around?"

"More than likely."

We got in the car and he stood on the curb, waving at us as we drove away. He reminded me very much of a lovesick teenager.

"Now I know how it feels to be invisible. I think he likes you," remarked Ernie.

"Ya think?"

"Maybe I should warn Tim."

"Nah, not my type. Too skinny. You up for a drink?"

"You read my mind."

§

We headed straight for the Monk's Habit, the neighborhood pub which inhabited the shell of an abandoned church. Although it was a Friday night, it was still rather early and the Monk wasn't crowded yet. The big-screen TV in the corner was tuned to a football game. A handful of faithfuls in green and gold jerseys were clustered at the end of the bar, staring intently at the screen. Farley, the owner, greeted us from behind the bar as we walked in.

Out of habit, we headed straight for our usual table under a stained glass window depicting the story of St. George and the dragon. We ordered beers from a waitress who cast frankly admiring glances in Ernie's direction. She was a pretty girl, but her tattered jeans and faded T-shirt were about a size too small.

"I'll just have a Guinness," said Ernie, without a glance at her. I ordered my usual Belligerent Bastard. "You know," he said thoughtfully after she left, "if I didn't know better, I'd say we have a serial killer in Throckmorton."

"I doubt it. Whoever heard of a serial killer that attacks middle-aged college professors? But there's certainly *something* going on. Should we have told those cops about the document—the one Holmes almost went ballistic over?"

"Maybe. I mean, I would have, if it'd been anybody but Kruszinsky. That guy suffers from a severe case of recto-cranial inversion."

"Huh?"

"He's got his head up his ass."

"I couldn't have put it better myself," I chuckled.

There was a buzz of excitement from the green and gold team's fans that culminated abruptly in a groan of disappointment. I looked at the giant screen in time to see a football bouncing off of a goalpost.

The waitress returned with our beers. It seemed to me she lingered slightly longer than necessary as she put Ernie's drink in front of him.

"You sure you don't want to talk about what's bothering you?" I asked, after a few minutes watching Ernie stare moodily into his beer.

"What makes you think something's bothering me?" he snapped.

"Well for starters, that girl practically shoved her cleavage in your face and you didn't even notice."

"Did she?" He looked over his shoulder and perused the crowd with interest for a minute. The waitress in question was at a table near the front door taking orders. "Son of a ..." I followed his gaze.

Elaine had just come in, and she was with a guy. He seemed familiar to me, but it took me a minute to figure out where I'd seen him before. It was the businessman who'd been sitting at the table next to Elaine and me when we stopped for drinks at the Pig and Whistle. How did she do that? I never saw them exchange so much as a word. He wrapped an arm around her and led her to a table out of our line of sight. Ernie looked like a little kid who'd just discovered that his iPod-shaped Christmas present contains socks.

He slumped in his seat and inhaled the rest of his beer. When, a few minutes later, the cute waitress breezed by, he waved his empty glass at her. "Can I get you another?" she asked, nodding in my direction.

"I'm fine at the moment, thanks," I said. Actually I'd barely started on my own beer. "Hey, we can leave if you want to."

He straightened up and squared his shoulders manfully. "And let her chase me out of my favorite hangout? No way. Have they seen us?"

"I don't think so. So are you going to tell me what happened between you two?"

The sad look returned to his eyes. "Margo, she's let me know in every way possible that I don't mean as much to her as she does to me."

"Well, didn't you pretty much know that going in? You should be working on changing that. It's not like you to give up so easily."

He pinched the bridge of his nose. "I was nuts about her for such a long time." This might have been the supreme understatement. For years, he had been walking-into-walls in love with her. "I think maybe the reality doesn't stack up against my fantasies."

"But I still don't understand. Why all the drama?"

He sighed. "She says I'm too possessive. Do you mind if we talk about something else?"

"Okay. Tim's coming out. I'm picking him up at the airport tomorrow."

His stormy expression changed to one of genuine delight. "What's the occasion?"

"Homecoming."

"Homecoming? You've got to be kidding!"

"Nope. Indian Springs' Homecoming is next week. For some reason he decided he wanted to go."

Ernie chuckled. "It should be a lot of fun. I've never been to homecoming. I haven't been to a football game since high school."

"You could go with us," I said. "You know, a double date."

His expression darkened. "Yeah, well I'd have to find someone to take."

"You don't think maybe Elaine would like to go?"

"It doesn't matter if she would. I have no intention of asking her," he said, glowering at me.

"Sorry I brought it up."

He perked up slightly. "I'm looking forward to seeing Tim. What time's his flight?" He was genuinely thrilled, but there was a certain wistfulness in his voice.

"He should be here by lunch time. Hey, why don't you ask Elaine to homecoming? We could double-date."

"Are you kidding? She's already moved on. Did you see how she was looking at that guy when they walked in?"

"Don't be a dork. You don't even know who that guy is. He could be her long-lost cousin for all we know. Kiss and make up. You'll feel better."

"They still there?"

"I think so. So are we hiding here until they leave?"

"The thought did cross my mind."

When the waitress returned with Ernie's beer, she deftly made sure their fingers touched as she set the glass down. This time the gesture was not lost on Ernie.

"You must be new here," he said.

"Yeah, this is my first week. How'm I doing so far?"

"No complaints. I'm Ernie." He offered his hand. "This is my friend Margo," he added as an afterthought.

"I'm Megan. Nice to meet you." She barely glanced in my direction.

I manufactured a sudden need to go to the ladies' room. As I was washing my hands, Elaine came in.

"Margo!" She enveloped me in a hug. "It's so good to see you. Hey, I heard about Dr. Holmes."

"Yeah, we're all pulling for him. He's a trooper, though; he'll be okay." I decided it was prudent not to say too much, but couldn't resist adding a little jab. "Ernie and I had a rough day, so we decided to stop in and decompress a little."

At the mention of Ernie's name, she stiffened a little. "Oh, is Ernie here? I didn't see you guys come in."

"Actually, we were here before you got here. We, um, saw you come in. But we'll probably leave soon."

As if reading my thoughts, she said "I ran into that guy at a seminar. He remembered me from the Pig and Whistle that day we were there."

"Well, he's kind of cute…"

"You think so?" she said, primping in the mirror. Stacks of bracelets jangled on her arm as she applied fresh lipstick. "Um…so how *is* Ernie?"

I decided to take a gamble. "He's fine, but I think he'd appreciate hearing from you. By the way, Tim's coming to town. For some reason, he got it in his head that he wanted to go to our high school's homecoming."

"Oh, doesn't that sound like fun!"

I couldn't tell whether she was being sarcastic. "I don't know if *fun* is the right word…" I said.

"No, really. It's something I always wanted to do. Sounds like a great time, in fact."

"Really?" It never would have crossed my mind that Elaine would want to do something as pedestrian as go to the Indian Springs High homecoming game.

"Yeah," she said wistfully. "I went to an all-girls school. We didn't even have a football team. You're going to have so much fun!"

"I'm not as optimistic. Well, I guess I'd better get back."

"Wait!" she said. "I need your opinion on something. I went with my friend Sally last weekend to investigate the bed and breakfast her boyfriend bought. You've heard me talk about her—she's the one that lives way out in the country. Anyway, we got a couple of EVPs, really good, clear ones, and I was wondering if you'd have a listen and give us your opinion."

"Sure thing. Email them to me. I can't promise I'll get to them right away."

"Oh, I understand," she replied with a wink. "Tell Tim I said 'Hello' if I don't see him."

"Will do."

On the way back to my table, I briefly pondered possible scenarios in which Ernie and Elaine might be maneuvered into a situation where they'd be forced to speak to each other. However, I came to the conclusion that it would only get me into trouble.

"Took you long enough," said Ernie when I got back to our table.

"There was a line."

"Really? There's hardly anyone here."

"You know how it is...always takes us longer. So, are we ready? To go, I mean."

"Yep, paid the tab already and everything." He seemed much more chipper than he had just a few minutes ago.

"Everything?"

He looked like the proverbial cat that swallowed the canary. "I don't suppose you and Tim want to take me up on my idea about a double-date for homecoming."

"Oh, Ernie, you didn't!"

"And why not?"

Out of the corner of my eye, I saw Elaine on her way back to the table where her date was waiting.

"Well for starters, she's barely out of high school herself."

"And your point is...?"

I sighed. "Look, you don't have to bring a date. Why don't you just come with us?"

"And be the third wheel while you two make goo-goo eyes at each other all night? Thanks, but no thanks."

"We don't 'make goo-goo eyes' at each other. Come on, let's go."

He waved jauntily at Megan on the way out, pointedly not looking in the direction of the table where Elaine was sitting.

"Ernie, why don't you just call her? I'm pretty sure she'd be happy to hear from you."

"I know you mean well. Don't worry about me. Things are looking up—honestly."

The Writing on the Blackboard

My alarm went off before the sun was even up. In my line of work, I'm seldom up so early unless I was out all night the night before.

When I sat down at my vanity table to get dressed, my stomach was churning. Even though we talk almost every day, I still get the jitters before I see Tim. I suppose this is normal for a long-distance relationship. On the other hand, you'd think I'd be over it by now, considering how long we've known each other. We met when I was a sophomore and he a freshman in high school. He was the kid brother I never had. Then I went away to college, and suddenly twenty years had gone by.

In high school, my friend Roxy, Tim and I were all but inseparable. Roxy and I were fiercely protective of Tim, and we spent a good many hours thinking of ways to wreak merciless revenge on those who dared to tease him. Perhaps because of his short stature, or maybe because he was a whiz-kid extraordinaire, it was inevitable, I suppose, that he attracted a certain amount of negative attention. The jocks called him 'Frodo' and played tricks on him—until Roxy and I came along, that is. Most of the bullies, once they realized we weren't going to back down, gave up and began treating him with grudging respect. But not all of them, and there were a few all-out wars between the three of us and the in-crowd.

After graduation, I couldn't get out of town fast enough. My personal motto was "Happiness is Indian Springs in the rearview mirror." Like most people, I lost touch with most of my old friends and Tim and I lived our separate lives. He married and eventually divorced, and I embarked on a career. After years of the manic frenzy of Boston, I moved back to Indian Springs.

Several months ago the team and I were right in the middle of what turned out to be our first high-profile case when, out of the blue, I got an email from Timmy. He wrote to tell me he was going to be in Indian Springs for a few days and wanted to know if we could get together.

When I agreed to meet him for dinner, I still had in my head a picture of the kid I'd known so many years ago—the short, chubby little guy with almond-shaped eyes hidden behind big aviator-frame glasses. I wasn't prepared to be completely swept off my feet by the tall, handsome man that he'd become. We did more than get back in touch—we fell head over heels in love. He confessed that he'd loved me since high school. Since then, the relationship has grown steadily stronger as we battled the highs and lows of a relationship between soul-mates who live almost two thousand miles apart. It hasn't always been easy. But we have the advantage of a solid base of friendship. He's the first man I've ever met that I think I could spend the rest of my life with.

As I studied my reflection, I decided that Tim would forgive me if I showed up at the airport with uncoiffed hair. It's an unusual shade of auburn that flatters my complexion (although I'm noticing the occasional gray strand these days), and I recently got it cut and styled. But on most days it does what it wants, so I rubbed a little bit of styling gel into it and left it at that.

Of more concern was a small, dark bruise at the corner of my mouth. I dabbed some concealer on it and examined the results. The results weren't encouraging. If I were lucky, he'd just assume it was because of my late nights stumbling around in the dark chasing spirits. Deciding I would cross that bridge when I came to it, I finished putting on my makeup. Glancing at the clock I saw that I still had plenty of time, so I turned the espresso maker on and got dressed while it was brewing. I slipped into my favorite jeans, which—I like to think, anyway—are comfy yet sexy at the same time.

I poured my cappuccino into a to-go cup and went out door with my stomach still fluttering.

§

Rush hour was over and traffic surprisingly light in San Guillermo, so I ended up at the airport in plenty of time, much to my surprise. I had time to drink another coffee, which possibly might not have been the most brilliant of ideas. By the time I was halfway through it, my stomach was turning cartwheels.

A tinny voice made an unintelligible announcement over the PA system. I could only guess that they must be announcing the arrival of Tim's flight. Eventually a few people started trickling out of the gate, then a few more. My hands were clammy and my stomach was all in knots.

Then a tall, delightfully gorgeous guy emerged, juggling a carry-on bag and an overcoat. He's a little taller than me and slender, although not as thin as Ernie. He usually wears contacts, but today he had on fashionable wire-framed glasses. His eyes have a slightly exotic look, from an Asian grandparent. It seemed like there might be slightly more gray in his black hair, just at the temples, but it was hard to tell.

He dropped his bag and I rushed into his arms. He wrapped me in a tight hug, then kissed me passionately. "God, Margo, I'm so happy to be here."

"That makes two of us. Oh, Timmy, I thought today would never get here. Did you check any bags?"

We held hands and chatted happily as we waited for his suitcase to arrive. I had that first-day-of-vacation feeling as we threw his stuff into the back of my car.

In the car, I filled him in on recent events. He knew about the murder, of course. But Dr. Holmes' accident, the break-in, and our trip to the police station were news. "There's a connection between the murder and the attack on Dr. Holmes—that much is obvious. Even the cops admitted that much," I concluded.

He tried to make light of it, but I could sense that he was concerned. "Two poky little country towns like Throckmorton and Indian Springs. I mean, the most exciting thing that ever happened when I was here was when Coach Sparkes married that cheerleader my sophomore year. There probably hasn't been a murder in a hundred years."

"Nineteen thirty-four," I said. At his questioning look I added, "Squabble over a barbed-wire fence that turned ugly."

"I think you should have told the cops about the phone call and the weird email."

"I will. Eventually. How was your flight, by the way? You tired?"

"Not much. I had to get up at an ungodly hour, but I'll be okay. What's on the agenda for today?"

I smiled wickedly. "I thought we might go home and just kind of ....relax."

He took my free hand and kissed it. "I was hoping you were going to say something like that."

We had just merged onto the freeway when the phone rang. With one hand on the steering wheel I fished the phone out of my purse. "Sorry," I said, "it's business—I should get this."

I barely had time to say "hello." On the other end was Principal Emily Golding, screeching at me hysterically.

I pulled over to the side of the road. "Emily, please calm down." I was holding the phone a good six inches from my ear, but she was screaming so loud we could both hear.

"You want to switch sides and let me drive?" whispered Tim.

"Good idea." I let her rant while Tim and I got out and traded sides.

"If this is your idea of a joke—" she steamed.

I interrupted her tirade. "Emily, I assure you, I don't have the slightest clue what you're talking about. What joke?"

"My classroom has been vandalized! Has one of your people been here?" By now she had calmed down enough that I could actually hold the phone to my ear without danger of damaging my eardrum.

"Trust me, no one's been there. Can you explain to me what's going on?"

"I think it would be better if you see this for yourself." She was starting to sound rational again.

I explained her request to Tim. "Do you mind if we make a stop on the way home?"

His eyes were twinkling. "Not in the slightest."

"We'll be there fifteen minutes," I told Principal Golding. I sighed. So much for the romantic welcome I'd planned for my boyfriend.

Next I called Ernie. "Can you meet us at the elementary school?"

"Be there in ten."

"This is kind of exciting," remarked Tim. "It's almost as good as going with you on an investigation."

"You wouldn't be as excited if it had been you she was screaming at. She seems to think we've resorted to some clever trickery to make our point."

I found a parking space in front in a one-hour zone and we went in. As Tim and I neared the school offices we could hear Emily, from all the way down the hall. "What could be taking her so long?" Of Ernie's reply I heard only bits: "...from the airport...you know how the traffic..." The receptionist waved us in and I prepared myself for the onslaught.

"I got here as soon as I could." I introduced Tim. Ms. Golding nodded curtly but didn't offer to shake hands. "I understand that you're upset; maybe it will help if you..."

She spun on her heel like a drill sergeant and began walking briskly down the hall. "Come with me," she barked. The sound of Emily's heels clicking on the linoleum floor echoed loudly around us as we scurried after her down the hall to the old wing. Classes were in session. I caught snippets of classroom discussions through open doors, the drone of adult and child voices punctuated occasionally by laughter.

A youngish woman was standing outside the door to Chester's classroom. Chester's teacher, Mrs. Cartwright, I presumed. She had obviously been crying.

Ms. Golding introduced us and threw open the classroom door. It didn't take much imagination to see what had set Mrs. Cartwright off. Scrawled across the entire blackboard in large, shaky letters was "MY NAME IS THEODORE."

Ernie passed a strange-looking gadget over the surface of the chalkboard, stopping occasionally to take a photo or speak into his iPad. The rest of us squeezed awkwardly into child-sized desks. Mrs. Cartwright eventually stopped crying. But then she looked at the blackboard and started sobbing again hysterically.

"You're absolutely positive," I asked "that no one else has a key? Or might have had one made without your knowledge?"

"Of course not," sniffed Mrs. Cartwright. She was a rather short, plump blonde with a pretty face. She didn't look old enough to have been teaching for very many years. I felt sorry for her. This sort of thing can be pretty unnerving for the uninitiated, and even for seasoned veterans at times.

"It will be easy enough to find out if anybody was in here last night. If anyone was here after hours, they'll be on the security tape," I said. "You won't mind letting us look?"

I thought for a minute she was going to say no, but ultimately she said, "I suppose we don't have much choice, do we?"

Somewhere a bell rang, followed seconds later by a stampede in the hall. A chorus of giggles and shrill voices grew louder. Three little girls, all attired in various shades of pink, started to walk in, but at the sight of the principal, they stopped short and did an about-face.

"Not if you want to know for sure whether this is a trick. This may not be what you want to hear, but I think you have a significant amount of paranormal activity here." I told them about the moving car and the conversation we'd had via EMF meter. "We also did a little conventional research and found out some things about the school that you might find interesting."

"I know about the orphanage," said Principal Golding gloomily.

"Would it help if we showed you what we found?" asked Ernie.

"I'm certain it would," answered the principal. Mrs. Cartwright was looking positively green.

"Then why don't we come back after school?" I said with a glance at the students hovering timidly in the doorway.

§

Tim had never been to the horticulture pavilion. We parked and he stared in amazement at the little throng of loonies lounging about the sidewalk with their tacky signs.

"Sorry. I guess I should have told you about our reception committee."

"Do you have to go through this every time you come to work?"

"Pretty much," I answered. "To be honest, I've more or less gotten used to it. You ready?" As soon as we stepped out of the car, the protesters began chanting and yelling. They waved their misspelled posters in our faces as we dashed down the sidewalk and up the stairs.

"I don't like it," said Tim. "They're all a little bit..."

"Crazy? Quite possibly. Of course, they think the same thing about me."

"They strike me as decidedly unstable. What if one of them tries to get at you? Those cops aren't going to be much help if something happens—provided one of them did actually happen to wake up."

"They're harmless. Stop worrying. You sound like my mother." We went down the hall where the usual cluster of people were milling about. I couldn't help but notice that some of the girls were checking Tim out appreciatively.

"A broom closet?" he asked incredulously as I pushed him through the door. "Did anybody really think that would keep this place a secret?"

"It seemed like a good idea at the time. Then we ended up on the news and that was the end of that." I swiped my access card and the door clicked.

"Electronic doors? Nice!" he mused.

"Yeah, they keep the riff-raff out."

"What if the power goes out? Wouldn't you be trapped inside?"

"Nah, it has all kinds of safety features. If the electricity goes off, it pops right open." Inside the lab, I pointed out the security monitor near the door. "So we can see what's going on in the hall outside...for what it's worth."

"Impressive."

Sandy was sitting at a computer with a frown on his face. He appeared to be studying something intently. "Hi, Sandy. You remember Tim. Ah, yes, and this—this is Willis."

Willis was now marginally less ugly than before. His toenails had been painted a fashionable blue. He looked, I thought, rather pleased with his new haircut, which closely resembled a mohawk.

Tim proceeded to make friends with the creature. "Has he met Fang?" he asked.

"Not yet," said Sandy.

Ernie came in, lugging his usual assortment of bags and boxes.

"Did you get the security vids?" I asked.

"Right here," he said, patting a backpack. "Give me a minute to set up, and I'll start running them through the video filter."

"Sandy, we could use your help." I said.

"Sure thing. I heard about the excitement at the school. What can I do?"

"We need to see what we can find out about a kid at the Throckmorton Township School named Theodore—pronto. We have until 3:00 p.m., when school lets out."

"That's not much time. I could use some help."

My visions of a little afternoon delight vanished.

"We'll be happy to help out," said Tim. "Surely three heads are better than one."

"Four," said Sandy. "Seamus is working at the library today. Ernie, would you mind if I leave Willis here with you?"

"It's what I live for," answered Ernie, rolling his eyes.

"Good man," said Sandy. "Come along, kids. I suspect we have our work cut out for us."

So Much for a Romantic Evening with Tim

"Did your, uh—entity give you any idea of the time frame we ought to be looking for?" asked Sandy as he plunked a massive leather-bound volume on the table in front of Tim.

"We've narrowed it down as best we could. But the responses we got didn't always make sense," I said.

We were in the Indian Springs library, where Seamus had escorted us proudly to the local history section. "I haven't seen the evidence from that night" said Seamus. "Any chance you could show it to me?"

"Well, I have it right here." I pulled out my iPad. "Will you be okay with this Sandy?"

Sandy shuddered. His aversion to anything paranormal was beyond reasoning. "If I must," he said, sounding braver than I suspect he was feeling.

"Well, let me know if it gets to be too much." I found the footage in question and propped the iPad up on a stack of books so we could all watch.

I watched myself ask *"Can you tell us what year it is? Is it before 1900? Is it between 1900 and 1910?"*

The flashing lights showed up clearly in the grainy black-and-white video.

Then Ernie saying, *"Doesn't really narrow it down, does it?"*

Then me saying, *"Let's try something else. Is the United States at war? Is the year 1918?"* and the hesitant flicker on the meter. *"Nineteen forty-two? Forty-three? I don't think this is working, Ernie. We're not getting anything."*

On the video Ernie said, *"Let's back up. Is it before 1920?"*

We watched until our question about the entity's name, when the meter's lights had stopped flashing altogether.

Sandy had been watching this all with an expression of extreme distaste on his usually cheerful face. "Something doesn't make sense," he said. "You got a 'yes' for 1910 through 1920 and 1920 through 1930. Twenty years is a pretty long time span to be uncertain about. Any theories?"

"It's not all that unusual for an entity to respond with inaccurate or conflicting answers. But no, I don't have a theory. Whether this is because they're confused about where they are, don't realize they're dead, or want to trick us is hard to say. Besides, there's only so much you can find out from yes/no questions."

"Well," said Sandy, "let's look at what we *do* know. You've got a boy named Theodore, eleven years old. We don't know what year it is to him, but my theory—if the response on your meter wasn't just a random EMF fluctuation—is that he's old enough to remember World War I. When was World War I?"

"It started in 1914 and lasted until 1918, but the United States didn't get involved until 1917," replied Seamus.

"Allow me to point out something," said Tim. "You asked if the year was between 1910 and 1920, then asked if it was 1920 and 1930. Suppose the year—as far as our entity is concerned—is 1920. In that case, 'yes' is the correct response to both questions. Maybe you confused him."

"Of course! It seems so obvious now." I stole a glance at my beloved, who was looking mighty pleased with himself.

Said Sandy, "If Tim is right, then your entity was born around 1909. If we're lucky, we'll find him in the census." He pointed to large two leather-bound books embossed with *Throckmorton County Census* in fading gold letters. One was stamped 1870-1910, the other 1920-1940.

"And if we're not lucky?" I asked.

Sandy shrugged. "Then we have to come up with a Plan B."

"I don't get it," said Seamus.

"It's very simple. We have to look through these for everybody named Theodore. In the 1910 census he'd be about a year old."

"Suppose we're off by a year. What if he was born in 1910 after the census was taken?" asked Tim.

"Then he won't show up until the 1920 census. Those are the breaks. If there's the slightest possibility it might be our Theodore, write it down. And let's hope Theodore wasn't a popular name," added Sandy.

"But there must be thousands of names here!" exclaimed Tim.

"Precisely. Which means you'd better get to work. In the meantime, Seamus and I are going to start looking through the newspapers for obituaries," said Sandy. They toddled off toward the microfiche readers.

"Happy reading," I said, flipping open the 1920 census.

§

A couple of hours and one massive headache later, I had found but one potential Theodore. Tim hadn't uttered a sound. He was hunched over the massive book rubbing his eyes. "How's it going over there?" I asked.

"Ugh. This guy's handwriting is next to impossible to read. And I think I'm getting a stiff neck," he said flexing his shoulders gingerly.

"Welcome to my world. Have you found anything?"

"Two Theodores, both around a year old in 1910," he replied

"Well, you're doing better than I am. So far, the only Theodore I have was 11 years old in 1920, living at home with parents and a younger sister. I don't think he's the one."

"Named Higson?"

"Yes. The father's occupation is listed as 'banker'"

"Yep, that's it. Did you look to see if he's in the 1930 census?"

"Not yet. Let's look." I flipped through the pages and scanned the 1930 census. "He's here safe and sound, and married by now. His occupation is also banker. I think we can safely eliminate this Theodore. Show me what you found."

He opened the volume to a page in the 1910 census he'd marked and pointed to the Higson family. They lived in Norton Township and the only child was a one-year old boy named Theodore. The other possible Theodore was ten months old in 1910 and had eight older siblings. The family lived in a rural area, at that time unincorporated, now part of Deerfield. The family name was Routledge. The father's occupation—farmer; the mother's—laundress.

"Good work," I said. "Let me see if I can find the Routledge family in the 1920 census." I flipped through the massive book looking for the large brood that ten years previously had been living on a farm outside town. Instead, I found only two Routledges listed—the mother, whose occupation was now seamstress, and a teenage daughter. A cross-reference with the names and ages on the older census confirmed that these were probably the same people. The daughter was now apparently taking in laundry, although she was barely thirteen years old. They were no longer living on the rural farm, but in Throckmorton.

"That's horrible," said Tim, as he scanned the pages. "I wonder what happened to everyone else. The father's not in here anywhere and neither are any of the other children."

It's amazing what you can deduce from a bunch of dry facts—names on a page of people long dead. "It's pretty obvious. Something happened to the father and most of the kids. Maybe there was some kind of epidemic. Without them, the mother couldn't keep the farm. Try not to get too caught up in it," I said, gently. "They lived a long time ago. "

"But they were just kids. What could have wiped out a whole family? There were nine children."

"It could have been anything—diphtheria, typhus, cholera. Infant mortality rates back then were simply staggering. If you made it to your tenth birthday you had a good chance of living to adulthood. But until then…"

"But Theodore isn't listed here," he reminded me.

"That's not a good sign," I said. "If he died before the census was taken, this is kind of a dead end."

Tim tapped the eraser end of a pencil on the table, lost in thought. I continued to examine my census book, but I was growing concerned that we'd exhausted our possibilities.

"Something occurred to me," said Tim suddenly. "Are the names of all the children in the orphanage listed?"

"I don't know. Let me look…yes, we got lucky on this one. Unfortunately, this census taker had lousy handwriting. It's all I can do to decipher it—but so far I haven't found any names that look like Theodore."

"May I see it, please?" he asked.

"Knock yourself out. I'm going to get a drink of water."

When I came back, Timmy was smiling, looking quite satisfied with himself. He crooked a finger at me. "Look."

"Look at what? Yeah, but we're looking for Theodore, not Ted...oh. Duh."

"Unfortunately we got a lazy census taker. He didn't write down most of the kids' last names, but this Ted is eleven. How much you wanna bet this is our Theodore?"

I was proud of him. "Not bad for a beginner. If Sandy ever decides to leave us, maybe I will offer you a job. Speaking of which, here he comes now." To Sandy I said, "Where'd you leave Seamus?"

"Shelving books, this being his day job."

"Find anything?"

"Quite possibly. You?" said Sandy.

"We think we have our Theodore," I said, flopping open the books.

Sandy studied the list carefully and pumped a triumphant fist. "I knew it! It makes perfect sense.

Look at this." He produced a printout. It was from the Indian Springs *Herald* from May 18, 1920.

> Routledge, Teddy. Age 12, succumbed Tuesday night at Norton Township Children's Home to ruptured appendix. Survived by mother Felicia and sister Rosemary. Funeral arrangements pending.

"That's all?" asked Tim incredulously. "A kid dies and that's all they have to say about it?"

"Here's something else I found, if it makes you feel any better." said Sandy, handing him another paper.

Tim read the paper and passed it to me without comment.

It was an article from the *Herald* dated October 25, 1951.

> The Throckmorton County Children's Home has been home to hundreds of children since it opened in 1891. For generations, it has provided shelter for children who otherwise would have doubtless have ended up on the streets. Our taxes guaranteed them a warm bed, three meals a day, and an education. But in recent years this venerable institution has come under intense scrutiny throughout the county as allegations of neglect and abuse surface with disturbing regularity. Saturday's death of yet another child has sparked a new call from citizens for a

thorough investigation.

Over the years it is, sadly, inevitable that some of the children will succumb to illness or accident. But investigations into the school's records reveal that the number of deaths per thousand children is far out of proportion compared to the population at large. The death Saturday of Elena Markovich, 7, has sparked outrage among the community. Peritonitis resulting from a ruptured appendix, once a not infrequent killer of young and old alike, has thankfully, become more the exception than the rule.

Which makes the tragic death of little Elena all the more heartbreaking, bringing to mind several similar cases going back as far as 1920. When Theodore Routledge died in May of 1920 after his appendix burst, a furor erupted. When it was revealed that prompt medical care could have potentially saved the child's life, it set off a storm of controversy. Critics have accused the orphanage's administrators negligence and greed, placing more importance on saving money than the welfare of the children in their care …

"This is a stern accusation," I remarked.

"Still, it doesn't tell us much," said Tim.

Sandy drummed his fingers on the table impatiently. "No, it doesn't. I wonder if the school keeps records or something?"

"The least we can do is ask, right?" I said.

§

Principal Emily Golding sternly ushered us into her office. She noticed we were short one chair and started for the outer office. Tim stopped her. "Please don't bother. I don't mind standing." Sandy and I sat while Tim stood quietly behind me, taking it all in.

"I hope what you have is good news. I could really use some good news about now," said Principal Golding.

"I guess it all depends on your definition of good news," I said. "Ernie examined the security video closely. The last person to leave the previous evening was the teacher in the room across the hall from Mrs. Cartwright, a man."

"That would be Mr. Mabry, the third grade science teacher."

"He left about 4:00 and the cleaning crew locked up shortly after. That's it. Nobody entered the building all night. The next person to enter that wing was Mrs. Cartwright at 7:39 the next morning, the morning you called us. The room has no windows or other doors that somebody could have used to get in without being seen." I paused to let this sink in. "We have a couple of things to show you."

I turned to the laptop we'd set up on her desk and played the video of the toy car moving. I couldn't help but notice as she studied the video that Principal Golding's hands were clenched into fists. Next, we played the recording of the EMF meter session. She watched it in stony silence.

When it was over, she said, "This is worse than I could possibly have imagined."

I put a hand on her arm. "Emily, please. It's really nothing to get upset about. Honestly."

"Nothing to get upset about? I'm responsible for the well-being of 284 children."

"Look at it this way. Nothing has happened to indicate that the children are in any kind of danger, right? Or the teachers, for that matter. This is a benign spirit. We believe it to be a child, a former student of the school. This entity means no harm," I assured her.

She sighed heavily. "Benign or not, isn't there something you can do? When word of this gets out, parents will start taking their kids out of school. My career will be over."

"We work in strictest confidence," I said. "Nobody outside this room will ever know. "

She smiled wanly. "I'm guessing none of you have kids. Trust me, if even one of them knows about it, they all do."

I pointed out that it was, according to Chester, common knowledge that the school was haunted.

"You have a point. But until we had professional ghost hunters on the scene and evidence to prove it, it was just a kids' story."

"I can promise you that none of this will end up on the evening news," I reiterated. In the meantime, there are a couple of other things we want to show you."

Sandy offered her the copies of the records he had printed. She studied every piece of paper carefully. "Theodore Routledge," she said thoughtfully. "It's kind of sad, isn't it? Makes you wonder what might have happened if they'd gotten him to a doctor in time."

"Yes, it is sad," I agreed. "Once you have a name, and know something about them, it kind of changes your outlook on things. Look, I'm sure Theodore wasn't the only kid that perished because the orphanage couldn't or wouldn't spend the money. But maybe we can at least make amends, after a fashion."

"How so?"

"Well, we'd like to do another investigation, to try and contact him again. Also, I suppose it's too much to hope that the orphanage's records might have survived somewhere, but surely the school still has its records from that era?"

She started to shake her head, then suddenly brightened up. "Yes, I think I might be able to help. Come with me."

§

We trekked back to the old wing past Mrs. Cartwright's classroom coming, finally, to a dark corridor. Principal Golding flipped a light switch. Ugly florescent ceiling lights hummed to life. The walls were scuffed and grimy, and I detected a faint smell of mildew. Principal Golding produced a key and unlocked a set of double doors. When she turned on the lights, which were dim or, in some places, nonexistent, we could see endless rows of bookshelves. Against the walls and scattered haphazardly about were dozens of filing cabinets, some metal and rusty; others were made of wood.

"This was the library in the original school. It's hopelessly inadequate now, of course, so we use it for storage. I seem to recall hearing a rumor that the school inherited some files from the orphanage when it closed." She must have noticed the hopeful expression on my face. "Before you get too excited, even if it's true I don't have the first clue as to where they might be."

"Fair enough," I said, looking around in dismay. "Talk about a needle in a haystack."

"I wish!" Tim smiled. "Needle in a hay*field* is more like it."

An astute observation—we would be here all night. I'm sure it wasn't exactly the kind of welcome Tim had been expecting. He didn't seem too perturbed, though. In fact, he'd already wandered off and was milling around, perusing the contents of the bookshelves.

"Where do you want to start?" asked Principal Golding.

"We don't even know what we're looking for," said Sandy with a sigh of resignation.

"I know that the old enrollment and attendance records are over there. I've no idea how far back they go, though."

I turned to a scarred and battered file cabinet. "Well, we have to start somewhere. This looks as good as any." The cabinet contained a jumble of cardboard folders and decaying ledger books of all ages. As I flipped through the contents, I discovered with dismay that nothing was in any particular order. I found student files from the 1940, report cards from the

1930s and a folder neatly labeled "Budget 1953-54 School Year." It was all fascinating, but quite irrelevant. I felt a sneeze coming on and was fumbling around frantically in my purse for a tissue when a whoop of excitement from Tim shattered the stillness.

We found him in a dark corner, sitting on the floor, surrounded by stacks of books. Without a word he held up a faded book with a gray cover and flaked silver letters and the title *Renegade 1920*.

"The high school yearbook? That's interesting, Timmy but…"

"Not just the high school. The entire Norton Township School. Turn to page 80," said Tim.

With Sandy peering over my shoulder, I flipped through the yellowing pages. "Fifth Grade." It was a photo of twenty or so unsmiling kids arranged in rows on what must have been the front steps of the school. Next to them a heavyset woman in long skirts glared at the camera.

"Second row, fourth from the left," said Tim triumphantly.

Theodore had an angelic face and a mop of unruly blonde curls to match. His expression was grave and his arm was around the shoulder of the little boy next to him.

"He doesn't have any shoes," said Sandy, sniffling discretely.

The Renegade was a strange little book by modern standards. Compared to the dusty Indian Springs High School yearbooks stashed in the depths of my bedroom closet, there were relatively few photos and a lot of text, including a "History of the Class of 1920." Norton Township School had housed twelve grades. Only the graduating seniors got individual photos, but there was a group photo of all of the other classes, including the lower grades, all the way down to kindergarten. I paged through the seniors, all 20 of them. How sobering it was to realize that they were most likely all dead now. Even the kindergarteners, if any were still alive, would be pushing 100. Near the front I came to a page that said "In Memoriam" and contained list of names of students, plus a few alumni, who had died during the school year. Under each name was a sentence or two. We found Theodore about halfway down. "A dedicated scholar and sympathetic friend, much lamented. Ruptured appendix. March 1920."

"Look at all these names. And in a school this size," said Tim. "There can't be more than 200 kids in the whole school."

"You think that's bad," said Sandy handing me another yearbook. It was the *Renegade* from the previous year. The list on the memorial page was much longer, taking up the entire page. Many of them were young men from the classes of 1917 and 1918, fallen at Chateau-Thierry, the Marne, or Belleau Wood. At least Theodore had been spared that agony. Out of curiosity I looked at the fourth graders. We found Theodore, standing with the same youngster. Both were wearing shoes. And—although it might have just been my imagination—their faces seemed not quite as thin.

§

"You know, I wasn't too enthusiastic about this case when Chester came to talk to us, but now I think it could turn into something big," I said to Tim as we finally headed home that night. When he didn't respond, I glanced at him—he was asleep. He woke up just as I pulled the car into the garage.

"Sorry," he said, sounding a little bit sheepish, "it's been a really long day."

"Don't be sorry. I'm the one who should be apologizing—this wasn't quite the welcome I had in mind for you."

I wheeled his suitcase in and deposited it unceremoniously in a corner of the bedroom. I was suddenly feeling unexpectedly shy. After all, it had been two months since we'd seen each other. It's one of the hazards of a long-distance relationship, and I was willing to accept it, but each time we were together again I worried that the magic would be gone. "If you want to unpack, I made some space for your things in the closet here."

He sat down on the edge of the bed and grinned wickedly. "Unpacking isn't what I really want to do. Hey, what's that bruise on your face?"

Oops. Somehow I'd managed to forget about my little souvenir from Seth. My industrial-strength concealer must have worn off. "Oh, it's nothing," I said airily. "I bumped into something in the dark during an investigation."

"Hmm. Seems like every time we're together you have a new bruise."

"One of the hazards of the job."

He stood up and took me in his arms. We kissed—finally—a long, delicious kiss that left me weak in the knees and hungry for more. When I went into the bathroom a few minutes later to brush my teeth and put on my sexy new nightie, Tim was puttering around in the bedroom, unpacking from the sound of things. I dabbed a bit of concealer on the bruise and silently cursed Seth. I shivered in anticipation.

When I went back into the bedroom, Tim was sound asleep and snoring softly.

Homecoming

The next evening we were sitting in a sunny spot on my patio. It had been a mild, unseasonably warm day. Tim and I were basking in the last of the sun's rays, sipping champagne. The sun was warm on my face, but an occasional breeze reminded me that it was indeed Fall.

"Who's taking care of Franklin?" I asked. Franklin was a stray cat that had taken up residence in Tim's building in San Francisco. There was little love lost between Franklin and me; we had taken an instant dislike to each other when I stayed with Tim for a couple of weeks early in our relationship.

"Oh, he can manage. Everyone in the building looks after him. He's sort of a community pet."

"But he seems to have taken a particular liking to you. Don't you consider him more or less your cat now?"

"Well, with cats I'm not certain it's ever totally cut and dried as to who owns whom. Have you ever thought about getting a pet?"

"Me? Are you kidding? I can't even keep a house plant alive. Anyway, my schedule is so hectic, it wouldn't be fair."

"You're probably right. By the way, I have some news. Kendra's getting remarried." Kendra is Tim's ex-wife. Rumor has it that she bears a striking resemblance to me, although I've only ever seen photos.

I wasn't sure exactly how to respond to this. "And how do you feel about it?"

"Couldn't be happier. Our marriage never should have happened, and I wish her all the best. What do you hear from Roger?"

"Poor Roger. I've seen him around town with at least three different women since we broke up. They're all half his age, and they dump him the minute someone more interesting comes along. I guess I can't blame them. I don't know how I put up with him as long as I did." Snarky of me, I know. But it's true.

"I kind of envy you your job," he said. "I get the strangest reactions when I tell people my girlfriend's a ghost hunter. It's one of the many things I find fascinating about you. I just can't picture you in a cubicle job."

"I did that for years," I reminded him. "But I don't miss the nine-to-five routine—it didn't take long to get used to being able to come and go as I please. And I like being able to take a few days off when I need to...like now, for instance."

"I can relate," he said. "I'm lucky in that respect, too. One of the perks of owning a business." He twirled a strand of my hair absently around his finger. "How's the other investigation going?"

I'd been thinking long and hard about whether I should tell him everything. I didn't want him to worry about me. On the other hand, it was good to occasionally get an outsider's perspective and I valued his opinion. He knew about the phone call and email, of course, and I'd given him a decidedly sketchy account of getting stuck in Pritchett's office. But he didn't know that we knew who the intruder was. Something told me Tim didn't need to know about Seth just yet. And I hadn't quite gotten around to telling him about the EVP. I made a quick decision said, "Well, there is something I haven't told you yet. We got an EVP that I don't know what to make of." I could see him growing concerned as I described the words we captured on the voice recorder.

"Has anything ever happened to make you feel uncomfortable around Dr. Holmes?" he asked, pouring the last of the champagne into our glasses.

"No, that's just it. He's like a father to me...I can't in my wildest imaginings picture him being in any way dangerous."

He pulled me to him and kissed the top of my head. "Look, I'm sure there's a perfectly logical explanation for all of this. But something's not right here. Please—*please* be careful. Maybe it's best for you to avoid being alone with Holmes, at least for a while."

"Well, that shouldn't be too hard to do, since he just got out of intensive care." The sun went behind a tree, and a sudden crisp breeze made me shiver.

"All the more reason to keep your eyes open, Margo. You need to consider the possibility that he's somehow involved in something he shouldn't be. And I don't want you getting caught up in it by association. I love you, and I couldn't bear it if anything happened to you." He put a finger under my chin and tilted my face to his. We shared an exquisite kiss.

"I can think of plenty of things I'd much rather be doing than talking about work," I said.

"Me too," he said with a smile. "Let's go inside."

§

On the night of the game, we were dressed and about to head out the door when Tim snapped his fingers and said "Almost forgot something...wait just a sec."

He returned from the bedroom with something concealed behind his back.

"What's that?" I tried to grab his hand.

"Just wait!" His eyes sparkled. "I was going through a box of old junk a couple of months ago when I ran across something, and I want you to have it. Do you remember when it was the thing for a girl to wear her boyfriend's ID bracelet?"

"Yes, of course." How could I not? Until we got our class rings, a girl wore her guy's ID bracelet to proclaim that they were going steady. It was the coolest fashion accessory a girl could possibly wear. It was not unheard of for a girl to go with a guy just because he had a cool bracelet.

He held out his hand. In it was a silver ID bracelet. TIMMY was engraved on the scuffed and scarred name plate. "You don't have to wear it," he said hastily. "I just wanted you to have it."

"Don't be silly. Anyway, they're coming back in style. But you have to put it on me. That was the rule."

He put it on my wrist and fastened the clasp. It was big and clunky, but it fit—just.

§

We could hear the marching band warming up long before we got near the stadium. By the time we were close enough to see the stadium, traffic had slowed to a crawl and the parking lot was filling up rapidly. We found a spot in a distant corner and joined the throng of people hiking in.

"I should have bought you a mum."

"Thanks, but I think I'm a little old for that." We got in line at the box office, in the midst of a churning sea of kids half our age. Some of the girls, many with multiple corsages pinned precariously to their chests, looked like walking piles of blue and gold ribbons and glitter. Indian Springs has an abundance of competing florists. We're well known in these parts for our over-the-top football mums. Hundreds of tiny bells tinkled around us, and the ground sparkled with glitter.

The lady in the ticket booth glanced at us and asked, "Parents or alumni?"

"Alumni," we said in unison. Tim slid some cash through the slot in the window.

"There's an entire section reserved for alums—section C, great seats. Enjoy the game," she said, pushing our tickets and change back through the slot toward us.

We climbed the step and found our section—beneath the press box, right on the 50-yard line. Somewhere out of sight, drums began beating. "Not bad," said Tim. "See anybody you recognize?"

"Just a bunch of old people."

"Those 'old people' are from my class. I recognize some of those faces."

I took a second look; he was right. "Wow. That's kind of depressing."

We found some vacant seats and sat down. The homecoming pre-game show had started, but I couldn't have been less interested in what was happening on the field. It was far more interesting to see who was there that I knew. I spotted a familiar face one section over. Two familiar faces, in fact. One of them was Ernie's Aunt Muriel. "There are some people I know over there," I said, pointing. Then I saw something that made me do a double-take. "Oh, my God!" I said. "I don't believe who Aunt Muriel is talking to!"

"Who's Aunt Muriel?"

"She's Ernie's aunt. She's the one I told you about."

"Oh yes, the one who sees angels and auras." Ernie's lovable but quirky Aunt Muriel is hard to describe. She specializes in reading auras and has been known to detect the presence of an angel or two. She tells me I have a guardian angel. I have to take her word for it, since he or she doesn't seem to do much to keep me out of trouble.

"That's her. And look who she's sitting with! That's Rollie."

Tim knew all about the time Rollie rescued us from Officer Kruszinsky. Tonight Rollie was looking comparatively dapper, all cleaned and pressed. He and Aunt Muriel seemed to be having quite an interesting conversation. He didn't take his eyes off her for a second, even when the Indian Springs High School band and dance team marched onto the field.

Aunt Muriel saw me and we waved at each other. The tune the band struck up was one that I didn't recognize, yet somehow it sounded like the same old band from my high school days. Why is it that high school marching bands always sound like a slightly warped tape? It was followed shortly by a tune I did recognize: the school fight song. Tim broke into a grin. "I feel like a teenager again." He wrapped an arm around me. He looked as happy as I've ever seen him.

"Hey, isn't that Ray Gilbanks?" Tim pointed to man who was navigating the bleachers toward us. The reflection from the stadium lights off his bald head was positively blinding, and he was preceded by a massive beer gut.

"Oh, my God!" I said. "I remember when every girl in school had a crush on him. He was senior class president when I was a sophomore."

"And captain of the football team, if I recall correctly. He and Buster Snellins once locked me in my locker. Tell me you didn't have a crush on him."

"They did? I didn't know about it. Why didn't you tell me?"

"Because I knew you'd do something diabolical to get even with him. Angie Kirkpatrick heard me yelling and let me out. It wasn't worth getting yourself in trouble over it. Besides, I got back at him."

"How?"

"I bribed the football team's water boy to pour an entire bottle of Ex-Lax into his Gatorade when he wasn't looking. My mom found out and grounded me for two weeks. But it was worth it—he was absent from school for three days."

We were waiting for the kick-off when I saw two more familiar faces—unfriendly ones this time. Lorena Gross, my high school arch-nemesis and her evil sidekick Patty Snypes. Patty has always been known to us as "Punkin," for reasons that have never been clear.

Tim did a double-take. "Hey, isn't that..."

"It is. And they're coming over here."

"Something's different about Lorena. She used to be flat as a pancake."

"An astute observation. Remember when she was voted Most Likely to Get a Boob Job? Well, she did."

Lorena looked better from a distance than she did close up. A do-it-yourself dye job in a painful shade of red gave her a somewhat brittle appearance. In spite of the chill in the air, she was wearing a skimpy sleeveless top about a size too small, a most unfortunate choice of garments. It only called attention to her skinny legs and rotund middle.

"She looks like a beach ball on chopsticks. With batwings," remarked Tim.

It was a given that you befriended Lorena at your own risk. She was known far and wide to be—how shall I put it?—rather generous with her favors. For Lorena, the challenge wasn't getting the guy. At an age when hormones speak louder than words, she seldom lacked for male attention, but it was only worth the effort if the attention was from another girl's boyfriend. When we got older she graduated to the husbands of friends. She was—and still is, if I may put it bluntly—a bit of a skank. Not much has changed over the years, except that now she's a skank with boobs.

"Oh, look, Patty. It's Margo!" exclaimed Lorena. Several people in the rows in front of us turned to stare. "But isn't it wonderful to see you, daahling?" she purred. "After all these years."

"Oh, hello, Lorena. What brings you to town? Other than homecoming, I mean." It was a trick question. I knew perfectly well what she was doing here. I'd heard through the grapevine that husband number three had packed up his toys and moved out. She was doubtless on the prowl for her next victim. To my horror, Punkin and Lorena found seats right in front of us. Tim looked at me with dismay.

Ignoring my question, she turned to Tim and stuck out a veiny hand adorned with an alarming number of cheap, sparkly rings. "Lorena Gross," she said.

"Tim Beckwith."

"Tim...*Timmy*! Oh my goodness, but I never would have recognized you. My, but didn't you turn out...*nice*!" Whether he was aware or not that she was already shamelessly sizing him up, I don't know. As an afterthought, she said, "You both remember Punkin."

Over her shoulder, Punkin shot us a predatory look. "What do you hear from Roxy these days?"

"Oh, she's fine," I answered. "Just became a grandmother. Lives in San Guillermo. I talk to her several times a year."

"A grandmother! My goodness, and so young!" exclaimed Punkin with exaggerated horror.

"Well, you know she got married right before graduation and started having kids right away."

"Yes," agreed Lorena. "Who would have guessed: mousy little Roxy. But, of course, she always was so... domesticated."

Tim sputtered indignantly but I stopped him before he could say anything. "I could really use something to drink." I dragged him to his feet and propelled him toward the aisle before they had a chance to say anything.

He was still fuming when we got into the drink line, which was actually something more akin to a thronging mass. "We'll be lucky if we get out of here before half time. Why did you let her get away with that snotty remark?"

"Because, Timmy, she only said it to get a reaction. The best thing to do around Lorena is to refuse to play the game. Trust me—after all these years I know what I'm talking about."

A petite blonde, looking for a shortcut through the throng, darted into the space in front of me with a mumbled "'Scuze me." Three mums embellished with candies, tiny footballs and all kinds of small tchotchkes hid the front of her completely. Some of the ribbons were as long as she was tall, almost touching the ground. She tinkled merrily as she squeezed past us.

"Jeez, the mums just keep getting bigger and bigger," said Tim.

"Homecoming is what keeps the florists in business. I'm not so sure I want to go back and sit with Lorena and Punkin. Maybe it's time for you to meet Aunt Muriel. I've warned you about her, haven't I?"

"You and everybody else. But anything beats sitting with Lorena." Miraculously, we had reached the front of the line. "I'll take a large Coke and a large Dr. Pepper, please."

Trying to avoid spilling our drinks, we worked our way carefully back through the crowd. We were skirting a throng of senior citizens wearing stick-on name tags that said "Class of '53" when I almost ran right into Ernie.

"Oh, there you are, Margo. I've been looking for you. Aunt Muriel said you were here."

"Oh yeah? Did she say who else was here?"

"No….oh, you mean Lorena and Punkin? Yeah, I saw them. Which is why I'm here and not in my seat. 'Sup, Tim?" The two men greeted each other with a bro-hug. We continued our trek through the bleachers.

"You here by yourself, man?" asked Tim.

Ernie suddenly seemed uncomfortable. "No, I'm here with a...date."

I had a premonition that Tim was about to ask after Elaine I caught his eye and shook my head. He shrugged and we followed Ernie up the concrete steps without further conversation.

"They won't mind if we sit with them. There seem to be plenty of empty seats," said Ernie, pointing toward Aunt Muriel and Rollie. "Class of '68. They do this every year," he added. There was a younger woman sitting with them.

"Ernie, I thought you were joking about asking Megan."

"Well, I wasn't," he responded snippily. "And before you say anything, yes, I know it was a dumb idea."

"Did I miss something?" asked Tim.

"He brought Megan to Homecoming."

"Who's Megan?" asked Tim. To me he said quietly, "What happened to Elaine?"

"I don't know. Neither of them will talk about it. Megan is a waitress at the Monk's Habit."

"She looks kinda...young."

Ernie glared at us. "If you're going to gossip about my love life, at least have the courtesy to do it when I'm not around."

Aunt Muriel spotted us. "Oh, look, Rollie, there's Margo," she exclaimed.

Tim sniffed at the air. "I smell something...it smells like burning plastic."

I poked him in the ribs. "Shhh," I whispered. "I'll explain later."

The rhinestones in Aunt Muriel's vintage cat-shaped glasses twinkled merrily. "Margo, darling!" She greeted me with a kiss on each cheek, Continental style. I've never known her to simply shake hands with anybody. She greeted Tim in the same fashion. He returned her air-kisses, but his eyes were watering.

Next, Ernie introduced first Rollie, then Megan. Megan glanced up from her phone long enough to mumble a curt greeting.

There were two vacant seats next to Aunt Muriel. I tried to take the one closest to her, but Aunt Muriel grabbed Tim's arm and gently pushed him into it. "I'm so happy that I get to meet you at last, Timothy," she exclaimed. She put a hand on either side of his face and gazed intently into his eyes. I could tell from his body language that this made him extremely uncomfortable, but to his credit he returned her gaze calmly. A lesser man would have freaked right out.

"Yes," said Aunt Muriel. "You have a very strong aura, my dear." She released my boyfriend and patted him on the shoulder. "I knew you would be here, of course. My guides told me to expect you." Then she leaned to him and whispered something that I couldn't hear. He grinned happily, blushing slightly, and gave Aunt Muriel a quick hug. She beamed back at him.

Rollie had been watching the exchange with interest. Last summer, when he rescued us from the clutches of Officer Kruszinsky, he'd asked me if Ernie was my boyfriend. I got the impression he didn't approve too much; Ernie, as sometimes happens, hadn't made a particularly positive impression on him. At the time I'd recently broken up with my long-term boyfriend Roger. It was before I started seeing Tim, and I was smarting from the humiliation of Roger and his new girlfriend seeing us being herded into the police station like a bunch of petty criminals. It was Rollie who'd reminded me that there were plenty of fish in the sea. Indian Springs is hundreds of miles from the sea, however. At the time, I despaired of ever meeting a man who could walk into my kitchen and not hyperventilate because the spices in my cabinet aren't arranged in alphabetical order.

I left Tim with Aunt Muriel and sat down next to Rollie. He gives, if I may be frank, the impression of someone for whom personal hygiene is something of an afterthought. But tonight he smelled of soap and aftershave and his hair—what was left of it—was carefully parted and combed. "I didn't know you knew Aunt Muriel."

"Know her? Why, we was big sweethearts plumb until she went off to college. It was me that exscorted her onto the field when she got to be homecoming queen," he said proudly.

Aunt Muriel as homecoming queen? Who knew? "Rollie, I've been meaning to ask you something. That day we got arrested, did you know Ernie was her nephew?"

He snorted. "'Course I did. Ain't hardly nobody in this town I don't know. I remember you was all in a tizzy on account of that old boyfriend of yours. That your new beau?" He nodded toward Tim, who was deep in a conversation with Aunt Muriel again. Actually, it was more like a lecture. Aunt Muriel was doing all the talking with Tim nodding occasionally.

"Yes. That's Tim. We went to high school together, too. But he lives in San Francisco now. He's just here for a few days visiting."

Rollie pondered this for a minute. "Big city boy, eh? No regrets about the ex?"

I smiled. "No, Rollie. None at all. I think it was more a case of wounded pride than anything. I mean, life with Roger was kind of like watching paint dry. Honestly, what's there to say about a man whose favorite Marx Brother is Zeppo?"

Rollie stared at me blankly for a moment, then burst into raucous laughter, rocking in his seat and slapping his thigh. "Zeppo!" he wheezed. His face turned red and I feared for a second he might be having some kind of seizure. But then he shook his head and whipped out a grimy handkerchief. "Zeppo!" he hooted again, wiping his eyes and chuckling.

On the field, the second quarter ended and the two teams jogged off the field.

Tim caught my eye. He'd escaped from Aunt Muriel. "Let's watch the half-time show. Should we go back to our official seats?"

I glanced over to our section. Trapped between Lorena and Punkin was a man about our age I didn't recognize. The look on his face plainly said "Somebody please help me."

"What?" I replied. "And spoil all Lorena's fun? She's got a live one there. Ernie looks like he could use some company, though."

Ernie was next to Megan, who was utterly absorbed in her phone. I watched him make a couple of feeble attempts to engage her in conversation. He didn't appear to be having much luck. "See you later, Rollie," I said. Tim and I squeezed past him and slid into two empty seats behind Ernie.

"How's it going over here, Ern?" asked Tim.

"Just peachy," he grumbled in reply.

"Cheer up," I said. "They're about to announce the homecoming queen."

The contenders, each on the arm of a beefy football player, were being escorted onto the field. A resonant voice boomed over the PA system, introducing the girls and their escorts. Excitement mounted, then the winner was announced. She was suitably overcome with emotion and presented with a enormous bouquet of roses.

"It amazes me that they still do this stuff in this day and age," said Ernie.

"Aww, the kids enjoy it," I said. "Don't be such an old grouch."

§

It was something of an ignominious homecoming for Indian Springs. We lost 14-40, never having gained the lead. Halfway into the fourth quarter there was a massive exodus for the parking lot. We stayed until the bitter end, but I noticed that the seats Lorena and Punkin had been sitting in were empty. A tidal wave of humanity swept us toward the parking lot.

"We have a surprise for you girls," said Timmy. "We're going to dinner."

"We're going out?" asked Megan. "Now?" It was one of the few things she'd said all evening. Ernie, who had been trying valiantly to keep a conversation going with her, had long ago given up and was strolling along with his hands in his pockets and a disgruntled look on his face.

"Well, of course. It's the tradition. Don't people still go out after football games?" he said.

She shrugged her shoulders. "I guess so. But every place is going to be packed. No matter where we go we'll have to wait."

"Nope. We have reservations," said Tim. From the startled look on Megan's face, I surmised that the concept of reservations was a new one to her.

"Meet you there in a few," said Ernie, ushering Megan politely to his car, which was parked several rows away.

Tim opened the passenger's side door of my car with a gallant flourish. At first it had been a little disconcerting being a passenger in my own car, but I had to admit that it was nice to let someone else worry about traffic and parking for a change.

"Aren't you going to tell me where we're going?" I asked, as we pulled out of the parking lot and into the river of cars creeping slowly toward the exit.

"Nope," said Tim. "It's a surprise."

Once we got past the traffic bottleneck, we headed in the general direction of downtown Indian Springs, if you can all it that. So I wasn't totally taken by aback when we pulled up at the stately Lawrence Hotel. Their restaurant, Chez Claude, is Indian Springs' one and only four-star restaurant. It's not bad for a town the size of Indian Springs, and people all the way from San Guillermo come here for their French desserts. Chez Claude had special significance for me—Tim and I dined here on our first date.

We pulled up and valets rushed to open our doors. I glanced back over my shoulder as we went inside; my aging station wagon looked a little out of place among all the sleek sports cars and BMWs idling at the curb. But then Ernie pulled up in his Mini. It looked equally out of place, so I didn't feel so bad.

We were shown to our table by an obsequious maitre 'd whose white tie and tails gave him a most unfortunate resemblance to a penguin. Everything about Chez Claude was carefully calculated to invoke visions of Old Money. The understated good taste was diametrically opposed to trendy. Spotless white tablecloths covered tables sparkling with the finest china, crystal, and silver.

"Look at the weird stuff on this menu! I don't even know what half of it is," remarked Megan.

Megan's attitude was beginning to irritate me and I felt an attack of cattiness coming on. "We had the escargot last time we were here..."

"Escar—snails? You eat *snails*?" asked Megan incredulously.

"Great idea," said Tim with a broad smile, thoroughly enjoying himself. "I remember they were some of the best I've had."

The men conferred briefly over the wine list, Ernie ultimately deferring to Tim on the grounds that he lived closer to wine country.

Waiters returned shortly with the escargot and wine. The waiter went through the customary ritual with Tim, holding up the bottle with a flourish, then splashing a taste in Tim's glass. Tim nodded and the waiter poured wine all around, starting with us girls.

Ernie speared a snail and maneuvered it carefully to his plate. "It's been ages since I've had a decent escargot."

Megan stared at him in horror. "You're actually gonna eat that?"

"Well, yes, that's the general idea."

She shuddered and reached for the bread basket.

"Aren't you even going to try it?" asked Ernie.

"No thanks," said Megan petulantly.

Worried that things might turn ugly, I decided a change of subject was called for.

"So what's with your Aunt Muriel and Rollie?"

Ernie shook his head. "That's a new one on me."

"It's not a match I would ever have predicted. Do you suppose it has any potential?"

Ernie's eyes grew huge. "I hope not. If they got married that would make Rollie...my uncle!"

"He's not as bad as all that. If it hadn't been for him we would have ended up in jail."

"I know. It's just that he's a little...strange."

"I'm pretty sure he thinks the same about you," I replied.

Ernie made a face at me, then addressed Tim. "I saw you and Aunt Muriel having quite a conversation."

"Yes, she's certainly a character."

"That's putting it mildly," said Ernie. "You seemed to be getting along with her." He put his nose in the air and sniffed theatrically. "Do I detect the lingering aroma of *Soir d'amour?*"

Tim's eyes rolled. "Great. So now I smell like an electrical fire, too."

Ernie grinned. "She's been wearing it as long as I can remember. You have a headache yet?"

"So that's where that came from."

"It tends to have that affect on people," said Ernie.

"So what did you two talk about?" I asked.

Tim smiled mysteriously. "Oh, you know, chit-chat. Life in the big city, the old alma mater, you know—stuff."

"I saw her whisper something in your ear," I said.

"Yes, she did."

"Oh come on. Tell us what she said," cajoled Ernie.

"I promised not to tell."

"It's okay. You can tell me later," I said.

"No, really. I promised I wouldn't. Besides, you'll just turn around and tell Ernie, and it's supposed to be a secret."

"Oh, for heaven's sake," I said with exasperation.

"I'll tell you some day. Maybe. So—what's everybody going to order?"

Security Breach

The next day, I finally got around to listening to the EVPs Elaine wanted me to hear. I plugged my best quality headphones into the iPad and opened the two files. Barely audible in the background were the flat, tinny snippets of what I was pretty sure was supposed to be "The Charleston." Elaine and Sally both swore they hadn't heard it until they listened to the tapes later. I had only to listen a couple of times to come to the conclusion that Elaine and Sally had found a fraud.

Tim was lounging on the sofa, reading. "How would you like your first lesson in how to spot fake evidence?" I asked.

Tim put down his book and regarded me with surprise. "Not the one at the school, I hope?"

"No, thank goodness. These are two EVPs Elaine sent me from a job in Sylersville. Her friend's boyfriend owns a bed and breakfast there, which he claims is haunted. I can just about guarantee you these are fake." I curled up beside him on the sofa. "Let's stream this to the television so we can both hear," I said, turning on the TV. "This is the first one.

I'm going to play it and you tell me what you think it is."

"The Charleston."

"That's right. Now here's the second one."

"The Charleston...again."

"Very astute observation," I said. "Now, does anything strike you as odd between the two?" I played both snippets for him again.

"No...wait—they're identical. It's the same part of the song in both."

"That's right. And what does that tell us?"

"That it's a residual haunting?"

"Wrong," I replied. "That it's not a haunting of any kind. Watch." I opened an audio program on the tablet and pulled up both files as sound waves. "Notice that the wave pattern matches exactly. Now, the music starts right about here." I moved the playhead to a point a couple of seconds into the file. "It's not just the music where the waveforms are identical—you have a second or two of static before and after the music. But even the waveforms for the static are identical. What are the chances that two legitimate EVPs would be identical? This, my dear Watson, is a recording."

"Well played," he said. "But why would someone do that? Do you think it's supposed to be a joke?"

"A publicity ploy, I suspect. People would travel from far and wide to stay at a bed and breakfast that's been declared haunted by the famous Margo Monroe, if I may say so."

"What are you going to tell Elaine?"

"That I want to go there and check out the place in person," I said.

"Why? Seems like an awful waste of time."

"Not necessarily. The speakers shouldn't be too hard to find, and it'll be worth the trip out there to watch this guy squirm when I call him on it. Few things make me madder than someone who fakes a haunting, especially if it's to dupe innocent people out of their money."

§

We spent the rest of the weekend putting new tiles in the guest bathroom. By lunchtime on Monday Tim was on his back, half in/half out of the kitchen cabinet under the sink, fixing a leaky faucet. He'd already installed a new garbage disposer that morning. Do I know how to show my guests a good time, or what? "Why don't you take a break and let's go get some lunch. It's my treat—I'll take you anywhere you want to go."

Before he could answer, the phone rang. "What can he possibly want?" I said when I saw who it was. "Hi, Sandy. This better be good."

"Sorry, Margo. I hate to bother you while Tim's in town and all, but there's been an incident and I thought you needed to know about it"

"Incident?"

"Somebody smashed a window. Threw a rock through it."

"Lovely. Just what we need. But the only windows on our side of the building are glass blocks. It must have been an awfully big rock."

"That's just it. It smashed out one of the windows in Irmalene's office."

"Well, that's certainly unpleasant, but I don't see how it concerns us—"

"There was a note attached to it. It said 'Freaks out now.' They spelled "freaks" f-r-i-e-k-s."

Tim had extricated himself from under the sink and was now sitting on the floor watching me.

"Oh dear, then it's probably safe to assume it's us our semi-literate vandals have the beef with." There are some colorful people in the horticulture department, but I can't in my wildest dreams imagine anybody would consider them freaks.

"Irmalene's fit to be tied," said Sandy.

"No doubt. She's bad enough on a good day. Do I need to come in?"

"Well, she's been chewing on Ernie's butt for the past half-hour. He could probably use some relief. I wish Dr. Holmes were here."

I sighed. "Okay, Sandy, I better see if there's anything I can do. Give us a few minutes."

"I'm willing to bet Irmalene will still be here when you get here."

I explained to Tim what happened. "I should at least make an appearance. Time to get cleaned up," I said, offering him a hand and hauling him to his feet. We scrambled to make ourselves presentable.

"I still don't understand Irmalene's problem with you," remarked Tim when, a few minutes later, we were in my car on the way to the lab.

"I think she feels like she's been used. And frankly, I might feel the same if I were in her shoes. To say she's a skeptic would be putting it mildly—she has absolutely no reservations about letting anybody in earshot know she thinks what we're doing is nonsense. We still have to deal with reporters because of the symphony case last fall. Every time she comes to work, she has to dodge a crowd of protesters. And now she gets a rock through her office window."

§

Two patrol cars were parked in front of the lab—one from the Throckmorton PD and one from campus security. The usual crowd was standing around. Maybe they were mellowing out; for once they watched us go in quietly.

A Throckmorton cop and a campus security officer were talking quietly to several people I didn't know; horticulture students, probably. It would have been hard not to recognize the Throckmorton cop—my fan on the police force, Officer Toby Garcia. "Good morning, Ms. Monroe," he greeted me cheerfully. But when he saw Tim, his expression clouded.

"Officer Garcia! Fancy meeting you here," I said. Garcia stared hard at Tim. "Um...I'd like you to meet my boyfriend, Tim Beckwith," I said when he didn't respond. "Tim, this is Officer Garcia of the Throckmorton PD." They mumbled "hellos" but neither man offered to shake hands.

"Are you the one in charge?" It took me a second to realize that the campus security officer was talking to me.

"Uh, I guess so. In Dr. Holmes' absence, anyway. I suppose it would be silly of me to ask if anyone has any idea what happened." I could hear Ernie and Irmalene arguing somewhere down the hall.

"No one saw anything, but we're hoping we might have something on the surveillance camera," he continued. I didn't even know there was a surveillance camera. When had those been put up?

The door opened and Ernie strolled in, Irmalene on his heels. In spite of having spent the last half hour being chewed out, he looked to be in a remarkably jovial mood. The same cannot be said of Irmalene. I swear steam was coming out of her ears.

As Ernie walked briskly past me he silently mouthed the words "Thank you." Spotting a larger target, Irmalene stopped and began to direct her wrath at me. I let her fume—the secret to dealing with angry people is to simply let them get it all out. Eventually Irmalene's rage balloon deflated to a point where she accepted my sincere apologies.

The two officers watched the exchange with detached amusement. "Is she always so charming?" asked Garcia.

"If she likes you, she can be very nice. She just doesn't like us," I said. "She and Holmes have been feuding for years."

The campus security guard nodded at Garcia, then me. "We'll be on our way now, but I'll be in touch and let you know if we find anything. Oh, and I almost forgot." He pulled some pieces of laminated cardboard about five inches square. They were stamped with a large letter "A."

"What's this?" I asked.

"Your new parking permits. The spaces out front —they're reserved now. Put this on your dash when you park. There's one here for Ms. Gibson, too. I'll see to it that she gets it. Maintenance will come out some time in the next few days and put up signs. You call us if somebody parks in one of your spaces. It's not much, but maybe it will help make things a little easier. Well, have a nice day, ma'am." He touched the visor of his hat and the cops left through the janitor's closet door. Garcia cast a backward glance over his shoulder at Tim on the way out.

Ernie had fired up the Monster and was contentedly tapping away on the keyboard, humming to himself.

"You're in an awfully good mood."

He smiled mysteriously. "Should we talk about tomorrow night's follow-up investigation?"

"So much for my day off," I replied. "Did you talk to Seamus?"

"I did. He's out," said Ernie.

"Oh no! Why?"

"Broken toe. Somebody dropped an amplifier on his foot."

"Lovely. " An idea had been brewing in my head for a while. I turned to Tim. "I don't suppose you'd be interested..."

"I was hoping you'd ask!" he exclaimed.

"Well before you get too excited, understand that you'll be doing the jobs nobody wants to do. Set-up, take-down, watching the monitors. Ernie, is there something you'd like to share with us? What'd you do? Put cayenne pepper in her Irmalene's coffee or something?"

"Hey, no, but what an idea! If you must know, Elaine wants to help us."

"So that explains the spring in your step. Who called the truce?"

"We ran into each other at the Taco Loco."

"That's certainly good news. What happened to Megan?" I asked.

Ernie shuddered theatrically. "Possibly not one of my better ideas. I took her to the fanciest restaurant in town and she ordered a hamburger and fries off the kids' menu."

"Well, Ernie," I said, as gently as I could, "you keep asking out these younger girls and you're always surprised when you don't have anything in common with them."

"Yeah, well," he retorted, "the one that's my age keeps dumping me."

"It's none of my business, but I think it was a mistake not asking Elaine to homecoming."

"Elaine? I can't picture her wanting to go to a high school homecoming game."

"Elaine is full of surprises. But it's too late now."

"Maybe next year," said Ernie with a rueful smile. "In the meantime, you remember I told you I have a friend who's...er, good with computers?"

"You mean your hacker friend?"

He sighed. "Call her that if you must, but I think you're going to want to know what she found out."

"Your hacker is a girl?"

"Margo, I'm surprised at you—automatically assuming a tech nerd is a guy. If I did that you'd read me the Riot Act. Anyway, it would appear our friend Seth has made numerous clandestine trips to the science lab in the middle of the night." He pulled up a cryptic-looking file.

"Who's Seth?" asked Tim.

"Ah, I see you have yet to meet the ever-charming Dr. Carling. Pritchett's temporary replacement. We hope he's temporary, anyway." said Ernie.

I gave him a dark look.

"Sorry, I know this is probably a blinding flash of the obvious, but why isn't he just logging in from home?" asked Tim. "Surely he's got a computer and a user ID on the network. Why sneak in in the middle of the night?"

"Give the man a gold star! It is my considered opinion that he's looking for a file or files that are not accessible from the outside," replied Ernie. "I did a little bit of discreet snooping and found out that the science department is rumored to have some computers that are not part of the school's official network and are not accessible from the outside. I haven't been able to find out where they are or what's on them, but few people know about it, even fewer have access, and the rumor is that it's protected by defense-level security."

"How would Seth know that whatever it is he's looking for isn't on the public network?" I asked.

"A very good question." Ernie opened another file. "And the answer is...because he's already looked. Someone tried to hack into the college's network remotely. Tried and succeeded, actually."

"And you know this how?" I asked.

"Because the college's network is protected by a firewall—multiple firewalls, actually."

"What's a firewall?" I asked.

"A firewall prevents unauthorized access to a computer. In our case, it's software that controls data traffic that goes in and data traffic that goes out. Everything on the science department's network servers is behind the firewall. When someone logs on to the school network remotely, they can only do so using a special application called a virtual private network. You have to have a user ID, which Tech Support assigns, and a password.

"Now, this file is a record of every remote login attempt." He scrolled down to a long list of user IDs, beside each of which it said ACCESS DENIED. "But here you can see where they actually did breach the firewall. Notice the date, by the way. It was a few days before Seth showed up."

"Is there any way to know where they were logging in from?" I asked.

"We've traced the IP address to a location outside Baltimore," Ernie replied. "Someone tries from the outside to get into the network. They finally hack in, but that's all for a while. Then suddenly Seth shows up and he loses no time before he's here in person, snooping around the department's files."

"You said you thought he was looking for something that's not accessible from the outside," I reminded him.

"I'm getting to that." He opened another file, a long list of dates and times. A very long list—I scrolled through it, but it was only so many numbers to me.

"Enlighten me."

"This," said Ernie patiently, "is a record of activity on the college of science's server. Here Seth is logged on as himself. What's interesting is that there's activity from someone logged in using the generic guest account—but it's the same date and location as Seth logged in as himself, just a few minutes later. Which doesn't make sense, unless you consider that different logins have different access privileges. He downloaded a couple of files off the server, but you can see here that there's one directory to which access was denied for both his account and the generic account.

"But here's the kicker." He scrolled through the list of user IDs, until we came to one that gave me goose bumps.

"NPritch?"

"Note the date," said Ernie.

I did a quick calculation in my head. "This was the night you and I were there! It couldn't have been

Professor Pritchett because he was already dead by that time."

"Yes, so while we were cowering under the desk of the only murder victim in Throckmorton since 1934—"

"Excuse me," said Tim. "Am I missing something?"

"Well, yes, actually," I replied. I told him about our close encounter.

He cast his eyes heavenward and shook his head. At least he didn't lecture us. "So when this Seth guy almost caught you and Ernie snooping around in the science lab, he was there trying to hack into the department's files by logging on as the late Nigel Pritchett."

"That's what it's starting to look like," said Ernie.

"Do you think that clunky old computer out in the lab is part of the secret network?" I asked.

"Well, it might explain why he was on the old computer and not on the spiffy new one in his office," Ernie replied.

"So what do you make of all this?" asked Tim. "One professor is dead and his closest friend almost. You've found the dead professor's replacement combing through the department's files. Does anybody else know about this?"

"Not yet.

"Don't you think maybe it's time somebody did?" said Tim, sounding a bit exasperated.

"Ahem, well," said Ernie, "I'd be happy to inform the authorities, if there was some way we could without getting ourselves in trouble." At Tim's questioning look, he continued. "It might be kind of hard to explain how we know all this."

"Good point," said Tim. "Margo said you got an EVP that night."

"Indeed we did. We're not sure what to make of it, especially under the circumstances. Have a listen."

Tim put the giant headphones on and was quiet for a minute while he pressed them to his ears. "Play it again." He listened to it a couple of times. "Tell me what you think it says, and I'll tell you what it sounds like to me."

"We think it's saying 'Look out for Ben,'" I said.

Tim shook his head. "I agree it's a little hard to make out. It's fuzzy right in the middle. Let's see what we can do to enhance it." He tinkered with the wave pattern for a few seconds and played it again. "Listen," he said, with a triumphant smile, giving the headphones to Ernie.

Ernie's expression changed. I could almost see a light bulb pop on over his head. "Yes, of course! It's so obvious now. Here, Margo." He passed the headphones to me.

I played the recording and listened carefully. I had to listen to it a couple of times, but now I could make out clearly what it said. "It's saying 'Look *after* Ben' not 'Look *out for* Ben.' It's pretty obvious, isn't it?"

"It would seem so. We didn't do a very good job, did we?" said Ernie ruefully.

"What I don't understand," said Tim, "is why you didn't hear it when it happened."

"We get asked that question a lot," said Ernie. "It's actually fairly straightforward. An EVP, by definition, is any sound that's picked up electronically that wasn't audible to the human ear."

"But why would your audio equipment be able to detect sounds outside the normal range of hearing? I would think it would more like the opposite—that you can hear things that the equipment doesn't pick up."

"It depends on the equipment, of course," Ernie replied. "But it helps to understand how sounds work. When you hear something with your ears, it's because something has vibrated the air. Those vibrations are interpreted by your brain as sounds. We think that, with electronic voice phenomena, an entity is somehow using generated energy to manipulate the mechanism of the electronic device itself to make the sounds, bypassing the ear completely. Two entirely different things—hey, that looks like Sandy." He pointed to the security monitor that gave us a view of the hall. On the screen, we could see Sandy at the janitor's closet door, holding the door open with one hand and awkwardly maneuvering his bike with the other. "I'll open the door for him."

"Does he ever go anywhere *not* by bike?" asked Tim.

Before I could answer, we heard Ernie exclaim from inside the broom closet, "Holy cannoli! What happened to you?"

Sandy, with an expression of murderous rage on his normally serene face, wheeled his bike into the lab. His jeans were torn and filthy. There was a hole in one knee, exposing an ugly, bleeding scrape. The rear tire flopped loosely about the wheel and the chain was clanking uselessly against the frame.

"Some asshole tried to run over me!"

"What!" "You're kidding!" "Are you okay?"

"Let me help you with this. You got some tools somewhere, man?" said Tim, taking the bike and deftly flipping it over on its handlebars.

"There's a toolkit in here," replied Sandy, fumbling with his ever-present backpack, which was dirty but still in one piece.

"Sandy, tell us what happened!" I said.

"Honestly, I don't really know. I just left class and was headed this way when suddenly this car comes out of nowhere. I didn't hear him until he was practically on top of me. If swear, if I hadn't bailed out onto the grass, he would have run right over me."

"Did you get a look at the car?" asked Ernie.

"Late model silver something. One of those luxury brands, a Lexus or BMW maybe...not sure, it happened so fast. He was gone before I could get a look."

"Well, there's no real damage done," said Tim. He had the chain back on its sprocket and was coaxing the tire onto the wheel. "You've got a few scratches and a dent on the fender, but it should ride just fine."

Gingerly, Sandy brushed flecks of dirt from his scratched knee. I handed him a first-aid kit that I'd found in the depths of one of the cabinets in the kitchenette. "I guess I should consider myself lucky," he said.

"I was just about to suggest we adjourn for lunch. Why don't you join us?" I said. "You'll feel better."

"No, thanks," replied Sandy hesitantly.

"You sure?" I pointed out. "My treat."

"I know, but I...um...there's something I need to look into."

"Well, I'm in," said Ernie.

"Me, too," said Tim.

"Well, all right. If we can't change your mind..."

"Thanks, but don't worry about me," said Sandy.

When we left him, he was working away at the computer.

Haunted School, Round 2

For our second investigation at the school, we set things up much like before. As we unloaded the cars and hauled the boxes and carts down the halls to the old wing, I waited for signs of friction between Ernie and Elaine, but they showed nary a sign that there had ever been anything between them but the most professional of relationships. Ernie was in a jovial mood, and a couple of times I caught Elaine watching him with an expression that was difficult to read.

I reasoned that we were most likely to make contact with our friendly entity in Mrs. Cartwright's room, but I hoped we might find more evidence in areas we hadn't yet covered and Principal Golding had given her okay for us to wander a little farther afield. Using as our reference the information Sandy had uncovered, we set up some cameras and sound recorders in a wing of recent construction that looked to be in the approximate location of the old orphanage dormitories.

We set up a table and some computers in Mrs. Cartwright's room and put Tim in charge of monitoring the half-dozen or so audio and video feeds.

He accepted his assignment with good humor and didn't seem to mind being low man on the totem pole.

"Before we turn the lights out we still need to capture our new recruit's voice for the VR program," Ernie reminded us. The voice recognition program is an invention of Ernie's, one that we've had a lot of success with. It uses voice recognition to identify voices that don't belong to anybody on the investigating team. The few minutes it takes us to set up and configure it saves us hours of tedium later when we review the evidence. EVPs, especially of the Class C variety, can be easy to miss during the review process—it's hard to stay alert after listening to hours and hours of recordings. Ernie's invention runs through the audio files in a few minutes and flags every sound, attempting to match the voices with recognized voices in the database.

"What do you want me to say?" asked Tim.

"Anything. It doesn't matter," said Ernie waving a microphone in his direction.

"This is Tim Beckwith. Testing one, two, three."

"Okay, got it."

Ernie produced a parabolic mike from one of his equipment bags. "Where do you want me to put the sonic ear?" he asked.

"Near the blackboard," I answered. "That's where we were when we got the responses on the K2 meter last time." Ernie parked the parabolic mike on a desk near the front of the room and pointed it toward the blackboard. He went back to the computer and pulled up another program. Giving Tim the headphones he said, "Put these on. We need to test it for volume levels." Ernie went back to the front of the room and whispered something I couldn't hear.

"Got it," said Tim.

"Great! Let me try again from over here."

"Ow!" Tim pushed the headphones away and grabbed his ears. "The last time I heard something that loud it was at a Ramones concert. And it's in stereo."

"Whoops...sorry," said Ernie, pushing a button on the sonic ear. "Now try it."

"WHAT?"

"I said 'Now try...' Oh, stop it!"

I left them squabbling and went to set up the video camera and toy car in the hall. This time I also went to a classroom in the new wing and put out a small rubber ball, a doll, and some jacks, marking their locations with chalk.

Before turning the lights out we did a quick sweep of the area for base readings. Ernie and Elaine went from room to room with EMF meters and temperature gauges while I concentrated on Mrs. Cartwright's room.

Tim watched with interest. "Why go to all the trouble?" he asked, as I moved around the room with various gadgets and an iPad.

"Well, we always do a sweep to find out what's normal for a location so that we can distinguish background radiation from potential paranormal activity. Same for the ambient temperature. I'm comparing tonight's readings with what we got last time we were here."

"I notice it goes off around the wall plugs and computers," said Tim.

"That's normal. These devices all give off electromagnetic energy. A strong electromagnetic field can come from any number of perfectly mundane sources. Old electrical wiring is particularly likely to cause a response on our meters. Which is why we do this. It helps us sort out the normal from the paranormal."

Tim chortled. "Come over here. You have to see this." He pointed to one of the monitors.

Ernie and Elaine were in a classroom in the new wing. By the light of their flashlights I could just make out two dark shapes—locked in a passionate embrace.

"Oh, for crying out loud! That's the last thing we need," I said.

As we watched, they separated and went on about their work. "It was just an innocent smooch. Much like this one," he said, pulling me toward him.

I dodged the kiss. "There's plenty of time for that later."

"Can't blame a guy for trying," he said with a good-natured shrug.

"Time to get to work for real. Ready for me to turn out the lights?"

"Ready as I'll ever be."

I turned out the lights. The computer monitors gave off an eerie glow that bathed one half of the room in a soft blue light. "I'm going to start with an EVP session using the sonic ear," I said. "It's got a wireless transmitter. You'll be able to see on the computer if it picks up anything."

Moving to the front of the room, I whispered "Testing, testing. Okay, Timmy, whenever I speak it should show up as a waveform on your computer."

He nodded. "It's working."

"Good. Okay here goes. I'm trying to contact Theodore, who wrote on the blackboard. Theodore, are you here? I bet you don't like to be called Teddy. I'm a friend of Mrs. Cartwright's. If you're here can you let me know?"

"I'm getting something!" exclaimed Tim.

"Play it back and let's see if we can hear what they're saying!"

Tim reached for the headphones and put them on. The look of astonishment on his face was almost comical.

"Margo!" he whispered. "I can hear voices. It sounds like they're saying 'We're here'. But there's more than one voice."

"Good! Just keep an eye on it and let me know what's going on. Is that you, Theodore? My name's Margo and that's my friend Tim. Do you want to play a little game? If you'll yell as loud as you can into this toy here, I might be able to hear you." I paused for a few seconds. "Is anyone else here with you? Do you like school? "

I waited for a few minutes, watching Tim, who signaled that sounds were still registering on the computer.

"Theodore, tell us why you stay here. Don't you miss your family? You don't have to stay here, you know. You can go with them now."

Suddenly there was a commotion in the hall Ernie and Elaine stormed into the room, deep into a heated argument.

"So much for that," said Tim with a sigh, removing the headphones. "I think we've lost them."

"Thanks a lot, you guys," I moaned.

"Sorry," they mumbled in unison.

Elaine gave Ernie a dirty look and said icily, "I'm going to see if I can get anything with the thermal camera." She stomped out of the room lugging the thermal camera. Ernie started after her, but I stopped him.

"I don't think she wants your help. Besides, we could use you here. This is—was—turning into a great EVP session."

"Sorry," he said in a stage whisper, perching on the edge of one of the desks.

Tim put the headphones back on and we waited for a few seconds until he nodded to us.

"Hey, Theodore. Remember me from the other night? My name's Ernie. Did you see the car out in the hall? I put it there again for you to play with."

Suddenly Elaine burst into the room, causing us all to jump. "You won't believe what I got!" she said breathlessly.

"Thanks for almost giving me a heart attack!" said Ernie.

"Well, *pardonnez moi!*"

Ernie bristled. Before he could start their argument all over again I said, "Enough already. What did you find?"

"I went over to the new wing where you put out those toys. Look!"

The four of us clustered around the thermal camera's tiny display screen. A thermal camera uses temperatures rather than visible light to display images. Unexplained cold spots are often a sign of paranormal activity and we've used the thermal camera to record them with sometimes startling results.

"These are the toys you put out," she said, pointing to some vaguely toy-shaped forms. "Now watch."

A small spot of red light appeared near the doll. As it grew larger it began to turn white. It formed a child-sized blob, then bent over the doll. Abruptly, it vanished, but there was a distinct heat signature that lingered on the doll. "Let me zoom in on it." As the camera zoomed in, the image of the doll filled the tiny screen. On the doll was a small handprint; it glowed red, lingering for a moment, then winked out.

Unfortunately, it was the high point of the evening. Although we stayed until the wee hours, we didn't hear another peep.

§

It was almost noon before we got up the next day. I was sitting on the bed drying my hair when Ernie called. "Hey, Ernie. What's up?"

"I couldn't sleep last night, so I started looking at the evidence....what's that weird noise?"

"Just Tim whistling in the shower."

"Hmmm. Sounds like a rusty hinge. Anyway, I started going through the files, and we got some stuff I think the whole team needs to hear. I thought it might be fun if we could all look at it together. Do you have plans for this evening?"

"Well, no, but..."

"Good. My place around seven, then. Nothing fancy, a small affair, just you and Tim, Sandy... and Elaine," he said casually. "She's bringing dessert."

"Dessert?" I sighed. "In that case, I guess I should bring something. What's she bringing?"

"I don't know. She's keeping it a secret."

"This ought to be interesting," I said. "I'll bring my usual." Tim came out of the bathroom, his dark hair wet, still whistling. "Just the person I want to see," I told him. "Ernie's invited us over tonight to look at evidence. Are you up for it?"

"Sounds great," said Tim.

To Ernie I said "We're in. See you tonight."

Tim got dressed while I finished drying my hair. I savored this little moment of easy domesticity, more than I would, I suppose, if this were something we could do every day. "What shall we do between now and time to go to Ernie's?" I asked.

"I don't care what we do as long as there's food involved. I'm starving."

§

Twenty minutes later we were sitting in a booth at the Empress of Siam.

"I still can't get over the fact that pokey little Indian Springs finally has a decent Thai restaurant," remarked Tim as he studied the menu.

"Yep, you can imagine how thrilled I was when this place opened up. It beats the heck out of having to go all the way to San Guillermo for Pad Thai."

"So that makes how many real restaurants in town now? Ten? A dozen?"

"If that. But there's always Throckmorton."

"It's a far cry from how it was when I lived here."

"Yeah," I said, "and that was a long time ago. The town has changed. A lot."

We gave our orders to the petite Asian woman who came around. She owns the place, and most of the time waits tables, too.

"You know," said Tim, "within a few blocks of my apartment there are half a dozen excellent Thai places, sushi bars, bagel shops. Margo, when you moved back here, did you think you would end up staying?"

It was a valid question, and one that was hard to answer. "You know, there's a certain feeling of security you get from being around familiar places and people. Of course, the place you come back to is never the same place that you left, is it?"

"No, I suppose not. You know, after high school my parents worked hard to convince me to live at home and go to college in Throckmorton," he mused.

"Really? I didn't know that!"

"Yeah, but I couldn't bear the thought of staying here. You'd already moved away and everything reminded me of you. Have I ever told you how miserable I was my senior year? Anyway, going away to school was possibly the best decision I've ever made. Except, of course, for getting back in touch with you. But don't you get bored here?"

"Oh, Tim. You know perfectly well I do. It would be nice if we had more than a handful of restaurants. I'd like to be able to go to a museum or see a play without having to drive for an hour. But I'd have to make tons more money...what do you think a house like mine would cost in San Francisco?"

He took my hand, seemed to be studying it intently. Then finally he said "But that wouldn't matter, 'cause you'd live with me."

Maybe I was just tired, but I suddenly felt a little teary. I summoned all my self-control and said, "As much as I'd love to live with you, it's just not time yet."

The moment was spoiled when the waitress/owner appeared with our food. Is it just me or do people who work in restaurants have some kind of uncanny ability to sense right when a conversation is getting intense?

"What else you need?" asked the waitress, seemingly oblivious to our discomfort. "You want fork?"

"We're fine for now, thanks," he said.

She nodded curtly and headed toward the next table, giving us a curious look over her shoulder as she left. An idea suddenly occurred to me. "Timmy, I know you love living in San Francisco, but wouldn't it be possible to manage your business from here?"

"You mean move? Oh, Margo, you know how I feel about this town…"

"I don't necessarily mean move—just…expand. I mean, you could manage your consulting business from anywhere, couldn't you?"

He thought about this for a moment. "Possibly. But I have an established client base on the west coast. Expanding into a new market isn't as easy as all that."

"Well, then we have to stick with our current arrangement for a while longer."

"But it works both ways. Couldn't you do paranormal research anywhere, too? I mean, it seems like if ghosts are everywhere, as you say they are, that some place like San Francisco would be the perfect spot."

"One of the things I like most about what I do is that I get paid for it, Timmy. Where else am I going to find a job like mine?"

"So convince some other school to start a paranormal research department."

"Look Timmy, you know I love you. But this job is the opportunity of a lifetime. And I love it. Now that you've been a part of it, can't you see how I feel?"

"Okay, Margo," he said, kissing my hand. "As long as it's the job and not me."

I took a bite of my curry and my tongue burst into flames. I reached for my water glass. "When they say extra spicy, they mean extra spicy."

"You think so? Mine seems kind of bland." He spooned a hefty dollop of sriracha sauce onto his noodles. "Better."

§

After lunch we ran errands, including a stop by the hardware store in downtown Indian Springs. By late afternoon, we had migrated to the Monk. Tim glanced occasionally, without much interest, at a skateboarding competition on the big screen over the bar and sipped a Scotch and soda. I was nursing a Belligerent Bastard and trying hard not to think about work when my phone chimed. "It's a text from Sandy. Says he went to the county records office and dug up some info on Theodore's mother. She remarried a few years after Theodore died, then died herself a couple of years later. He found her grave; says there's no record for Theodore or the surviving sister. Here's a photo." I held up the phone so Tim could see the photo Sandy had sent, a gravestone in the small cemetery plot.

"She was so young!" he exclaimed. "She was younger than we are now when she died. And she outlived all of her children but one."

"Life was hard," I reminded him. He got quiet after that, sipping his Scotch moodily, not saying much.

I was consider going over my customary two-beer limit, when the door opened and in strolled Seth. He glowered darkly as he scanned the room. When he saw us, his entire demeanor changed. He strode purposefully toward our booth, an obviously forced smile plastered on his face.

"Hello Seth. Won't you join us?" I said, more to be polite than anything.

But he replied, "Don't mind if I do," and plopped down in the seat next to Tim, offering his hand. "Seth Carling."

"Tim Beckwith."

"Seth is the interim professor of chemistry," I said.

"Oh yes, of course. Replacing the late Dr. Pritchett," said Tim.

"Only temporarily. Big shoes to fill. Whatever you've heard about me, it probably isn't true." Seth chuckled with delight at his own joke. "You must be the lucky man I keep hearing about."

"I like to think so," said Timmy, catching my eye. "Actually, we were just about to leave, soon as we pay our bill."

"We were? I mean, yes, we were." I found the waitress and waved her over. "We'll take the check, please."

"Can I get you anything, sir?" asked the waitress, a girl I hadn't seen before. I wondered idly if Megan still worked here.

Seth ordered a beer. "So, how's the ghost hunting business?" he asked suddenly.

"Oh, there've been a couple of breaks in a big case we've got going." I replied. "But I can't talk about it. You understand."

Tim pulled out his wallet and slapped a bill on the table. "We probably need to get going."

"What's the rush?" asked Seth.

"We're due at a friend's house shortly." Tim stood up and handed me my jacket.

Seth slid out of the booth to let me out. "How exciting," he smirked.

"Well, it was nice to meet you. Sorry we can't hang around," said Tim, propelling me toward the door.

"Timmy, why..."

"The guy's a jerk. I want you to stay away from him...hey, don't you know that guy?" He nodded in the direction of the bar.

Officer Toby Garcia was perched on a stool, alone and out of uniform. On the bar in front of him was a large, frosty beer that looked like it hadn't been touched. When he saw me his face lit up; then he saw Tim and his smile faded abruptly.

"Officer Garcia! I didn't know you came here," I said.

"Oh, I stop in for a cold one every now and then." There was an uncomfortable silence.

"Um...Officer Garcia," I said hastily, "you remember Tim." They shook hands, a tad awkwardly, then Garcia nodded at Seth. "You know that guy?"

"Who? You mean Seth? He's a professor at the college. Taking the place of Dr. Pritchett. Why do you ask?" I answered.

"Oh, it's nothing, I guess. His face looks familiar, that's all." He forced a smile that didn't quite go as far as his eyes.

"He's all right," I hastened to add. "A bit annoying maybe, but the students seem to like him."

"Is that so? I'm probably just imagining things, but he's a dead ringer for somebody. Well...you folks enjoy your weekend."

"You know, you were kind of rude to Seth," I said when we got outside.

Tim stopped short and gave me a look of pure exasperation. "And I think you're being naive. Something's not right about the guy. I want you to stay away from him. Please."

Normally it would have irritated me to no end that he was telling me what to do. But in reality I kind of liked it. Besides, I was inclined to agree with him.

"You sure you're not just being overly possessive?"

"I'm not being possessive, Margo. It's common sense," he answered.

"Well, I think all of you men are jumping to conclusions."

"Jumping to conclusions? Margo, he tried to hack into the school's network using the user ID and password of a dead guy. I don't trust him, and apparently neither does this guy Garcia. You really ought to tell the cops...why don't you talk to Garcia?"

"You're probably right," I said with a sigh. "But later. Right now we have to go home and get ready for Ernie's party."

Sandy Earns His Paycheck

"Elaine's already here," I said. "That's a good sign." I parked my trusty Subaru station wagon behind her shiny red BMW. An ear-splitting racket started before we even reached Ernie's front porch. Our gracious host appeared in the doorway, holding the door open a few inches while trying to restrain a tiny white dog with one foot. To no avail; Fang squeezed between Ernie's foot and the door with room to spare and bounded down the front steps. He made a beeline for Tim, yapping furiously. Tim was trying valiantly to pet the maniacally squirming ball of white fluff with one hand while balancing a bowl of guacamole in the other as Sandy rode up on his bicycle. Willis sat in a large basket attached to the handlebars, surveying his surroundings with regal disdain.

"Maybe I should take that," I said. I rescued the guacamole and handed the bowl and a bottle of wine to Ernie.

"Man, that is one homely dog," remarked Tim, watching as Sandy extricated Willis from the basket.

"And that's post-makeover," I said.

Sandy put Willis on the sidewalk and he trotted purposefully toward Tim. "Hey there, Spuds!"

"Stop calling him Spuds!" Sandy groused.

Fang had lost interest in Tim and was staring at the canine newcomer, completely still except for his quivering ears.

I whispered to Sandy, "Are you sure this was a good idea? I mean, he's twice Fang's size."

"They'll be all right."

The two canines regarded one another for a moment, then greeted each other in the customary manner.

"See? I told you," said Sandy.

Fang escorted his new friend into the house, his entire body wagging frantically in the absence of a discernible tail, and we followed.

§

"Sandy, you haven't said much this evening. You feel okay? There's still some guacamole left. You want to finish it?" said Elaine pushing the bowl toward him.

He scooped a small bit of the remaining guacamole onto a chip and nibbled at it absently. "It's nothing. Just tired, I guess."

We were in Ernie's den, sitting around an enormous television screen that displayed an endlessly looping video of a cheerfully crackling fireplace, complete with sound effects. We'd polished off the first bottle of wine and had just opened a second. Fang and Willis, growling playfully, were alternately wrestling and chasing each other.

"If you're not going to finish the guacamole, I will," said Tim.

Sandy shook his head. "It's all yours."

Elaine stood up. "Who's up for dessert?" Everyone raised a hand. "Back in a flash," she said on her way to the kitchen.

"I'd better go help," said Ernie and followed Elaine.

"Point me to the bathroom," said Tim.

"Down that hall and to the right," I said.

As soon as Tim was out of the room, Sandy got up abruptly and sat down next to me. "Margo, listen, I found something out that I think you need to know about. It's about Seth," he said quietly.

"Well, out with it, then. It sounds serious."

"It might be. I found this at the library." He whipped out his phone and showed me a photo of the cover of a book. *Biological Chemistry and You*, by Dr. Seth Carling.

"So he's published a book. College professors do that occasionally, you know."

"Yeah, well, imagine my surprise when I flipped it open and found this." He swiped to another photo, the back cover, complete with author photo. The author of *Biological Chemistry and You* bore no resemblance to the Seth Carling of my acquaintance. The man in the photo staring back at me was probably at least 60, chubby, and bald with a white walrus mustache and glasses. Below the photo was a short blurb about the author.

> Professor Seth Carling is a professor of Organic Chemistry at the Sheldrick Institute. His previous works include *Practical Chemistry for the Scientifically Challenged* and *Fun with Organic Chemistry*. A native of Louisville, Kentucky...

That was all I needed to read. I'm pretty sure the Seth of my acquaintance was not a native Kentuckian. "Father and son?" I asked, trying to sound lighthearted.

"That idea occurred to me, too, so I did a little snooping. I called around on the pretext that I wanted to interview him for an article for the school newspaper."

"And?"

"Professor Carling is indeed on sabbatical. And he's currently in a remote village in Kenya helping build a school. My timing couldn't have been better. I only managed to catch up with him through email because he was in Mombasa for a few days taking a break. He's 67, married, no kids, never heard of Throckmorton College. What do we do?"

"I don't know," I sighed. "But don't bring it up tonight. Tim and Ernie will go ballistic, and I'm not in the mood to deal with it right now. Thanks for telling me."

"There's something else...maybe it's just a coincidence, but when my roommate got home this afternoon, he scared off a guy hanging around in the alley."

A sick feeling started in the pit of my stomach. "A homeless person?"

"Yeah, probably. I'm sure that's all it was."

Down the hall, the bathroom door opened.

"Hope I didn't spoil your evening," he whispered, then jumped up and began hastily gathering up plates and glasses. Tim, returning from the bathroom, looked at him quizzically but said nothing.

"I'll take these." I took the stack of dishes from Sandy and went into the kitchen. "Can I help?"

"Nope. We have it all under control. Just set those over here," said Ernie on his way into the den with a stack of small plates and a container of ice cream.

"Tim seemed to enjoy his first investigation," remarked Elaine as she sliced bananas and arranged them in a pan. "You think he'll want to do it again?"

"I hope so."

Elaine poured the brandy, and blue flames flared in the pan. "It's ready!" Elaine maneuvered the flaming pan carefully as we went back into the den, to appreciative mutterings from the guys. She waited until the flames died down, then spooned bananas and sauce over the bowls of ice cream.

Sandy's appetite had evidently returned—he finished his Bananas Foster and had seconds. Tim allowed himself to be talked into a second round as well.

Ernie topped off everyone's wine glasses. "Maybe we should look at the stuff from the school before we all go into a food coma," he said, tapping on his iPad. The cheery fire vanished from the television screen, replaced by a virtual media console. "This is everything we have so far from both school investigations." He tapped an icon. "What you'll hear is the audio from the parabolic mike. You can see the waveform scrolling along the bottom of the screen there. And here," he said, swirling the cursor around a frozen image of us in Mrs. Cartwright's room, "is the video from the DVR. They're time-synched, so we'll be able to see and hear everything as it happened on different equipment." He started the playback.

I heard myself saying *"Theodore, are you here? I bet you don't like to be called Teddy. I'm a friend of Mrs. Cartwright's. If you're here can you let me know?"*

The response was a soft giggle and some excited whispering. The words were too indistinct for us to make out any words, but the voices sounded like little girls.

"That doesn't sound like anybody whose name would be Theodore," said Ernie.

"Listen, whoever's here, do you want to play a little game? If you'll yell as loud as you can into this toy here, I might be able to hear you."

"Pause it for a second," I said. "Tim, you thought they were saying 'We're here,' but to me it sounds like 'They're here again.'" Then I heard, very distinctly, a voice say *"Theodore."* "Wait a second! I think they're saying 'They're here again, Theodore.' Play it back!"

We listened to it several times. "I think you're right," said Ernie. "You okay, Sandy? Not getting creeped out?"

Sandy's face had gone a funny shade of gray. "Don't worry about me," he replied. "I'll be okay...in a week or two."

"You're a trooper," said Ernie, clapping him on the back. He turned back to his iPad and tapped the Play icon. "There's plenty more where that came from."

I heard myself ask *"Is this your classroom? Are there others with you? Tell me about yourself."*

We heard more giggles and whispers, then a different voice said *"Mother says...mother says to stay here."*

"Do you like school?"

There were more giggles, then a different voice, one that sounded distinctly like a little girl, said *"Theodore likes school."*

"Theodore, tell us why you stay here. Don't you miss your family? You don't have to stay here, you know. You can go with them now."

"Mother says....back for..."

"Wow! Stop it right there," exclaimed Tim. "Ernie, is there anything you can do to clean that up?"

"Let me see what I can do." He isolated the sound clip and worked on it for a few seconds. "Let's try it again."

This time it was easier to understand. *"Mother says...stay here. She will...come back for me."*

We listened to it several times. "That made the hair on my arms stand up," I said.

"Me, too," Tim confessed.

"There's more," said Ernie. "Are you sure you're up for this last bit, Sandy?"

"I guess so," Sandy mumbled.

Ernie tapped his iPad. The next voices we heard were Ernie and Elaine arguing. On the video playback, we saw them burst through the classroom door. "I'll just fast forward through this part, shall I?" he said, looking a bit sheepish. Next, we heard his voice say, *"Did you see the car out in the hall? I put it there again for you to play with."*

The response was not at all what I was expecting. A voice, the one that I'd come to think of as Theodore, answered, "Thank you, sir." There was a few seconds of silence, then the same voice said *"Sir, my stomach hurts."*

"I am *so* creeped out," said Sandy.

We listened to the rest of the file, but aside from a few barely audible giggles, heard only our own voices.

"Well, that's going to keep me awake for a few nights," said Elaine, after a long, uncomfortable silence.

I was inclined to agree with her. I drained my glass, but it failed to dispel the lump in my throat.

"I wish we could figure out a way to help him," said Ernie.

"His mother evidently took him to the orphanage —probably as a last resort—with the intention of coming back for him as soon as possible. It sounds like he thinks he'll get in trouble for disobeying his mother if he leaves," said Tim. "You seem to have established a rapport with him, Ernie. Maybe you can convince him he won't get into trouble for leaving the orphanage."

"Me?" asked Ernie, surprised.

"Well, yeah," Tim replied. "We weren't making any progress at all until you showed up."

Ernie tapped on his iPad. The media console vanished and the virtual fireplace filled the TV screen once again. "Let me think about it a bit. I'll see what I can do."

"You know," said Elaine, "I'm not sure whether I could classify this as an intelligent or residual haunting."

Ernie looked surprised. "How so? The entity is clearly aware of our presence."

"Yes, the definition of an intelligent haunting. But the fact that his stomach hurts, armed as we are with the knowledge that Theodore died from a burst appendix, makes me think that to him, he's reliving—so to speak—a specific moment in time."

"You have a point. Any theories, Margo?" asked Ernie.

My colleagues and Tim are well acquainted with my theory of paranormal activity. My opinion is that time and space are not the smooth continuum we envision when we learn about relativity in school. Instead, they're all crumpled and wrinkly, rather like a wadded-up piece of paper, occasionally bringing different times in contact with one another. Add in an extra dimension or two beyond the three physical dimensions we're familiar with, and it all starts to make sense—sort of. "I see Elaine's point," I said "but we encounter plenty of entities that are aware of our presence, yet aren't aware they've passed on. It must all be terribly confusing, especially to a child."

Everyone was silent for a moment. I sipped my wine and pondered the implications of what we'd just heard.

"So, Tim," said Sandy suddenly, doubtless relieved at the opportunity to change the subject, "how does it feel to be back in the old home town? It must seem like a wide spot in the road after San Francisco."

Tim smiled. "A little bit. But things have improved since I lived here back in the Dark Ages. We had lunch at Empress of Siam today. Imagine! A Thai restaurant in Indian Springs! When I lived here a big night out meant a trip through the McDonald's drive-through," he said.

"Yeah, and until a few years ago we had to go to Throckmorton just to get a beer," mused Ernie.

"Which reminds me. You'll never guess who we ran into this afternoon," I said.

"Hmmm...don't tell me...was it Seth, perhaps?" said Ernie.

"How did you know?" I asked.

"He seems to have a knack for showing up where you happen to be."

Ernie's matter-of-fact statement startled me, and suddenly a chill that wasn't there before seemed to hang in the air. I tried to shrug it off. "Oh, Ernie, don't be paranoid. Indian Springs is a small town. It's hard *not* to run into people you know."

"Hmmm. Maybe. How many times does that make now? By my count, three at least. Where were you?"

"At the Monk's Habit. I didn't see Megan. Does she still work there?"

"Don't know," said Ernie. "I haven't seen her since homecoming."

Elaine stopped in mid-sip to stare at him over her wine glass. "You went to homecoming?"

"Yes," replied Ernie, seemingly oblivious to her frosty tone. "It was fun to be back, rooting for the old team. Didn't you think so, Tim?"

Elaine got up and began gathering the dessert dishes, with a bit more gusto, perhaps, than absolutely necessary. She stalked off into the kitchen without a word, juggling a stack of bowls.

Ernie looked genuinely puzzled. "Did I say something wrong?"

§

The party broke up around midnight. Tim didn't seem to mind when I insisted on following Sandy home, even though it meant going several miles out of our way. But nothing out of the ordinary happened, and when Sandy cycled safely to his front door he dismissed us with a jaunty wave.

Back at my house shortly thereafter, I was about to fall asleep, curled up next to Tim in bed, when he said suddenly, "What was it that you and Sandy were talking about that you didn't want anyone else to hear?"

The cozy sleepy feeling vanished, and I was suddenly wide awake. Should I tell him? Part of me said 'no,' but I thought better of it. "That Seth Carling isn't really Seth Carling."

Tim sat up and switched on the light. "Please explain."

"He found out that the real Seth Carling is currently in Africa building a school."

"So who is this guy, then?"

"You tell me and we'll both know. The dean certainly thinks he's Seth Carling, and that he's here from the Sheldrick Institute."

He sat up in bed. "Okay, are you convinced now? Margo, people don't just go around impersonating dead guys for chuckles and laughs. Promise me you'll talk to the cops."

"I will, but…"

"Soon."

"I will. But I want to talk to the dean first."

"Then do it. I have a bad feeling about this."

I sighed. "If you want to know the truth, so do I."

§

The next morning Tim cooked breakfast for us. Did I mention he's an excellent cook?

"What do you want to do today?" I asked.

"I don't care as long as it doesn't have anything to do with hunting ghosts."

"Well, now! Where did that come from? I thought you were having fun."

"Sorry," he said, smiling ruefully. "I can't stop thinking about Theodore. And I wish I didn't have to go home so soon."

"That makes both of us." I picked up my iPad and opened it to the weekend guide. "There's a street fair in San Guillermo to celebrate the opening of the new park. Crafts, jugglers, face painting—the usual stuff."

"Sounds wonderful," he said, standing up and clearing the table. "You get ready. I'll take care of this."

An hour later we were strolling amidst pine cone Santas and hand-painted pottery, not saying much. We stopped to watch a group of kids in colorful costumes dance before an appreciative crowd. When they finished, we applauded politely.

"Margo," he said suddenly, "do you think I should start working out? I mean I get plenty of exercise, but maybe I should start lifting weights."

"What on earth brought this on?"

"Oh, I don't know. I guess I'm just feeling my age today."

"You don't need to start lifting weights, Tim. You look marvelous the way you are. Hey, maybe I'll get one of those temporary tattoos. I've wanted one for a long time."

He didn't have a chance to answer because my phone rang.

"Of all the...sorry, I'd better answer it. What's up, Sandy?"

"Sorry to bother you on a weekend, but I wanted to run something by you." Sandy's face filled the screen of my phone. "Where are you?"

"At that street fair in San Guillermo."

"Ah yes. The new park. I thought about going to that. Anyway, I thought you might want to know that I found the Routledge family home. We're in luck. That area hasn't been developed yet and the building still stands."

"Some of those old houses have a family burial plot. Can you find out?"

"I already thought about that. I can't be sure but on the satellite image there's something that might or might not be a small graveyard."

"It certainly sounds like we need to check it out. Shall I meet you at the lab bright and early tomorrow morning?"

I turned to Tim and said, "How much of that did you catch?"

"Enough to know that there's a trip to a graveyard in my immediate future."

§

"Whose idea was this, anyway?" grumbled Ernie.

"I think it was yours," answered Sandy. "Okay, I brought bug spray, a first aid kit, a cooler full of drinks...I think we're all set. Is everybody's phone charged up? By the way, cool tattoo, Margo."

"Thanks. Okay, looks like we're good to go," I said. "We'd better get a move on. The weather is supposed to get bad later."

The drive took the better part of an hour. Once he finally woke up completely, Ernie kept up a running stream of chatter, pausing only to send an occasional text. By the time we got to the lonely country road that intersected with the farm-to-market road we were on, I would gladly have strangled him.

I almost missed the turn, obscured as it was by waist-high weeds. We rattled down the gravel road and parked in front of a crumbling abandoned farm house. Much of the wood siding was gone or rotted, and what remained had turned a ghostly silver-gray. The entire structure listed crazily to one side.

Ominous dark clouds did nothing to dispel the gloom, although I suspected that the Routledge family farm wasn't a cheerful place even on the brightest sunny day.

"Wow," whispered Ernie. "It looks like a good strong wind would just flatten it."

We piled out of the car, being careful where we put our feet. The ground was littered with brush, tangles of barbed wire, and broken glass. It was utterly silent. The only sound was an occasional distant roar of a motor on the main road. Even the birds weren't chirping.

"Watch out for snakes, everybody," said Sandy.

Ernie made his way purposefully toward the front porch of the house. Tim followed him.

"You know, if you get hurt or something, we're pretty much out of luck if we need to rush somebody to the hospital," I said.

"Don't worry, we're just going to have a quick peek," said Ernie, brandishing an EMF meter. As they navigated the front porch, I could almost see the house sag.

Sandy and I worked our way carefully through a tangle of brush to the back. When we got to the back, Tim was standing on the back porch—what was left of it—surveying the surroundings. An ancient washing machine with a wringer stood rusting in the middle of the yard. The hull of a tire dangled on a chain from a tree limb; an occasional gust of wind caused it to swing wildly. The tree limb had grown over the chain, engulfing it completely. Across a clearing was the rusted hulk of an old pickup truck.

"Any idea what kind of car that is?" I asked.

"1936 Ford," said Tim.

Sandy, looking dubious, went in for a closer look.

"It's a Ford, all right. We'll take your word on it about the year."

Tim climbed carefully down the rotten porch steps and came over to examine the car. "I know my cars," said Tim. "Much too late for the Routledges. I wonder who lived here after they died."

"It'd be the perfect movie set for a gangster hideout," I said.

"People have certainly been here," said Sandy, kicking at a plastic drink bottle and the shell of an eight-track tape. "Come on. We're wasting time. Where's Ernie?"

We called to him and Ernie poked his head through the back door. He was holding an EMF meter in one hand, a voice recorder in the other and had his phone pressed against his ear with his shoulder. "Look, I gotta go," he said, sounding exasperated.

Juggling the gadgets, he jabbed at the phone fiercely and shoved it into his back pocket, shaking his head.

"Did you get anything?" I called to him.

He shrugged. "A few EMF spikes is all." He started across the crumbling porch.

"Careful, Ernie," called Tim. "One of those boards is..." There was a loud pop as the board Ernie stood on cracked. "...rotten."

"Thanks for the warning," replied Ernie, somehow managing to stay on his feet. He crept gingerly to the edge of the porch, the boards groaning under his weight. When he jumped off the porch, I held my breath for fear that the entire rickety structure would collapse. It didn't, and he joined us, still in one piece, as we set off through the underbrush in what we hoped was the general direction of the Routledge family burial plot.

We climbed a small slope and, after coming to a couple of dead ends, found a grassy clearing dotted with a few gigantic, gnarled trees. A rusted gate hung awkwardly on one hinge, swinging forlornly in the gusts of wind. A few posts marked the boundary of what had once been a fence.

We trooped around, gingerly clearing vines and weeds away from the small collection of headstones. Many of the graves in the small plot were completely overgrown and several headstones were broken. Ernie was unusually quiet and I caught up with him as he stood lost in thought, mulling over a small cluster of unmarked gravestones. "Everything okay?" I asked.

"Huh? Oh, yeah. It's nothing. Just...Elaine again. Seems like there's always something. Sorry, I didn't mean to let it get to me. Look at this one." He pointed to a headstone with an exquisitely carved angel. "Some of these are really sad. Look how young she was."

Most of the people buried here were Routledges, but there were a few other names here and there. I found one whose occupant had been born before the Civil War. It was a small place and didn't take long to find the lonely cluster of graves we were looking for.

"Theodore's not here," said Sandy. "It's just the dad and the other kids." The writing on the gravestones was badly eroded. Some of the inscriptions were unreadable. What we could tell, though, was that these people had all died within a few weeks of each other.

"Here's a scan of the page from the census," said Sandy. "The names match. These are Theodore's brothers and sisters."

"That's disappointing," said Tim. "Now what do we do?"

"We go for a pizza," said Ernie.

The Storm

By the time we got to Umberto's, the afternoon rush-hour crowd was starting to dissipate. We were led to a booth in a far corner. We ordered drinks, which we all slurped down in seconds.

"So this is a typical weekend for you guys, is it?" asked Tim.

"Insofar as there is such a thing," said Ernie.

"I'm disappointed that we didn't find Theodore's grave," I said.

"Me, too, but we found the house where he lived before he went to the orphanage. That's something at least," said Ernie. "Did you notice that old tire swing? I wonder how long it's been there. Maybe Theodore and his brothers and sisters played in it." I heard a chime that sounded like it was coming from somewhere in the vicinity of Ernie's back pocket. He ignored it.

Sandy peeled the wrapper off of a breadstick and munched it thoughtfully. "There's something none of us has considered so far."

"And that would be...?" I asked.

"Another likely place where Theodore and others like him might be buried. He can't have been the only indigent child that died in the care of the orphanage, right? Back in those days, if you were in an institution when you died, you were probably buried there—somewhere on the property," said Sandy.

"Property which is now part of the Rhonda Q. Mills Magnet for Gifted and Talented Children," said Tim.

"Exactly. I'm willing to bet money that they were interred somewhere on the orphanage grounds. It's my hypothesis that the graves of children are under the new wing of the school. Possibly lots of them," said Sandy.

"Which would go a long way toward explaining why there seems to be so much paranormal activity there," Ernie pointed out. "I hope you're wrong."

"Well, I hate to sound callous, but there's probably not much we can do to right that particular wrong now," said Sandy.

"He's right," I said. "We need to focus on finding a way to help Theodore find peace."

"I sure wish I could be there when you do," said Tim.

Ernie poked me in the ribs. "What...?" He nodded toward the door. Toby Garcia was at the hostess station. He was out of uniform and conspicuously avoiding looking in our direction. The hostess took a menu and led him toward a table in a secluded corner.

Sandy raised an eyebrow.

"Tim has competition—that's Margo's admirer," Ernie explained.

"Not to worry, though." I said "Too skinny for my taste."

"Whew, you had me worried there for a moment," said Tim with exaggerated relief. "So what are we going to get on the pizza? Anybody else like mushrooms?"

§

That evening, just as we got back to my house, the bottom fell out of the black clouds that had been gathering all day. The storm pounded my roof and rattled the windowpanes.

"This kind of weather calls for a fire," said Tim, and promptly set about lighting one in the fireplace. It was such a treat—I seldom use the fireplace. I'm usually alone and it seems like such a lot of effort to go to for just one person. We curled up on the sofa with a bottle of wine. We sipped in silence, basking in the toasty glow. Tim seemed lost in thought.

"Hey, stop worrying about Theodore." I said, snuggling up to him.

"Hmm? No, I wasn't thinking about Theodore. Look, I have to leave in a couple of days, and I really don't feel right about leaving you here."

"Relax. You have nothing to worry about. This is Indian Springs. The most exciting thing that ever happens here is when somebody's cat gets stuck in a tree."

"Except that somebody tried to murder your boss and succeeded in murdering his best friend."

"Well, there is that," I admitted.

"Look, something really fishy is going on, and everything points to your pal Seth, or whatever his name is. I'd feel a lot better if you'd distance yourself from it."

"You know that's asking a lot, right? Imagine that you get a phone call from someone whose funeral you just went to and tell me you'd drop it," I huffed.

"You know, Margo, I just might if I thought somebody might be trying to kill me. Someone has already tried to run over Sandy..."

"Oh, for heaven's sake, Timmy! It was just a drunk driver."

"Then folks around here sure get an early start," he said, his eyes flashing angrily. "It wasn't even lunch time yet!"

"I admit you have a point. But whatever else is going on doesn't involve me."

"Correction: *didn't* involve you." He closed his eyes and took a deep breath. Controlling his voice carefully, he continued, "Look, somebody wants something badly enough that they're willing to kill to get it." The memory of the look in Seth's eyes when he told me the story about the jellyfish made my skin crawl. I shivered, and Tim pulled me closer to him. "Has it ever occurred to you," he continued, "that maybe the bizarre email you got has something to do with what Mr. Mystery Guy is looking for? Do you think it's a coincidence that you found him snooping around the lab in the middle of the night? Promise me you'll go to the dean and tell him everything."

I groaned. "But that could get me in so much trouble. We weren't supposed to be in the science lab that night. I'll be lucky if they don't cancel the program!"

"Good. Then you can come to San Francisco and move in with me. Promise me one more thing," he said.

"What?"

"I don't want you to be alone with Seth."

"Timmy, don't you trust me?"

"This is not about trust. Of course I trust you. It's just that we have no idea who this guy really is."

"I'm not arguing with you. I'm just trying to figure out the best way to handle this without getting myself into trouble."

"You'll think of something," he said. He reached for the coffee table and picked up *Haunted Pubs of England*. "Where'd you get this?" he asked, flipping through it.

"There's a new bookstore next to Empress of Siam."

"A bookstore...I can't remember the last time I was in a bookstore," he mused.

"What happened to the one just down the street from you?" I asked, surprised.

"Oh, it's still there. But I buy books online and read them on my tablet." As he flipped through the book, Tim continued, "Some of these places look interesting. They'd be fun to investigate. Margo, we should go on a trip somewhere..."

"Paris."

"Excuse me?"

"I want to go to Paris."

Tim looked at me and raised an eyebrow. "Okay, Margo, if you want to go to Paris, then you shall go to Paris."

§

Normally, I'm secretly relieved when my visitors leave and happy to have my house back to myself. But on Tim's last day here, I dreaded every passing minute.

We had no plans for the day, and after analyzing our options we decided to have a picnic at the park. We lugged the drink cooler and picnic hamper to a sunny spot near the creek and found a dry bench. The day was pleasantly warm and sunny. As often happens in this part of the country, the only sign of last night's storm were soggy grass and a few broken limbs here and there.

Hungry ducks surrounded us before I had even unpacked the picnic hamper. They huddled just out of reach, waiting patiently. I pulled out some bread and a box of cat food.

"Cat food?" asked Tim.

I shrugged. "They love it." I tossed out a handful of the cat food and some bits of bread. In seconds, twice as many ducks seemed to have materialized out of nowhere.

Tim crumbled a slice of bread and placed the crumbs a few inches from his feet. A couple of the boldest ducks waddled over and gobbled them up greedily. "They seem to know you," he said. "You must come here a lot."

"Oh, I don't know about a lot. A couple of times a week maybe. Sometimes it's nice to be able to get away from the computers and gadgets—and the ghosts. Pour us some wine?"

He uncorked a bottle of chardonnay and filled some plastic glasses. "You know, being here has been really strange. When I left for college, I couldn't wait to shake the dust of Indian Springs off my feet. But when I come here, it still feels like home. I get nostalgic, I guess. Especially when I'm around you. Do you ever get nostalgic?" he asked.

"Not for my childhood especially. But sometimes I still feel like I'm in touch with my inner teenager."

"Whatever happened to that guy you used to go with? The one who was in class with us? He played guitar, I think."

"You mean Corey? He's a video producer now. Lives in L.A., last I heard."

"You and Roxy used to sit around and moon over him. I never let on, but I used to get so jealous." He had a melancholy look in his eyes. "I remember when I sat with you and Roxy at lunch one day and listened to you describe your date with Corey in gruesome detail. You went to Chandler's Union, if I recall. It was killing me."

Chandler's Union—a legendary place when we were kids. I hadn't thought about it in years. An undeveloped tract of land between Throckmorton and Deerfield, it was supposed to be haunted by the spirit of an escapee from the lunatic asylum. To question the whereabouts of this supposed lunatic asylum never occurred to anyone. If it had, we would have learned that there was not, nor had there ever been, a mental institution anywhere within a 100 mile radius of Throckmorton County. But it was dark and creepy, and out in the middle of nowhere, and there was never any delusion as to why your date was taking you to Chandler's Union. You went there to make out, and as far as I know nobody ever once saw so much as a shadow of the escaped convict's ghost.

"I know it's a little late, but I'm really sorry, Tim. I would never have knowingly hurt you."

He brushed my apology off with a little laugh. "I used to daydream about taking you out. In my dreams we always ended up Chandler's Union. I wonder if the kids still go there."

"I doubt it," I answered. "A developer bought the land a few years ago, and now it's covered with suburban housing pods."

He shuddered. "Who'd want to live there? The very idea gives me chills." Abruptly, he got up and walked to the edge of the creek. It had overflowed its banks because of the rain, and the receding water had left behind a jumble of garbage. "Look at this! This creek used to be pristine." He began angrily gathering up plastic shopping bags and drink bottles. "How can people be so thoughtless?"

We spent a few minutes picking up the soggy debris—fast-food wrappers, an occasional tennis ball, but mostly lots of plastic. Tim stormed around, grumbling every time he shoved more junk into the lone—and now overflowing—park garbage can. I'd never seen him so angry. Something was definitely bothering him.

"Tim, is something wrong? Besides the trash, I mean."

He stopped suddenly and took me gently by both shoulders. He searched my face for a moment, looking into my eyes. "Margo, there's something I need to know and you have to promise to answer me truthfully."

"Of course, Tim, anything," I said. But my stomach was suddenly doing flips.

"What happened between you and Seth?

§

I sniffled and dried my eyes on a paper towel. "And that's all, I swear."

It was one of the few times I've seen Tim angry—I mean *really* angry—and it was a somewhat formidable sight to behold. "It's not your fault. And I promise I'm not mad. Not at you, anyway." But his hands were clenched into tight fists, and an unfamiliar fire flashed in his normally serene brown eyes.

"In retrospect, I should have seen it coming," I said ruefully. "And I should have told you."

He took a deep breath and flexed his shoulders. "No, it's probably a good thing you didn't tell me until now." The storm in his eyes faded into hurt. "I'm sorry for ruining our picnic."

"You didn't ruin the picnic. In fact, I feel much better now."

He was back to his old self. "Let's pack this stuff up before the ants get to it. I want to try to figure out where the squirrels are getting into your attic, and this is my last chance for a while."

§

"You see?" said Tim. "You might as well have a sign outside that says 'Squirrels Welcome'." He tugged cautiously at an ancient piece of wire mesh over a vent on the gable. One entire side was loose. Flakes of old paint crumbled off of it. "Who knows how long this has been here...probably long before you bought the place. Hand me the hammer, please."

I left Tim to his squirrel-proofing and grabbed a flashlight. I hadn't spent much time in the attic since I bought the place several years ago. Apparently neither had the previous owners. I shone the flashlight in dark nooks and crannies that I'd never explored, but found only a box of vintage Christmas tree ornaments and a stack of magazines from the 1970s. I was perusing a recipe intriguingly called Astronaut Fruitcake, when my phone rang. It was Sandy.

"I've been down at the county records office," said Sandy. "It's just as I expected—the orphanage had a cemetery."

"I don't know if this is good news or bad news," I said truthfully.

"I made copies of the plat maps if you'd care to have a look."

"Yes, of course. We'll stop by in the morning on the way to the airport."

Tim was inspecting his handiwork, making a few taps with the hammer here and there. "This will hold you for a while, but really, all this old wooden stuff needs to be replaced."

"It's a project for next time," I replied, making my way carefully across the ceiling joists. "I have no intention of spending our last evening together crawling around in the attic."

Enough Excitement for One Day

The next morning, Tim and I stopped by the lab on the way to the airport. In spite of the hour, a few protesters were already there, but their cars were presumably parked somewhere down the block. Sandy's bike and Ernie's car were already in their new designated spaces right in front. Feeling smug, I parked next to Ernie and tossed my parking permit on the dash.

"They get an early start," remarked Tim.

"Yeah, kind of makes you wonder what they'd be doing if they weren't harassing us. At least we don't have to hike from down the street anymore. You know it's kind of scary. I'm starting to recognize some of them."

In the lab, Sandy and Ernie were looking unusually cheerful when we walked in.

"My goodness," I said. "Aren't we a couple of happy campers this morning. What happened? Did Irmalene turn in her resignation?"

"Better," said Ernie. "The dean's office called...Dr. Holmes is home from the hospital."

"Well, that's the best news I've heard in a while," I said. "So show me what you found." We gathered around the computer and looked over Sandy's shoulder as he pulled up the files. "Here's a plat map of Norton Township in the 1900s." On another monitor, he opened a different file. "Here's a satellite image of the same area today. "This is obviously the original school building, and here's where the orphanage was. Look at this area right here."

"Burial grounds," said Tim. "Right where the new wing is now. Honestly, who builds a school over a graveyard?"

"It happens all the time," I reminded him. "If they wouldn't spend the money for a doctor for a little boy with a burst appendix, I doubt if they spent much on grave markers. By the time the orphanage was torn down, probably nobody remembered that a cemetery was ever there. This goes a long way toward explaining why there's so much paranormal activity in that particular spot."

"And nobody ever thought to look into it. Until we came along," mused Ernie.

Sandy unrolled some papers. "There's more. I found these aerial photographs—the precursor to Google Earth. Here's the area in the 1930s. It's a bit fuzzy, but if you compare it with the plat map, you can see the orphanage buildings. It's not much different than the plat map from thirty years earlier. But in this photo from the 1950s, most of those buildings are no longer there." He pointed to an area of the grainy black-and-white photo. "This building here, for example, looks recently demolished—only the foundation remains."

"I wonder," said Ernie, "if any of these graves could be moved now. If I'm reading the old map correctly, this entire area was a cemetery. The new buildings cover only part of it."

"You're right," said Tim. "It doesn't make up for everything, but it would at least be a step in the right direction."

"It's worth looking into," said Sandy. "I have to go. I have a class in ten minutes."

Tim glanced at his phone. "Guys, as much as I hate to say this, I probably need to get going, too."

"Seems like you just got here," said Ernie. Tim said his goodbyes to Ernie and Sandy.

"Hope we see you again soon," said Sandy on his way out the door.

"That makes two of us," replied Tim.

Tim wrapped an arm around me as we walked, rather reluctantly, back to my car. The overweight woman with frizzy hair rushed toward me shaking a tattered sign. "Oh, give it a rest," I snapped.

§

When the San Guillermo airport was built in the 1960s, it was was well and truly out in the boonies. It's now in the busiest part of town. Traffic can be brutal, but we'd missed the worst of rush hour—to my disappointment. I had secretly been hoping that we would get stuck in traffic and Tim would miss his flight. I had no such luck, though, and we pulled up to the curb with time to spare.

"Are you sure you don't want me to go in with you?"

"You see that policeman over there? Giving you a ticket would make his whole day."

It was true; the burly cop patrolling the drop-off lane stared at us with a look that suggested he was itching to whip out his citation book.

We got out and I was helping Tim get his bags out of my car when he suddenly took me by both shoulders and looked into my eyes. "Margo, promise me that some day we won't have to do this."

"I'm working on it—honestly."

"I mean soon. And you're going to go to the dean and tell him what Sandy told you."

"Don't worry...I will."

"Today."

"Okay, today."

He kissed the top of my head. "I don't feel right about leaving you."

"There's nothing to worry about—really. I'll be careful."

We shared a lingering kiss.

"I love you, Margo. I always have."

"I love you, too, Timmy. Text me when you get home. I'll see you soon—I'll take a long weekend. We'll talk about Paris." I wanted to say much more, but I just couldn't. I was afraid if I opened my mouth I would start bawling like a baby.

Tim had tears in his eyes, too. He looked deep into my eyes, squeezed my hand, and turned away. Forlornly, I watched him go through the doors.

In the privacy of my car I allowed myself to give in to the tears, but only for a few minutes—the policeman was strolling nonchalantly in my direction. "This is silly," I told myself. "We talk almost every day. It's almost as good as him being here." But it isn't —not by a long shot—and I missed him already. The cop was moving along the line of cars idling at the curb, rapping on car windows, telling drivers to move.

I took a certain childish pleasure in driving away just as he was about to pound on my window. Going home, however, was the last thing I wanted to do. I knew I'd just mope around the house and feel sorry for myself. So I decided to go to the lab; it would help take my mind off of Tim. I had plenty of reports to write—it's part of my job, after all—and the ones I started before Tim came had been languishing.

Driving back from Sam Guillermo gave me time to mull over the events of the past few weeks. Not for the first time, I found myself wondering how long Tim would wait for me while I chased specters. But it's my dream job, and the thought of going back to being a cubicle dweller made my blood run cold. Yet I knew that one of us would have to move if the relationship were going to survive in the long run. Which one of us would make the sacrifice? Experience has taught me that the person who makes the sacrifice usually ends up resentful.

The more I was with Tim, the more I realized how lucky I was. It wasn't just that he was smart and handsome and loved me for who I was; we had a solid relationship, a real history together before we became more than friends. He was a part of my life like few other people would ever be.

The darkly overcast sky matched my mood. Here it was, twenty minutes after I dropped him off at the airport and I was still fighting tears. I glanced at the clock on the car's dashboard. His plane probably hadn't even taken off yet. A voice in my head said, "Get hold of yourself, Margo."

I remembered how I'd been mooning over Seth, and felt sick at my stomach. If Tim had ever had the slightest inkling that I'd been attracted to Seth, he didn't let on. But I knew how hurt he would have been, and the very thought made me want to cry. How could I have almost jeopardized my relationship with him over a smarmy slimeball like Seth?

§

When I pulled up in front of the horticulture pavilion, Ernie was about to get in his car. "Gotta make a run to the electronics store in Deerfield. Don't look for me until after lunch."

Inside the horticulture pavilion it was unusually quiet. A couple of students were in the greenhouse in front, working industriously on some interesting-looking plants; otherwise, the place was deserted.

Inside the lab I found a barely-legible note that Ernie had scrawled for me. Not being in a sociable mood, I was happy to have the place to myself. Sandy had classes and wouldn't be in until the afternoon. It seemed like a good time to catch up with what was going on in the paranormal world. Promising myself I would walk over to the dean's office after lunch, I went to one of my favorite blogs from a team in the UK, and was absorbed in reading about a particularly interesting case when someone pounded on the service door.

Annoyed, I went to the door, assuming Ernie had forgotten something and had to come back. I wondered for the briefest of instants why he chose to go to the back door. There was another knock, louder this time, and more persistent. I yanked the door open. "Ernie, I swear you'd forget your head if it wasn't attached..." But it wasn't Ernie standing there. "Seth...oh, for heaven's sake! You should have let me know to expect you."

"Good morning, Margo," he purred. "I trust I didn't catch you at a bad time." In retrospect, the way his eyes didn't meet mine should have been a red flag. He seemed to be studying the metal doorframe, running a finger along the edge.

"Well, Seth, actually, this isn't a good time..."

"But I see you're all alone. Surely you wouldn't mind some company? Aren't you at least going to offer me a coffee?"

Exasperated, I stepped aside and let him in. "Fine. One coffee. But then I really have to get back to work."

"No worries."

Although my instincts were telling me something wasn't right, I went to the kitchenette and slopped some grounds into the filter. "Cream? Sugar?"

"Neither for me, thanks. I see there are others like you out there...chasing ghosts and all, I mean." I looked up to see Seth seated at my computer, mouse in hand. My stomach did a flip-flop.

"Well, yes, of course. Surely you didn't think we're the only ones doing this kind of research? But, um...if you don't mind," I said, trying to keep my voice calm, "a lot of the stuff we do is confidential.

"How rude of me."

I returned with two miserly cups of coffee in small styrofoam cups. "What other fascinating stuff is on here?" he said, studying the computer's screen intently. He took the coffee and, without tasting it, set it down. He made no move to get out of my chair.

"Oh, nothing particularly interesting," I replied, trying to sound casual. "Just the usual administrative stuff."

"Well," he said, finally tearing his eyes away and vacating my chair, "that's disappointing."

I glanced at the computer and noted with relief that nothing was open except the blog I'd been reading. Calm down, Margo, I thought to myself. He's creepy but you don't know for a fact that he's dangerous. Your imagination is running away with you.

Seth clasped his hands behind his back and strolled casually toward a table strewn with bits of the electronics project Ernie had been working on. He picked up a circuit board and looked it over. "Where's Stapleton this morning?"

"He had to make a quick run to the store...but he should be right back," I added hastily.

"Is that so?" I cringed a little bit as Seth tossed the circuit board roughly back onto the table.

I watched him continue his leisurely stroll around the room. "Look, Seth, I was just about to start working on the budget. I don't mean to be rude, but really, I don't have time right now," I said.

"Oh, but you do, Margo. You have all the time in the world." The pseudo-British accent was gone, replaced by one that was one hundred percent New Jersey.

My stomach lurched. Then my brain started working again and I made a lunge for the door, knocking over my chair. It clattered to the ground with a harsh metallic clang. Seth was between me and the door in two steps. He caught me by the arm in a grip like a vice.

"Margo!" he exclaimed, "how careless of you!" There was cold fury in his eyes. Still holding my arm, he set the chair carefully upright without taking his eyes off me. Twisting my arm painfully, he shoved me into the chair with a savage grunt. I started to struggle, and suddenly found myself staring down the blade of a knife. A really big knife.

"My goodness, Margo, but what *has* happened to your manners today? Let's have a look at your email."

"My email? Look, Seth, I don't know what this is all about..."

"Call it a hunch...humor me."

Out of the corner of my eye I could just see the security monitor and noticed, wistfully, that the hall outside the janitor's closet was bustling with activity. I was only a few feet from the door, but it might as well have been a mile.

"You know, Seth, Ernie will be back any minute."

"I doubt it," he answered matter-of-factly. "That precious little shit-heap of his will have broken down long about the time he got on the highway. My feelings are very hurt that you think I'd let a detail like that slip by."

A muffled shout came from the direction of the front door. Seth froze, tightening his grip. On the security monitor I saw Toby Garcia and the horticulture student I'd seen in the greenhouse earlier —whose name escaped me—running down the hall. They dashed into the janitor's closet and a second later, Officer Garcia pounded furiously on the lab door. His voice through the door was muffled but clear: "Open this door—police!"

Relief washed over me. It vanished just as suddenly when Seth chuckled. "I see local law enforcement has arrived." He turned to look at the monitor; I contemplated taking the opportunity to try to break free, perhaps aided by a well-placed kick to his manly parts. But it was as if he read my mind and he tightened his grip on me, wrenching my arm tighter behind my back. I could feel the tip of the knife in my ribs. "I wondered how long it would take him to show up. He's been trailing me ever since I got to this rat hole." He leaned closer to me—close enough that I could feel his breath on my neck. "You don't suppose he's seen my handsome face somewhere before, do you, Margo?"

"Seth, listen to me. Whatever it is you're looking for, it's not here," I pleaded.

"Shut up and open your goddamn email!" he hissed.

I was now thanking my lucky stars that I'd done as Holmes had instructed and deleted the file. My hands shook so badly that I had trouble typing my password, but after several tries I managed to log on.

I must have been hallucinating—on the monitor, for the briefest of moments, I thought I saw someone that looked just like Tim. The pounding stopped abruptly. Garcia and the student ran down the hall out of view of the camera and my hopes faded.

I mustered up as much bravado as I could. "Don't be stupid. Surely you don't think Garcia is the only officer on the entire Throckmorton police force? How long do you think it'll be before the entire Throckmorton police force is here?"

He dug the point of the knife into my ribs and slowly released his grip on my arm. Then he leaned forward and whispered so softly into my ear that I could barely hear, "And so what? Do you really think I'm worried about a bunch of small town cops? Solid steel doors, several inches thick...really, Margo! In the time it will take Barney Fife and his pals to get that door open, we can have all kinds of fun." My thoughts drifted to my recent brief encounters with the Throckmorton and Indian Springs PDs. In my mind's eye, I saw Kruszinsky strutting like a banty rooster around the interrogation room at the police station and conceded that Seth might have a point. "This may surprise you," Seth continued, "but I do have some experience in these matters. We have plenty of time. Well, *I* have plenty of time. For you'd, I'd say time's running out." He cackled with delight. "I'm doing you a favor. What more could a ghost hunter ask for? You'll be the ghost! But my patience is wearing thin."

I made a show of scrolling through my email messages, as slowly as I could. "Look! See for yourself. There's nothing here of interest to you."

He opened a few emails, then snarled angrily. "Then you're not much use to me, are you? Time for some fun. It's a shame that slant-eyed boyfriend of yours isn't here to enjoy it...oh, hey, there's a camera on this, isn't there?" Still holding my wrist, Seth put the knife down, taking care to place it well beyond my reach, and picked up Ernie's iPad, which had been lying on the counter. He was mulling over it thoughtfully when everything went abruptly dark and eerily silent. In the wake of the constant background noise from all the computers and the fridge, the sudden silence was more unnerving than the sudden plunge into murky semi-darkness. For decades, this wing of the horticulture building had been used for just about every conceivable purpose except growing plants. A couple of long horizontal windows might once have provided light, but they had long since been replaced with glass blocks that were now too grimy to function as windows.

Seth muttered, "What the...?"

Being more familiar with the layout of the lab, I reasoned that I had a momentary advantage over Seth until his eyes adjusted to the darkness. I took the opportunity and slid out of the chair, shoving it into him with every ounce of strength I could muster. I heard a satisfying "Ooof!" and the chair clattered to the floor noisily. I heard what I was pretty sure was Ernie's iPad sail across the table and crash to the floor. Making a mental note to myself that if I got out of this in one piece I would personally buy him a new one, I ducked under the tall lab table and scrabbled around frantically in the gloom until I found my purse. I grabbed it and stuck my hand inside it quickly, searching wildly for my phone as I dodged Seth's grasping hands. Every second that passed seemed like minutes. My fingers touched my wallet, keys, assorted lipsticks, but no phone. Suddenly Seth made a powerful lunge for me. He grabbed my wrist with one hand and sent the purse flying with a sweep of the other, just as I remembered where the phone was—right where I'd left it: on the table beside my bed. I heard stuff fly out of my purse and clatter across the floor.

Then I realized that with the electricity out, the door was no longer locked. Surely it was just a matter of seconds before the people shouting excitedly on the other side of the door figured it out, too. It certainly occurred to Seth. Cursing furiously, he hauled me to my feet and started dragging me toward the back door. My feet refused to cooperate, but that didn't seem to bother him at all. With one hand he jerked me toward the door.

We were a few feet from the back door when it burst open and banged hard against the wall. A man appeared in the doorway, silhouetted against the glare of the late morning sun. It was Toby Garcia, his gun drawn.

Simultaneously, across the room, the janitor's closet door flew open and people—I couldn't see who or how many—tumbled into the room, tripping over each other and shouting my name.

The next thing I knew, I was flying across the room. I landed in a heap on the floor, my head missing the corner of a lab table by inches. I got my wits about me just in time to see Seth give Garcia a powerful shove and leap out the door. Garcia crashed against the door frame with a painful-sounding thud. He staggered but stayed on his feet. Someone stormed out the back door after Seth.

Outside, I heard agitated shouts. Another man appeared in the doorway. All I could see was a silhouette, but it looked for all the world like...Tim? Before I had time to wonder how Tim could possibly be here instead of at the airport where he was supposed to be, the florescent lights flickered on and the lab hummed back to life, computers chiming a chorus of boot-up sounds.

I felt an arm around my shoulder and somebody helped me to my feet. It was Seamus. Tim rushed over and gave me a quick but gentle hug. "You okay?"

"Probably not. Timmy, what are you doing here?"

"I'll explain later. What happened? Are you okay?"

"We have to go after him," I said, staggering unsteadily away from him.

"Margo, honey," said Tim "just slow down..."

"Help me find my keys. Seth threw my purse across the floor."

A muffled, tinny tune began playing from somewhere. I watched through a mental fog as Seamus fumbled in his jeans pocket and whipped out a blinged-out phone. "Dude," he said, by way of answer. "Way to go, Rod! That's my boy." Now I remembered—the horticulture student whose name I couldn't remember was Rodney. He must have been the one that went after Seth on foot. "He's headed toward Founder's Plaza."

"Come on," said Tim, taking my hand. "Forget about your keys." He led me urgently out the back door. Outside, the small crowd out front was growing as curious passers-by rushed over, many of them talking excitedly into their phones. There was an excited murmur when we rounded the corner. "Hey! Wait up!" exclaimed Seamus. He was wearing a high-top sneaker on one foot and a cast on the other and hobbling toward us as fast as he could go.

Tim pulled me gently down the sidewalk toward a taxi idling at the curb. It was painted garishly in red, green and yellow. Airbrushed on the door were the words "Dread Lion" in an ornate script.

"You have to be kidding," I said. "You came all the way from airport in that?"

"I wasn't in any position to be picky. Come on!"

I got a small bit of satisfaction from walking on a trampled sign that had a "Ghostbusters" logo on it, marked out with a giant red X. Some of the protestors had thrown down their signs and had taken off after Seth, some on foot; others on bicycle. We could see them in the distance, speeding across the expanse of grass behind the horticulture pavilion.

As we limped to the cab, I realized there was something wet on my left sleeve. With detached horror, I saw that the cuff of my sleeve was wet and my fingers were puffy and starting to swell. Tim opened the door and helped me into the back seat, then climbed into the front with the driver. Seamus clambered in after me, and had barely made it into the back seat when the taxi peeled away from the curb with a screech.

To the driver, Seamus said "Turn here."

"Seamus, where—?" I started to ask.

"Just trust me. Be ready to jump out."

The driver was attired in the same red, green and yellow color scheme as the outside of his taxi and had dreadlocks that were pulled back in a ponytail almost as thick as his head. The taxi smelled ever-so-faintly of ganja, and attached to the dashboard was a photo of Haile Selassie in a cheap plastic frame. As we careened around the corner heading toward the center of campus, I had to hold on to keep from being slammed against Seamus.

"Okay, turn here," Seamus instructed, pointing in the direction of Founder's Plaza, a sterile concrete and brick plaza ringed by concrete benches too uncomfortable to sit on. At the far edge of the plaza was an abstract metal fountain, long ago rusted to a brilliant shade of orange. A tired jet of water spouted from the center. The plaza sat smack in the middle of what in the distant past must have been an intersection. The fountain backed up to an alley that ran behind a motley assortment of buildings.

"I can't go dere, mon. What you tryin' to do—get me in trouble?"

"Anybody says anything to you, you send them to us," said Tim. "Just go."

With a shrug, the driver switched into low gear and sped across the plaza, startling a flock of pigeons and a guy whose attention was focused on his phone.

We screeched to a stop by the fountain, as far as the taxi could go. We were scrambling out almost before the taxi came to a stop. Or perhaps "lumbering" would be a better word, although Seamus moved surprisingly fast for a guy with a broken toe.

"Hey!" yelled the taxi driver. "Somebody gotta pay me, mon."

"We'll be back!" yelled Tim over his shoulder. "Wait right there!"

Tim skirted the fountain and dodged into the alley. I ran after him and Seamus followed me, trying valiantly to keep up.

But when I got to the alley, it was empty except for Tim and Rod. The alley dead-ended into a blank wall where two buildings on what was once either side of the alley had been merged into one. Rod was systematically checking back doors, all of which were locked. I watched as Tim kicked an empty cardboard box in frustration. Seamus caught up with me and surveyed the scene. With an expletive, he limped toward Rod and Tim.

Sirens wailed in the distance. I took the moment to have a look at my injured arm. The left sleeve of my favorite blouse sported a ragged gash. I pushed the sleeve back, revealing a nasty-looking cut that ended abruptly at the wrist. My wrist was becoming stiff and my hand was starting to resemble a plate of bratwursts. I fished a tissue out of my jeans pocket and cleaned up the blood. I finally concluded that it wasn't as bad as it looked at first, and went to the nearest Dumpster to toss the tissue.

Before my brain could quite register what was happening, somebody had me by the hair. I shrieked, and suddenly there was a knife in my ribs again. Tim started toward me, in slow motion, it seemed. Seth yelled, "Surely you're not that stupid."

The alley was suddenly ablaze with flashing red and blue lights as a police car wheeled between two buildings and stopped barely a few feet away. Toby Garcia leaped out, gun drawn. Seth was now cornered between the squad car and Tim on one side, Rod and Seamus on the other. His only way out was the plaza. He maneuvered me between himself and Toby's gun.

I took a deep breath and squelched my rising panic. Seth was breathing so fast he was almost hyperventilating. The hand holding the knife was trembling, and he seemed to be having trouble keeping his grip on my hair.

Tim caught my eye and looked pointedly at Seth. I tried to follow his gaze, but turning my head to get a better look was not an option. But out of the corner of my eye, I thought I detected, with some satisfaction, a smear of blood on his hand. Apparently I wasn't the only one that was injured. See, kids, what happens when you play with knives?

"Get out of my way...I'm getting in that cab, and if anyone tries to stop me I promise I will slit her throat." He gestured wildly toward the cab, still parked beside the founder's plaza fountain, then repositioned the knife next to my throat.

"Let her go," said Tim. "You want a hostage, take me."

"No! Tim..." I started to yell.

Seth dug the knife harder into my skin. "Shut up." Toby's gun was still pointed at Seth. I hoped like hell he wasn't going to fire the thing.

Tim took a step toward us. Seth lashed out viciously with the knife. Tim sidestepped it nimbly, ignoring him. "Margo," he said quietly. "Spuds." His eyes bore into mine as if willing me to understand something.

"What?" I stared at him trying to understand.

"Spuds" said Tim, widening his eyes.

If I weren't so terrified, I would have been furious. What kind of a guy would make jokes while a crazed maniac held a knife to his girlfriend's throat? Then, suddenly, I got it.

"Get the hell away and let me through, if you want to see her alive again." Seth lashed wildly at Tim again with the knife and, in one fluid motion, I fell. Seth lost his grip on my hair and I hit the ground— like a sack of potatoes. Tim lunged for me, dragging me away. Almost instantaneously, there was a gunshot. It missed Seth by inches. "Freeze or the next one goes between your eyes. Drop the knife!"

With a resigned look, he said, "If you insist," and dropped the knife, point down, where it lodged firmly in the ground right where my foot had been barely two seconds before.

Almost immediately, Seth disappeared under a dogpile. When Rod and Seamus got off him and Toby yanked him unceremoniously to his feet, his hands were cuffed behind his back.

More squad cars arrived, and soon the alley resembled an outdoor disco of flashing colored lights. Seth shot me a look of pure venom but put up no resistance as he was shoved unceremoniously into the backseat of a police car.

With Seth safely in custody, the police officers started taking statements. I was approached by two policemen. One of them was carrying a notepad and pen. He appeared to have been stuffed into his uniform; the seams of his polyester pants strained to the breaking point. I gave my name and did my best to explain what happened. When he asked me what I did for a living, I sensed a subtle shift in his attitude.

"I'm a paranormal researcher."

Evidently it finally dawned on him that we were the people who had caused the furor at the college campus. "And what, exactly, does a paranormal researcher do?" he asked. I might have detected a bit of condescension.

"I'm a ghost hunter."

"A ghost hunter?"

"That's right. I try to make contact with the dead."

"Well." He exchanged looks with one of the other cops. "Well, all right, then. Any idea what he was after?"

"He, um... seemed to think I had a file he wanted." I said. "He threatened me with a knife and made me log onto my email."

"I see. And how did that happen?" He pointed to my wrist.

"Not sure, it all happened so fast. He was holding a knife to my ribs, but when the electricity went off and the doors opened he sent me flying and took off."

"You might want to get that looked at. And you, sir," he said, turning his attention to Tim. "I understand you happened along at the same time as the officer on the scene."

"That's right. I was worried that Mar—Ms. Monroe might be in danger. Call it a premonition."

"A premonition." The officer arched an eyebrow and wrote everything down with an exaggerated flourish.

"Officer Garcia was already there when I got there. He asked if I knew how to get into the lab where Ms. Monroe and their team do their research."

"Did he indicate why, sir?"

"We didn't have time to chat," said Tim curtly. "But I think he felt Ms. Monroe might be in danger—apparently with good reason."

The cop scribbled down Tim's statement, then said, "I think you need medical attention, Ms. Monroe."

"Thanks, but I think it's okay."

"Maybe you should stop by the clinic when we're finished here," he insisted, politely but firmly. Actually, I was pretty sure I was going to be a walking bruise the next day and doubted there was much the campus clinic could do for me.

The policeman turned his attention to Rod, writing down his name and information. "I was working on my semester project when a cop—I mean, a police officer—came in. He asked me how to get to the ghost lab. Then we heard a loud crash coming from their room," said Rodney breathlessly, in response to the man's questions. "When I knocked on their door—their door's always locked—nobody answered. That guy there," he continued, pointing at Tim, "asked me if I knew where the main electrical box was."

"So you tripped the breaker?" asked the policeman.

"I did!" he said proudly.

"And whose idea was that?" asked the cop.

"His," said Rod and Seamus in unison, pointing at Tim.

I let Rod and Seamus tell their stories and pulled Tim aside. "You're supposed to be halfway home by now. Not that I'm complaining, mind you."

He kissed my forehead and brushed my hair back from my face. "I know this is going to sound really crazy. I just got in line to check my bag when my phone rang. A man's voice said 'Margo's in danger,' and then the line went dead. When I couldn't get you on the phone, I started calling everyone whose phone number I knew. Incidentally, if I may explain the concept of the cellular phone to you: being the portable devices that they are, you're supposed to take them with you."

"Sorry," I mumbled.

"I grabbed the first cab and got back here as fast as I could. I gambled that you'd go to the lab instead of home. Garcia was there—no surprise—and told me he'd seen Seth sneaking around to the back door. We both came to the conclusion he had to be up to something. Then we heard a crash and nobody answered the door... oh my God! Look at your arm!"

I pushed back the sleeve so he could see the cut. A deep and shiny new scratch shone on Tim's ID bracelet, which was growing uncomfortably tight on my arm.

"We'd better take this off," he said, gently unfastening the clasp. The links had left marks in my puffy skin.

"Sorry about the scratch." I slipped the bracelet into the pocket of my jeans.

"It's the least of my worries," he said. A gust of chill wind caused me to shiver. "Where's your jacket?"

"At the lab."

"Here, take mine." Tim took off his jacket and draped it around my shoulders.

"But you're going to be cold now," I protested.

"I'm wearing a sweater," he pointed out. "And you're not. I'll be okay. I'm more used to the cold than you are." Suddenly Tim's eyes got huge. "The taxi! I hope he hasn't had his meter on all this time!"

We hurried across the plaza, which was now crowded with onlookers. The Dread Lion was right where we'd left it when we got out. The driver was telling a story and seemed to have his small audience enthralled. When he saw us, he stopped abruptly, his eyes wide. "Are ya okay, mon?"

"I think so. Maybe a few bruises here and there." Bit of an understatement, but never let it be said that Margo Monroe is a drama queen. Tim pulled the driver aside and was negotiating with him over the cab fare, when I heard a wild shriek.

"EXCUSE me...let me through, please!" It was Irmalene, elbowing her way through the crowd toward us. As if my day could possibly get any worse. She stormed toward the cab driver. "Rufus, what are you doing here? You're supposed to be working today!"

When he saw her, the cab driver's face turned ashen. "Auntie Irmalene!" He was about a foot taller than his aunt, but he cowered before her like a naughty child.

Irmalene   stopped short, hands on her hips. "Rufus, I swear I'm going to..." Then she saw me and her eyed widened. "Margo! Oh, what happened? Thank God you're okay!" She threw her arms around me and hugged me like a lost child.

Another Message from Beyond the Grave?

Officer Garcia insisted on dropping us off at the campus clinic. I considered it a waste of time, but Tim agreed with him, so I was outnumbered. At the clinic I was X-rayed, stitched up, and lectured by a stern-faced nurse about the proximity of the wound to my artery.

As I was paying for the punishment that had been inflicted on me, I could hear Tim talking quietly in the waiting room.

"...No, but she should be out any minute now....I think it's just a cut, she'll be fine...There she is now. We'll be along in a minute...Okay, bye. How's my girl?"

"I had to have a couple of stitches. It'll leave a scar, but I'll live." I showed him the bandage and the gash in my shirt sleeve. Look what he did to my favorite blouse."

"I'll buy you a new one. Margo, you were lucky. This could have been a lot worse."

"Yes, I know. I just got lectured on that very subject...oh my God! Timmy, what if I hadn't been wearing your bracelet?"

He wrapped his arms around me, and for a few moments I was content just to let him hold me. "I don't even want to think about it. I could kill Seth with my bare hands right about now. That was Ernie on the phone. How far is it back to your car?"

"Not very. Unless you're schlepping a week's worth of luggage and it's starting to get chilly and you don't have a jacket."

"I can manage," he said stoically, shouldering his laptop case. We cut across the campus, walking briskly and trying to stay in the sun. I offered Tim his jacket back but he gallantly refused, even though he shivered when the wind blew.

"Tell me about this phone call you got. Who was it?" I asked.

"No idea. There was no caller ID. I wasn't going to answer it, but I got a feeling that it was important."

"Do you have any idea who it might have been?"

He sighed and stopped walking for a second. "Don't think I'm crazy. Remember that EVP you played for me? The one you got when you investigated the chemistry lab? That's exactly who it sounded like."

A white van from the local news station was parked outside the horticulture pavilion. So were Ernie's Mini and Sandy's bicycle. A decent-sized crowd milled around the front steps but they didn't seem to be the usual protesters. I surmised that they were simply curiosity seekers.

"Oh, lovely. Jessica Sharpe—what have I done to deserve this?" I exclaimed.

"Who's Jessica Sharpe?"

"The local TV station's one and only anchor person. I'm not in the mood to talk to reporters. Call Ernie and tell him to open the back door for us."

We slipped around to the side of the building before anybody spotted us and pounded on the back door. The door flew open and Ernie squawked, "What the heck happened?" and embraced me in a brotherly hug. He was holding the remains of his iPad.

"It's kind of a long story," I said. As tempting as it must have been for him to say "I told you so," he kindly refrained.

Inside the lab, Sandy was pacing the floor. "Margo! Are you all right?" He rushed toward me, stopping short when he saw the bandage. He gave me a sort of long-distance hug, being overly careful not to jostle my injured arm.

"Sorry about your iPad, Ernie. I'll replace it," I said.

"At a time like this you're worried about an iPad?"

My purse had been rescued from the floor and was on a lab table, surrounded by a small pile of cosmetics and assorted odds and ends. "This is your purse, right? I found this stuff scattered around and figured it was yours," said Sandy solicitously.

"So are you going tell us what happened?" asked Ernie as I shoveled my belongings back into my purse.

"Yes," I replied, "but all I've had to eat today was a blueberry muffin and that was at 6:30 this morning. I'm hungry enough to eat this lab table. Can we continue this conversation over food?"

I handed Tim the keys to my car and snuck out the back with Ernie and Sandy. Ten minutes later we were still waiting for him in the parking lot of the fine arts building.

"Sorry," he said when he drove up at long last. "First I had to dodge Jessica—she's not one to take "no" for an answer, is she? Then I had to squeeze your car past the news van and half a dozen cars. Where to?"

"How about the Taco Loco?" I asked.

There were no objections—not that I anticipated any.

"Are they usually this crowded so late in the day?" asked Tim when we went in.

"It's always busy," replied Ernie. "At meal times they're packed."

We sat down and a busboy brought a huge basket of tortilla chips and some little bowls of salsa.

"I'm still trying to piece together what happened," said Sandy. "I got a text from Seamus, who said for me to get to the lab pronto. So I get there not five minutes later to find the place in shambles, no sign of Seamus —or anybody, for that matter, and all these people hanging around. I asked probably ten different people what happened, and every single one of them told me something different."

"I had stopped in on the way back from taking Tim to the airport," I said, grabbing a chip and dipping it in the salsa. "Seth knocked on the back door —it never occurred to me to wonder why he didn't come to the front. I let him in and he took me completely by surprise. Then he pulled a knife on me and made me log onto my email. I'm eternally grateful that Officer Garcia has been hanging around."

"Garcia?" asked Sandy.

"You know, the skinny policeman with the Buddy Holly glasses."

"Ah yes, your friend on the force," he said.

"Yeah," I said, "all this time he's been keeping an eye on Seth. If it hadn't been for him, who knows what would have happened?"

"But if Margo dropped you off at the airport, Tim, how did you get back here?" asked Sandy.

"I was breaking speed records across Throckmorton County in an airport taxi called the Dread Lion," replied Tim. "It's a miracle we didn't get pulled over."

"And it turns out the driver is Irmalene's nephew," I said.

"You have got to be kidding," said Ernie. "There are others like her?"

"Apparently so. Speaking of which, how much did that taxi ride end up costing?"

"You don't want to know," replied Tim grumpily.

"Well, I'm grateful to Officer Garcia, but shutting off the electricity to the doors was probably what saved the day—and me." Seth's voice echoed in my head and I shuddered. Tim squeezed my good hand under the table.

"You know," remarked Sandy, "if things had worked out only a little bit different, he might have gotten away with it. They found his car in the parking lot behind Throckmorton Hall. He could easily have made it, even holding Margo at knife point. It's not that far."

"But Tim, when you got that phone call at the airport, why didn't you just call Margo to warn her?" asked Ernie.

"Great idea. Wish I'd thought of that," said Tim with mock sarcasm.

"Huh?" said Ernie.

"I left my phone at home," I said sheepishly.

"Oh, for heaven's sake, Margo. You could have been killed!"

"Thanks for reminding me," I said.

"You never told us who it was on the phone," said Sandy.

Tim hesitated, then looked at Sandy with a pained expression. "Don't think I'm nuts, but it sounded like the same voice in that EVP you got in the science lab. I think it was Dr. Pritchett."

"Why am I not surprised? Any idea what Seth looking for?" asked Sandy.

"Not exactly. But I'm pretty sure it had something to do with an email I got," I said.

"An email from...?"

"Dr. Pritchett. Which I got the day after his funeral."

"Sorry I asked," said Sandy.

"It had an attachment," I continued, "and when I showed it to Holmes, he freaked out. He shredded the copy I printed and made me promise to delete every electronic copy and not to breathe a word about it to anybody."

"What makes you think it's what Seth was after?" Sandy asked.

"We don't know anything for sure, but we do know that he spent quite a lot of time hacking into the department's email servers," said Ernie.

"Whoa, that's really scary. Now I wish I'd told Ernie what I found out," said Sandy.

"Told me what?" asked Ernie.

"That Seth was using somebody else's identity. Margo made me promise not to tell!"

"When were the two of you planning on sharing this little tidbit of information with me?" asked Ernie indignantly.

"I didn't want you to worry. I was going to tell you today," I said.

"Margo, you came *this* close to having to tell me via EVP!"

Our food arrived. Tim and I were still hungry, in spite of having already finished off a basket of chips and two bowls of hot sauce. I tackled my massive burrito with gusto, only slightly impeded by being able to use only one hand.

§

By the time we left the restaurant, my arm was starting to throb. We dropped Ernie and Sandy off at the lab.

"We need to stop by the pharmacy on the way home so I can get these prescriptions filled."

"Point the way," said Tim.

"Downtown. That way."

"You know we pass half a dozen drugstores between here and your house."

"Yeah, but I like the old one downtown. I've been going there since I was a kid."

The pharmacy is in an old red brick building right on the main square in the center of town. A pharmacy has been in this location since the building was built in the 1880s. On the sidewalk outside is a mosaic of a black "Rx" spilling out of a mortar and pestle.

"This brings back memories," said Tim. "That mosaic used to fascinate me when I was little. I loved coming here."

"Me, too! I thought I was the only kid in town that actually wanted to take medicine."

Tim opened the heavy oak door for me and we stepped back in time several decades.

"This place is still looks like something out of a black-and-white movie," remarked Tim.

We made our way to the back past a handful of customers seated at the lunch counter that ran along one wall. The pharmacist—the same one who has been filling prescriptions for me since forever—greeted us. Like his establishment, he hadn't changed much, except that the fringe of hair around his bald head was white now. He had kids about my age; I knew one of his sons from high school.

"Hello, Margo...Timmy Beckwith! Is that you?"

"Hello, Mr. Schneider," said Tim shaking hands with the pharmacist. "I'm impressed. You have a good memory."

"Heard you were in town. But I wouldn't forget you. I remember when you were in here every couple of weeks for something or other, seems like." Mr. Schneider chuckled softly, then his tone grew serious. "Margo, I heard you had quite an encounter today."

"Word travels fast." I handed him several scraps of papers scribbled with illegible hieroglyphics.

"Won't take but a minute," said Mr. Schneider, disappearing into the back.

Tim wandered off to look around. I found a chair and sat down, and promptly dozed off. I woke up to hear Mr. Schneider explaining to Tim which pills to give me. "And try to keep her out of trouble."

§

The next morning, we got up at a respectable hour. I felt surprisingly chipper, all things considered. Tim was trying—in vain, it would seem—to get through to a living human being at the airline, when a video call came in on my computer. It was Ernie.

"How long is Tim here for this time?"

"I don't know. He's on the phone now trying to get a flight. Still on hold?" I asked Tim, who was pacing the floor, cell phone to his ear.

"Yep. Going on ten minutes now. At this rate I'll...Yes, I'm here. Yes, I need to rebook a flight...Yes, I know. But it was an emergency." He was silent for a few seconds, then said, "Yes, that would be great." Nodding at me, he slipped into the bedroom and closed the door behind him.

"Well, if he can't get out today, perhaps you can recruit him," said Ernie. "We could use some help tonight."

"I gather Elaine's mad at you again."

He shrugged. "I guess. She usually is. I'll ask Seamus if he's available." He looked over his shoulder and was quiet for a moment. "Somebody's knocking at the back door."

"Well, be careful who you let in. I'll see you shortly—we should be there by lunchtime."

We disconnected the call. A few minutes later Tim emerged from the bedroom, smiling.

"Success?" I asked.

"Yes, finally."

I felt a pang of regret. "When?"

"The earliest flight I could get is tomorrow afternoon."

"Good. I have a job for you. We're going back to the school tonight."

"Another investigation?"

"Sort of. We're going to try to talk to Theodore again. So I'm putting you to work."

"Happy to be of service," he said.

§

"Jade dumplings—this is yours, Ernie. Buddha's Delight for Margo, so this should be my Hunan stir-fry." Tim passed out little white boxes as the tantalizing smells of take-out from Lim Yee's, the local

Chinese take-out dive, filled the lab. Ernie distributed napkins and packets of wooden chopsticks all around.

"Not bad," said Tim. "Almost as good as that Chinese restaurant around the corner from me."

"You see? This place isn't the last outpost of civilization you seem to think it is," said Ernie, spearing a dumpling with a chopstick.

"You forget, I grew up here," said Tim with a derisive snort.

"Things have changed."

"They haven't changed that much. Hey, could I hear that EVP again? The one you got when you investigated the science lab?" asked Tim.

Ernie fired up The Monster and opened the file on the chemistry lab investigation. "Here goes," he said, clicking Play.

"Look out...Ben."

"Yep, that's it. I'm certain. That's the person who called my phone when I was at the airport."

"You know," I remarked, "this is one of the most bizarre cases we've ever had."

"It is," Ernie agreed. "And it isn't even official! What a shame. You can't make this stuff up. How's the stir-fry, Tim?"

"Better than expected."

"I don't believe what I just heard!" crowed Ernie. "So, Margo, what's our plan for tonight?"

"There'll be four of us," I replied. "Seamus is helping. We're not covering any new territory, just trying to make contact with Theodore. I want cameras at all entrances and under observation at all times. We don't know who's still out there that might be taking an interest in us—better safe than sorry."

"Sounds like a plan," said Ernie. "Fortune cookie, anyone? Mine says 'An admirer is concealing his/her affection for you.'"

Tim cracked his fortune cookie open and rolled his eyes. "'Never play leapfrog with a unicorn.'"

They looked at me expectantly. "'Forgive your enemies but never forget them.'"

§

We had some time to kill that afternoon, so Tim and I went back to the house to relax before the investigation. While Tim got his laptop out and started slogging through a backlog of emails, I turned on the television. I'd been mentally bracing myself for a media onslaught, but it didn't seem to be happening. "Don't you think it's odd that there hasn't been anything on the news since the night after the attack?" I asked.

"I know. It's like the story just kind of died."

I flipped through the channels, but local news had only stories about the Indian Springs basketball team, who were set to go to the state championships. I dug through a stack of unread newspapers from the past week or so and found one short article titled "Disturbance at Throckmorton U" tucked away on page 5. However, a headline caught my eye. "There's an article in last week's *Herald* about homecoming," I said. The sound of clacking keys ceased. "Did you know that it's been 17 years since Indian Springs High School won their homecoming game?"

"Is that so?" said Tim. "They must have had a winning streak after we graduated, then. I don't remember us ever winning a game, homecoming or not."

"This reminds me of something I've been meaning to ask you about," I said. "What did Aunt Muriel say to you at homecoming?"

"I'm not sure I should," he said. "I did promise, after all."

"Aw, come on," I coaxed. "She won't know."

"From what you guys keep telling me, she will know."

"Okay, maybe. But she won't care."

"Fine. You win," said Tim with a sigh. " She said 'It will take a strong man to make Margo happy.'"

"Is that all? That sounds like typical Aunt Muriel to me."

"There's more. She said 'I can see by your aura that you're that man.'"

"Aunt Muriel has an uncanny knack for articulating the blindingly obvious. I don't need to see your aura to know that." I picked up a book and Tim went back to his computer. The soft sound of his keys tapping rhythmically was about to lull me to sleep when he said suddenly, "You know, Margo, Indian Springs isn't so bad."

"I can't believe what I'm hearing!"

"No, really. It's changed a lot in the last twenty years. There's a lot more going on here than there used to be."

"True. But it's nothing like San Francisco."

"No, no place is like San Francisco. But no place is like Indian Springs, either. Because you're here. What I'm saying is, I think I might—*might*—be able to live here without dying of boredom." I was rendered momentarily speechless. "If these last few days have taught me anything, it's that San Francisco without you doesn't quite stack up against Indian Springs with you. Hey, when your arm's healed, are you gonna put the bracelet back on?" He looked so eager that it was almost comical. For the tiniest of moments, I was seeing the teenage Timmy again.

"No. I'm going to—*we're* going to put it back on right now. That's the rule. You have to put it on for me."

I found the bracelet and used a fingernail to scrape off a few flakes of dried blood. The scratch from Seth's knife glinted, just a little bit shinier than the area around it, as a reminder of this latest adventure.

"How does it feel?"

"A little snug, but it should be okay in a day or two. See? I can flex my fingers now."

"Congratulations. But I think you have a long way to go. Hey, don't we need to start getting ready to go to the school?"

"Nah, it's early yet." I pushed him down, gently, onto the sofa. "We have plenty of time."

§

"I'm beginning to feel like a bona fide ghost hunter," remarked Tim as we carried our equipment once again down the hall of the school.

"True, but I wouldn't call this an investigation so much as a..." I couldn't think of exactly the right word. We weren't looking for new evidence this time;

just trying to fix something that should have been set right the better part of a century ago.

"An exorcism?" suggested Ernie.

"Absolutely not. There's nothing demonic here. Just a confused little boy." I turned to Seamus. "You can set up your command center in the classroom next door. I want to try out our new infrared and ultraviolet flashlights and I don't want the glow from the monitors interfering"

"Right-o," he responded jovially. I had to give him credit—he was a trooper. In spite of the broken toe, he managed to keep up with us without getting in the way.

Tim offered a hand and they set about moving tables and computers into the adjoining room. I handed Seamus a two-way radio with a reminder to call if he needed anything.

"I'll set up the DVR cameras. I'm thinking one in the hall and one in here," said Ernie. He started unwinding what seemed like miles of extension cords while I set up webcams at each end of the hall. These were the wireless cameras we usually set up with a view of all the entrances and exits. The idea was to allow Seamus to see immediately if there was anyone there who shouldn't be. He was also going to keep an eye on the feed from the infrared cameras and let us know if anything appeared on the night vision cameras that we needed to get a closer look at.

We put Tim in charge of setting up the audio equipment. He set up the parabolic microphone as we'd done previously, once again streaming the feed to the computers wirelessly where Seamus could keep an eye on it. But Ernie had rigged up something new. A small electronic gadget sat next to the sonic ear—a speaker, which we hoped would allow us to hear in real time any EVPs we might pick up.

"We need to test the sound levels," Ernie reminded us, setting the parabolic mike in the middle of the room. "If it works the way I intend, we'll be able to hear a mouse tiptoeing across the floor and record it on the computer at the same time." He backed away a few feet and murmured something. I couldn't hear him speak from where I was, but his words came through the speaker clearly. "Roses are red, violets are blue."

Ernie picked up the two-way radio. "Seamus, you there?"

"Ten-four," came the reply.

Ernie rolled his eyes. "Did you get that? It was the feed from the sonic ear."

Static, then "Roses are red, Ern."

Ernie shook his head, but couldn't stop himself from smiling. "So far so good. I think we're all set."

"Then I guess it's time for the lights," I whispered.

When we turned the lights out and got quiet, the atmosphere in Mrs. Cartwright's classroom changed almost immediately. Part of it was certainly our own expectations. But there was also an undefinable feeling that I knew from experience meant we weren't alone.

Ernie began, "Okay, I'm ready. Hello to whoever's here with us. We're here as friends. I was here not long ago and I spoke to Theodore. Theodore, if you're here I'd like to speak to you again. My name's Ernie... maybe you remember me? Theodore, are you here?"

We waited in silence for a few seconds, then we heard a soft giggle from the speaker. It sounded like a little girl, although it was very faint.

"There's nothing to be afraid of, Theodore," I added. My voice coming through the speaker startled me; it sounded unnaturally loud. "You've spoken to us before, Theodore," I said as quietly as I could. "Do you remember us?"

Another little girl's giggle came through the speaker, then a second voice—Theodore's voice. "I'm Theodore. I'm scared."

Ernie swallowed hard before continuing. "Listen, Theodore, there's nothing to be scared of. But we want to explain something to you." He paused, but the speaker remained quiet. "I know you don't know us, we're not your parents or your teachers or anything, but I want you to listen and do your best to understand. This isn't the right place for you to be anymore. Your mother, your brothers and sisters—they're all waiting for you on the other side."

"I promised..." Then static, followed by something that was impossible to understand.

"Theodore," I whispered, "this might be hard to accept, but your mother's not coming back for you. Not here anyway. She's waiting for you on the other side. It's okay for you to leave. You have our permission, and I promise your mother won't be angry with you." We listened tensely, but the only sounds from the speaker were occasional unintelligible whispers and a few girlish giggles.

"Don't be afraid. If you leave here, your stomach won't hurt anymore. Your mother's waiting for you, Theodore. She's on the other side and she's been waiting for a long time," Ernie said. "Theodore, are you listening?"

We waited, the silence in the room was like a brick wall. Then, just as I was coming to the conclusion that we'd lost him, we heard a whisper from the speaker. It was very faint, but very clear. "Yes, sir. I understand."

§

"Why don't you kids run along home. Seamus and I can take care of this." Ernie slid a fold-up table into the back of my car and closed the hatch door.

"But there's so much left to do," I answered.

"It will take just a few minutes," replied Ernie firmly. "You need to put that arm up. Besides, aren't you supposed to be taking some medicine?"

"I feel fine."

"Then why is your face the color of freshly poured cement? Trust me, we'll have it wrapped up in no time. Seamus lives for this stuff. Besides, you're just getting in the way."

"He's right," said Tim. "It won't hurt to let someone else finish up."

I was too tired to argue. Anyway, they were right. It was all I could do to keep my eyes open and my arm was starting to throb. Tim opened the passenger side door for me. "I'll just say goodbye to them and we'll be on our way. Won't take long, especially since I've already said goodbye once this week."

I got in and buckled up. The next thing I knew, we were pulling into my driveway.

Parents' Night

All too soon, we were driving to the airport. Neither of us was completely awake. Traffic picked up as we neared the outskirts of San Guillermo.

"Are you sure you're going to be able to handle driving?" he asked.

"Stop worrying. I shift gears with the good arm."

"Just be careful, please. In half an hour this freeway will be a parking lot. You sure that medicine doesn't make you sleepy?"

"Positive. Anyway, that cappuccino I drank should kick in any minute now."

"Well, text me when you get home anyway so I won't worry. Is this my exit?"

An airport security officer—a different one from last time—was herding cars as Tim pulled up to the curb. We got out, and Tim opened the hatch door of the station wagon.

He wrestled his bag onto his shoulder. "Wish I didn't have to go," he said morosely, shrugging his laptop case onto his shoulder.

"Me, too. But at least you got to go with us to talk to Theodore. That was an unexpected bonus. Anyway —admit it—you'll be happy to get home."

"It would seem more like home if you were there."

"I'm working on it."

"I know you are. I am too." He kissed me, and turned away abruptly.

"Bye, Timmy. I love you."

Just before he got to the automatic door, he paused and looked back over his shoulder. He blew me a kiss, and I blew one back. Then he disappeared inside and I felt as alone as I'd ever felt in my life.

His prophecy about the freeway was correct. A traffic jam—for no apparent reason that I could discern—had the freeway snarled up for miles. I just missed an enormous SUV when it darted into a tiny space in front of me. I slammed on the brakes just in time and uttered a few choice epithets. The driver, a young woman cradling a phone to her ear, seemed blissfully oblivious to the mayhem she'd come within inches of causing.

The drive home took twice as long as it should have and I spent most of that time riding my clutch, creeping along in second gear. By the time I got home, my arm was throbbing relentlessly. Fatigue hit me like a brick wall when I finally turned down my street. My house had never looked so welcoming. The hoped-for caffeine buzz never kicked in. I sent Tim a text and went back to bed.

§

"How was the flight home?"

"Oh, you know, the usual torture. We sat on the plane for an hour before we took off. I'm beat." Tim was sitting at the desk in his study. His face filled the display of my iPad.

Franklin chose that moment to jump onto Tim's desk and positioned himself squarely in front of the camera. "Get off of there!" exclaimed Tim, sweeping my ragged feline nemesis into his arms.

"Franklin seems happy to see you."

"For now, anyway. I got a fairly frigid reception when I got home."

"Hmmm, I thought that was how cats always act," I replied.

"Not Franklin. He's no ordinary cat, are you, buddy?" He scratched the flea-bitten beast behind its tattered ears. "Any news from our phantom friend Theodore?"

"No, it's a bit soon to know anything. But we have a meeting at the school tomorrow night. Principal Golding asked us to talk to the class and some of the parents about what we found. I'm a little nervous," I admitted.

"Nothing to be nervous about. You'll do fine. Are you gonna show them the evidence?"

"Funny you should mention it. I had a discussion with Ernie on that very subject. He thinks that letting a roomful of nervous parents listen to EVPs wouldn't be the smartest thing to do. He doesn't want to play any of the evidence for them."

"He might have a point," said Tim.

"Oh, it's not that I disagree with him. It's just that—as far as spirits go—Theodore's about as sympathetic a character as they come. But Ernie's afraid it might backfire on us."

"I'm inclined to agree with him. Most of us haven't conquered our fear of the unknown. Do you suppose we were able to help Theodore?"

I sighed. "That's the bad thing about this job. We may never know."

"Well, I'll be thinking about you. I wish I could be there."

"You and me both." I promised to call him after the talk with the school, and we said reluctant goodbyes.

§

I was putting in my contacts, getting ready for our meeting that night with the Rhonda Q. Mills PTA, when a cheery ting on the tablet informed me I had a message. It was from Ernie.

"Pls listen to attached. Is something we should share with tonight's audience?"

When I listened to the sound file he sent, it gave me chills.

"Powerful stuff." I wrote back. "Might be more than some of them bargained for. Let's see how it goes."

§

When Principal Golding ushered us into Mrs. Cartwright's classroom, several children were already there with their parents. Principal Golding was more relaxed than she'd been at any of our previous meetings. She greeted us warmly and said, "I can't thank you enough for agreeing to do this."

More parents and kids were filtering in; it looked like it was going to be a full house. I mentally swatted at the butterflies flitting about in my stomach.

"Has anything unusual happened since we were here last?" I asked.

Principal Golding laughed. "Margo, this is an elementary school. What's unusual is when unusual things *don't* happen. But nothing that I can't explain, unless you count the hamsters that escaped from their cage and are still at large. You know, the kids seem to be taking this all pretty much in stride. They're not the ones who have issues with all this—it's the parents. Anything you can do to calm their fears..."

"We'll do what we can," said Ernie.

Mrs. Cartwright introduced us. About twelve kids and twenty or so adults were present, slightly more women than men. I spotted Chester among the crowd —he gave me a thumbs-up.

Ernie began by describing some our methods and equipment, then explained our theory about Theodore. I scanned the room and thought I saw a few skeptical faces in the audience, among the grownups anyway. The kids, not surprisingly, were mesmerized.

Ernie concluded by explaining—without going into much detail—that we believed we'd been successful in convincing the entities to move on. It looked like we were going to be able to wrap things up when a thin woman dressed in workout clothes and sneakers raised her hand. She was not unattractive, but her hair had been subjected to chemical abuse to the point that it resembled straw. "You mean, like an exorcism?"

Ernie looked at me beseechingly and I jumped to my feet to rescue him. "No, not at all. I like to think of it more as helping a lost soul find its way home.

Exorcisms have traditionally been associated with demonic entities," I said. "Although we do encounter an occasional malevolent entity, I can assure you that's not what we're dealing with here—just a confused and frightened kid."

A tall black man in a business suit started to speak, but the bleached-hair woman cut him off. "How can I be sure that there's nothing here that can harm my child?" She sounded defensive, bordering on belligerent.

"Ma'am, I understand that you're concerned for your child's safety. But please believe me when I tell you that the paranormal is nothing to be frightened of. These are just ordinary people that lived ordinary lives. The only difference between them and us is that they no longer inhabit a body. If I may be frank, you have more to fear from the living." The crowd murmured. "Sir, were you about to ask a question?" I said, nodding to the man she'd interrupted.

"Thank you. I'll be honest, Ms. Monroe—I don't believe in all this ghost stuff. In my opinion, there has to be some kind of logical explanation for all this. But I was wondering if you have some kind of scientific theory that might explain it."

"Well, yes, actually. This is a gross oversimplification, of course, but I can offer you my theory, and scientific evidence backs it up. My belief is that many different paranormal phenomena can be attributed to anomalies in the time-space continuum. Picture the universe as a piece of crumpled paper, rather than smooth and flat like we tend to picture it. We are also exploring the possibility that there considerably more physical dimensions beyond the three that we detect with our senses, plus the fourth dimension, which is time. This isn't my imagination running amok, by the way. Far greater scientific minds than mine have hypothesized on these subjects. My mission—that is, our mission—is to communicate with these entities and help them move on."

I paused to survey the faces before me and see if it seemed like any of this was sinking in. I saw mostly puzzled looks on the faces of the parents, but several of the kids were nodding sagely.

The woman with the bleached perm spoke up again. "You can try to rationalize it all you want, but this...this ghost or whatever it was is frightening my child." She wrapped an arm protectively around a little girl whose face bore an expression not of fear but of mortification. "You say this Theodore is harmless, but we only have your word for it," she huffed indignantly.

Ernie was staring at the woman, his hands on his hips and one eyebrow arched. "I think it's time for the heavy artillery," he whispered to me. "Change of plans?"

"Go for it."

"If you'll give me just a second here while I get this ready..." Ernie set a small wireless speaker on the edge of the desk. He tapped on his new iPad and played a few seconds of our conversation from that night.

"Can everybody hear this?" asked Ernie.

The adults in the crowd nodded in agreement, and the children wriggled in their seats, a few of them clapping excitedly.

Ernie began, "Before we listen to the recordings, I want to show you something. This appeared on the blackboard here, the morning after our first investigation." He picked up the iPad and touched the display, then held it up for the assembled crowd to see. The children crowded around, exclaiming eagerly. "Chester, would you mind passing this around?"

Chester was barely able to contain his excitement at being selected for such an honor. "Sure thing, Ern— uh, I mean Mr. Stapleton." We gave everyone a chance to look, then Ernie was silent until we had their attention again. "With this little bit of information we were able to find out more about our entity. Theodore was an ordinary little boy, about the same age as many of the kids right here tonight. And he was a good kid, who'd made a promise to his mother. I want you to hear this. Please, everyone be very quiet." He clicked a button and we heard Theodore's voice: *"Mother says...mother will come back for me."* There was a collective gasp from the audience.

Satisfied that we had their attention now, Ernie launched into his spiel. "Some of you may not be aware of this, but for decades the county children's home stood on this very spot. To call it an orphanage isn't really accurate—most of the kids here probably weren't technically orphans. Some of them had been abandoned, but many were brought here because their parents had fallen on hard times and just couldn't care for them. They attended school here along with other local children, and the buildings in the old wing date back to that time. After a series of scandals in the 50s, the children's home was closed. The building stood vacant for a few years, then was torn down. Several of the old Norton Township school buildings remain, but the newest part of the current school was built over the site of the old orphanage. We believe, in fact, that some of the structures in the new wing were built over the graves of children who died here." The woman with the bleached hair gasped.

Ernie continued. "Through our research we were able to track down Theodore's family. The Routledges lived on a farm just outside of town. We think the father and most of Theodore's siblings died in some kind of epidemic. Theodore's mother was unable to take care of him, so she entrusted him to the care of the orphanage with the intention of returning for him when she was able. Theodore promised her he'd wait there for her until she could come back for him, and that's exactly what he's been doing since 1920. But unfortunately, Theodore died not long after he got here. His appendix ruptured, and he died because he didn't get to a doctor in time. It's possible it was a simple matter of the orphanage refusing to spend money on a doctor. We don't really know. What we do know, however, is that over the years several children died under similar circumstances, and eventually the children's home was shut down under allegations of neglect and abuse."

Ernie paused and surveyed the room, arms crossed. Some of the women in the audience sniffled, and even a couple of the men were misty-eyed. A large man with a white walrus mustache cleared his throat and said gruffly, "That's heartbreaking, and I think what you're doing is just great." There was an appreciative murmur. The man continued. "I don't know about these other folks, but I'm behind you one hundred percent."

"Well, as it happens," said Ernie, "we think this case has one of our happier endings. Have a listen." He pulled up another file and clicked Play. Theodore's voice whispered from the speakers: *"She's here. Thank you, sir, and goodbye."*

§

"Well, that went well. Feel like going somewhere to celebrate?" I asked.

"I guess," said Ernie.

"What do you mean, you guess? You had them eating out of your hand. We keep this up, and our names will be enshrined in the Paranormal Research Hall of Fame."

"Oh, I'm always up for a beer. But I'm not celebrating."

"I thought you seemed awfully subdued for someone who had a roomful of soccer moms reduced to tears. Elaine again?"

"Yeah," he admitted. "She broke up with me."

"Again? How many times is this now? Three? Four?"

"I don't know, but I can tell you that it's the last time."

"That's what you said last time. And the time before. How many times have you been through this..."

"Margo, I've had it. We're history. You know something? I *do* feel like celebrating. Let's go to the Monk. I'll call Sandy." He pulled out his phone and poked at it savagely.

It was a weeknight and the Monk's Habit was quiet. As our eyes adjusted to the dim light, we saw that Sandy was already sitting at our usual table. He raised a glass in salutation as we approached. "Wow. I've seen more cheerful people coming back from a wake. Am I to deduce it didn't go well?"

"Oh, no. Not at all," I said. "Couldn't've been better. We've just been discussing Ernie's personal life."

"Ah, well then your despondence is entirely understandable."

That Ernie didn't take Sandy's bait was a testament to how miserable he really was. He ignored Sandy as he pored over the drinks menu, using the glow from his phone for illumination in the cavernous interior.

"What's that you're drinking?" I asked Sandy.

"Belligerent Bastard Irish Cream Ale. Thanks for turning me on to it."

"Great minds drink alike," I said.

"How's the arm?" asked Sandy.

"Much better." I pushed up a sleeve to show him the bandage that still covered the cut.

"You're gonna have one doozy of a scar."

A tiny girl with shocking pink hair appeared out of nowhere. "What can I get you?" She had a dainty, childlike voice that contrasted oddly with her multiple tattoos.

"A Belligerent Bastard, please." I said.

"Excellent choice. And for you, sir?"

He slammed the menu shut with a grimace. "A martini."

"A martini? What kind? We have peach martinis, pear martinis with a caramel reduction sauce, Mexican martinis..."

"Just a regular old, ordinary martini. Extra dry, shaken—not stirred, with olives and the whole bit."

"Sure thing," she said, giving Ernie a look that clearly indicated she thought he was a bit odd.

"So are you going to keep me in suspense forever?" asked Sandy.

"About the meeting tonight or Ernie's personal life?" I asked.

"Both."

"Look, you two, my personal life is none of your business."

"Au contraire!" I said. "You promised me when you and Elaine started dating that it wouldn't interfere with your work."

"Well, it hasn't," he responded hotly.

"Not so far, but we have a dilemma. You have enough trouble working together when you're getting along, much less when you're at each others' throats. And Elaine was the one who got me into ghost hunting in the first place. I can't just kick her off the team."

"Not to worry. She said she'd rather be off the team than put up with me," said Ernie gloomily.

A rough-looking guy with a mohawk and multiple facial piercings approached with a tray. "Martini?"

"Me," said Ernie, raising his hand like a school boy. The guy raised an eyebrow as he set a rather generous martini in front of him, then plunked my beer unceremoniously in front of me and disappeared without a word.

"Charming character," I said as he retreated.

"I wonder what happened to the girl with the pink hair," remarked Sandy, looking around.

"Which reminds me, does Megan still work here?" I asked.

"Don't know," replied Ernie. "I haven't talked to her."

"You're striking out left and right, aren't you, bud?" said Sandy.

"Thanks for your kind sympathy," retorted Ernie.

"Okay, you guys. Enough," I said. "We're all supposed to be on the same team. If Elaine's out of the picture we're an investigator short. What are we going to do?"

"I'm pretty sure Seamus would be game. He hasn't stopped talking about the investigation he went on with you," said Sandy.

"He has potential," added Ernie.

"Then it looks like Elaine and I need to discuss it. I'll talk to her."

"Somebody has to, and it isn't going to be me," said Ernie.

"Okay, so tell me about the meeting," said Sandy.

"It went better than anticipated," I said. "Ernie single-handedly converted a roomful of die-hard skeptics."

"With a little help from Theodore," Ernie added.

"I thought you decided not to show them the evidence," said Sandy with a shudder.

"The natives were getting restless. We didn't have a choice."

"There wasn't a dry eye in the house," I added. "Except for Chester. He was in his element."

The conversation turned to lighter topics, otherwise known as gossip. The martini had the desired effect on Ernie, and he finally relaxed and began to enjoy himself. Some of Sandy's friends came in and joined us. Before long, the evening had turned into a party, and Ernie and I didn't leave until last call. As we were going out the door I caught a glimpse of Sandy deep in conversation with the girl with the pink hair.

A Meeting with the Boss

"Observe, and be amazed." Ernie was about to demonstrate a new invention he'd been working on for some months, to a captive audience consisting of Sandy, Willis, and me. "This, my friends, is my *pièce de résistance*, a contribution to the science of paranormal research that is destined to bring us—especially me—fame and fortune beyond our wildest imaginings."

"Get on with it," growled Sandy. "I have a class in 20 minutes."

"Just remember, you saw it here first." He tapped on the keyboard of a souped-up laptop that we use for investigations and an image began to build slowly from the bottom of the screen.

"I don't get it," said Sandy. "What am I supposed to be seeing?"

"Be patient, my friend."

I suddenly realized what I was seeing. "I recognize it," I exclaimed. "It's a 3-D model of this room."

"Right you are!" crowed Ernie, rubbing his hands together gleefully. "Now watch." He clicked a button and another layer began building itself over the first image. Some areas were darker than others. The pattern it was forming looked familiar.

When I looked at it from a different angle, it all made sense. "It's a 3-D representation of the temperatures in different areas of the room. Look," I said. "Here we are and this smaller blob is Willis. And here are the computers—they give off significantly more heat than the surrounding areas."

"Correct!" Ernie. "But wait—there's more." He clicked another button, and a different layer appeared. Darker areas outlined the room and floated seemingly in mid-air.

We studied the image for a moment, then Sandy blurted out "EMFs! Those dark areas are concentrations of electromagnetic radiation!"

"Well done," said Ernie. "You've really outdone yourself, Ernie. Is it ready to use?" I asked.

Ernie looked quite pleased with himself. "Yes, I believe so. Hopefully on our next investigation. It will be a monumental breakthrough in the science of paranormal research..."

"Spare me," said Sandy. "It's nothing more than an EMF detector on steroids."

"Are you crazy, Sandy? It's going to be every ghost hunter's dream!" I said.

"Leave it to Sandy to miss the point entirely. 'Mediocrity knows nothing higher than itself, but talent instantly recognizes genius.'"

"Whose profundities are you spouting now?" asked Sandy grumpily.

"Sherlock Holmes," Ernie replied.

"You know, don't you, that Sherlock Holmes was a fictitious character?" said Sandy.

"Entirely beside the point. Allow me to explain this to you, my phantasmophobic friend. This nifty invention of mine will make spotting EMF and temperature anomalies a snap. In fact, if I tweak the sensitivity levels just a bit, I begin to be able to see the shape of the hot spot. It's the next best thing to being able to see an entity."

"If you say so."

"I *do* say so. By the way, Sandy, you could contribute to tonight's investigation."

"We've been over this. It will be a cold day in August before I go on a ghost hunt."

"Yes," I replied patiently. "We know this."

"Well, then what—wait! No, keep your grubby mitts off my dog!"

"Aw, come on, dude. Just this once," coaxed Ernie. "He's a natural, I'm telling you, and there's no possible way that anything will happen to him. You wanna go on a ghost hunt, don'tcha boy?"

In response, Willis snorted and scratched behind his ear.

"Use your own dog!"

"Are you crazy? You know what a drama hound Fang is!"

"What if he gets, like, possessed, or something?" whined Sandy.

"That only happens in the movies. Look, we'll be sure that anything we encounter knows it's not to follow any of us home."

Sandy rolled his eyes. "I just know I'm going to regret this. Okay! But just this once. And if my dog comes home levitating or spitting up pea soup or something…"

"Then we'll call a doggie exorcist," replied Ernie with exasperation.

Sandy conceded he was fighting a losing battle. While he gave Ernie strict instructions regarding the custodianship of his dog, I turned to my computer in a futile attempt to ignore them. Perusing the blogs of the other investigation groups, I found some good news. The team that was helping the little girl who'd suddenly started having problems at school reported that she was making a remarkable recovery. Their investigation turned up what sounded like multiple entities, and my contact on the team felt that they had been successful in convincing them to leave the child alone. Her grades were improving, and according to her teachers she was getting along better with the other children.

Just when I thought I had managed to tune Ernie and Sandy out, I heard Sandy say, "...and don't let him have people food! It gives him gas. You don't want that —trust me. Gotta go. I'm late for class as it is."

As Sandy dashed out the door, my phone rang. "It's Dr. Holmes! Hello? Dr. Holmes, it's really you! How are you!"

The voice on the other end of the phone sounded a little tired, but otherwise Dr. Holmes pretty much sounded like his old self. He got straight to the point. "I'd like to have a little team meeting. It's of the utmost importance. And since I'm not particularly mobile these days, I'm extending an invitation to you and Ernie to come to my home. Shall we say tomorrow evening around 7:00?" He gave me an address in Indian Springs not far from the town square.

"Certainly, sir. We'll be there." When I hung up, the guys were staring at me expectantly. "Well, here's one you won't believe—we've been summoned. Dr.

Holmes invited us over to his house. I hope you don't have any plans for tomorrow, Ernie."

Ernie whistled quietly. "Either we're moving up in the world or we're in big trouble over something."

§

The address that Professor Holmes had given me turned out to be a rather imposing house with a grand neoclassical façade. I doubled-checked to be sure we were in the right place. "This is it. Impressive," I said as I pulled into the spacious circular driveway and parked in front of a flight of steps. A pair of massive stone lions, one with a raised paw, flanked the steps.

Ernie fiddled nervously with his tie. "I'm not overdressed, am I?"

"You look fine. No reason to be nervous. Holmes is a teddy bear." But my hands were more than a little bit clammy, and my stomach was churning. We'd never been to his house before, and given the current circumstances I was a little apprehensive.

"I bet he's gonna tell us he's retiring."

"Oh, for crying out loud! You're just being paranoid. Anyway, no point in speculating. We'll know soon enough. Come on, this is not the occasion to be fashionably late," I said as I climbed out and shouldered my purse. We climbed the steps, Ernie stopping to pat one of the lions on the head. The door opened in response to my ring, and a stout woman wearing sensible shoes and a white nurse's uniform ushered us inside.

Her shoes squeaked on the marble floor as she showed us into a large room lined with bookshelves. By the fireplace sat our boss, in a wheelchair and looking a trifle thinner than when I'd seen him last. A fire crackled welcomingly. On a table beside him was a dainty china tea cup, a bottle of cognac and some glasses.

"Thank you, Mrs. Gilbert."

"No more than half an hour, Dr. Holmes," she responded sternly.

"No worries, Mrs. Gilbert. Margo and Ernie will keep me in line." She looked us over dubiously on her way out. "Margo, Ernie...welcome!" Dr. Holmes continued. "Please, have a seat. Forgive me for not getting up."

Ernie and Dr. Holmes shook hands, and I gave him an awkward little semi-hug. "Dr. Holmes," I said, "you gave us quite a scare. Are you sure you're up for this?"

"Don't be put off by the wheelchair," he replied. "The doctor says I'll be good as new by the end of the semester." He smiled placidly. "I'm tougher than people give me credit for. How's the arm, by the way?"

"Still a little stiff, but I can manage."

"From what I hear you were quite lucky," said Holmes. "May I offer you a little drink? Unfortunately, I'm temporarily on the proverbial wagon, myself—doctor's orders and all that. He's something of a tyrant, I'm afraid, and I don't want to get on his bad side." He chuckled and Ernie and I nodded mutely while Holmes poured us each a generous portion of the cognac. "We have much to discuss," he continued. "I know you're wondering why I called you here—cheers! Here's to happier days ahead." He raised his teacup and we followed suit with our cognac glasses. When we tapped them together they made a dainty tink. "Now then, where shall I start?" He sipped some tea, then set the cup down carefully. "The fact is, I feel I rather owe you both an explanation. I hold myself responsible—at least in part—for some of the recent...unpleasantness. I wonder how much of it might have been avoided if I'd been honest with you up front."

Ernie and I exchanged startled glances. I started to protest, but Holmes held up a hand. "Hear me out. Where do I start? Nigel Pritchett was like a brother to me, but I think you both know that. What you don't know is that his life's work was a project that could have affected everyone on the planet."

"I'm not sure I'm following you," said Ernie.

"Bear with me a moment. Hopefully it will all make sense. You probably knew that Nigel was a passionate environmentalist, but I assure you he was not just another crazy tree-hugger, as some people thought. His pet peeve was plastic, which he regarded as a form of pollution. It never biodegrades, you know. Just breaks apart into ever-smaller pieces. It can be particularly lethal to sea life."

I stole a glance at Ernie, who looked as mystified as I felt.

Dr. Holmes paused to pick up his teacup and ran a finger absently around the rim. "Long before either of us ended up here at this obscure little institution, Nigel dreamed of finding a practical solution to the problem of waste plastic. He wasn't entirely alone in this. Scientists in Japan have had some success reclaiming the petroleum used in the manufacturing process. Nigel's process is similar, but goes one step further. The petroleum is reclaimed, and the plastic is broken down into a harmless biodegradable substance. Quite by accident, he discovered it generates a considerable amount of energy in the process. It's clean, cheap, and efficient."

"But that's brilliant!" I exclaimed. "Think of all the problems it would solve!"

"You're absolutely correct, Margo. As a viable alternative energy source, his project would neatly solve multiple problems. There's enough plastic garbage floating in the world's oceans to potentially free us from dependence on fossil fuels, at least for the foreseeable future."

"So why hasn't this been front-page news?" I asked.

"The cost had always been a major stumbling block. But recently he'd hit upon a strategy that would bring costs down considerably, and he felt it was only a matter of time before he arrived at a practical solution. He was focused particularly on empowering the developing world and felt that with proper backing, everyone on earth could eventually have free electricity."

Holmes paused to sip from the china tea cup before continuing. "You know, his discoveries could have made him a very rich man, but his driving ambition was to use his intellectual gifts in a way that would benefit others."

"But think of the implications!" Ernie sputtered. "A discovery like that would be worth..."

"A man's life," responded Holmes with a melancholy little smile. "Although Nigel was something of an idealist, he realized that not everyone shares his altruistic visions. Corporations generally aren't too tolerant of anything that adversely affects their bottom line. Or worse yet, puts them out of business."

"Huh?" asked Ernie.

Dr. Holmes shrugged. "Why pay the utility company when you can generate your own electricity from the packaging you used to toss in the trash? Nigel knew his only chance for success was to stay out of the limelight. So he was content to toil away in his obscure little corner of academia until the time was right."

"So if I understand correctly," I asked, "you feel somebody murdered Dr. Pritchett to get his project?"

"Yes. It's a distinct possibility."

"But I don't understand," said Ernie, "Why come after you?"

"My theory is that someone out there wants to make sure this idea never sees the light of day. Only a handful of people know about this. Not long before your big case last summer, Nigel, with the approval of the dean of the College of Science, put together a committee consisting of a few of his most trusted colleagues on the faculty—one of them being myself. Our first order of business was to put together plans for a pilot project. We had sent out a few tentative feelers in search of funding when the story about your big discovery broke. Before long, reporters were lurking in every nook and cranny of this campus."

"Yeah," said Ernie, "they were an infestation of Biblical proportions. One of them even followed me home once. I guess the 24-hour news channels have to find something to talk about."

"They were nothing if not persistent," agreed Holmes. "Once Nigel caught someone in the lab after hours. At the time it seemed like a minor irritant. But when he came home one night to find his home alarm system compromised, he realized he might be dealing with something rather more serious than a reporter trying to pass herself off as a college student."

"Did he call the police?" I asked.

"Of course. But since nothing was stolen, they rather condescendingly dismissed him as a stereotypical absent-minded professor."

"How much you want to bet it was Kruszinsky?" Ernie remarked.

Holmes smiled. "It would have been worse. We're lucky to still have Sandy with us and in one piece.

When he discovered our friend wasn't the real Seth Carling, he put himself in grave danger."

"What about the remaining committee members?" I asked.

"They will no doubt be relieved to learn that the man passing himself off as Seth Carling won't be going anywhere for a while. Interpol has had an eye on him for years. He's a master of disguises and has multiple aliases, but the general consensus is that his real name is Digby Briggs. The truly sobering part, though, is that he's almost certainly part of a larger organization. Whoever it is is well-organized enough to orchestrate his impersonation of the real Professor Carling."

"Sorry, I don't mean to be rude, but how do you know this?" I asked.

"No offense taken, Margo. I may be living a quiet life, sequestered here in my little corner of academia, but that doesn't mean I don't have friends. I can tell you that Briggs' arrest raised a red flag among various law enforcement agencies. An astute observer at the police department noticed a striking resemblance between Briggs and a face on an FBI wanted poster. I get the impression that someone on the Throckmorton PD has taken a special interest in our little operation."

Ernie smirked. "Margo has an admirer on the force."

"Indeed?" Holmes raised an eyebrow. "I should have guessed."

"But what about Professor Pritchett's project?" asked Ernie. "It could change everything..."

Holmes shook his head sadly. "Let me stop you right there, before you get too enchanted with the idea. The board of trustees has decided it's too dangerous."

Ernie was dumbfounded. "You mean they're..."

"Pulling the plug on it," answered Holmes.

"But...but..."

Holmes held up a hand to silence him. "We're out of our league on this one, Ernie. We don't know who's behind this, but whoever it is, not much escapes them. The number of people who have any knowledge of Nigel's project could be counted on one hand. Yet look what happened to me. How could I live with myself knowing I put your lives in danger?"

"But we can't just let them get away with it!" exclaimed Ernie, obviously agitated now.

Holmes sighed wearily. "Ernie, this is an institute of higher learning tucked away in quiet little corner of nowhere. Involvement in matters of international espionage is not part of the charter. I assure you, I am in complete agreement with the trustees on this one.

"Don't be discouraged. It's an idea whose time will come. In the meantime, the responsibility I have been charged with is to bring respectability to the science of paranormal investigation. I intend to see that to fruition. Are you with me or not?"

"We're with you," we mumbled in unison.

"Good. I knew I could count on the two of you. Now then, we don't have much time. I assure you Mrs. Gilbert is as formidable an opponent as any you've faced to date, living or otherwise. So let's use our time wisely—is there anything you need my assistance with?

"Um...well, yes, there is. But first I have—that is we have—a confession to make," I said.

"Is it about your clandestine visits to Nigel's office?"

Ernie slumped in his chair. "How'd you know?" he asked gloomily.

"Very little happens around here that I don't know about. In fact, I would have been rather disappointed in you both if you hadn't gone in there."

"Well, then," I said, "you won't be mad at us for asking if we can do another investigation. Just a follow-up. Maybe you could help us get whatever permission we need."

"Consider it done."

"Where's Seth—I mean Briggs—now?" I asked.

"In a maximum security facility under suicide watch," replied Holmes bluntly. "He's facing indictment on multiple counts of murder and attempted murder, both here and abroad. I doubt if he'll see the light of day again any time soon. I'm very sorry you had to get mixed up in all this. It's not what you bargained for, I know. I'm very impressed with the way you handled it."

"Thanks, Dr. Holmes. We really appreciate it," said Ernie, beaming. I nodded, touched at this display of warmth, which was uncharacteristic of our boss. "We're just glad you're going to be okay."

"There's one more thing," said Holmes. He pulled a scrap of paper from his shirt pocket and handed it to me with an enigmatic smile. "I'd like you both to meet me at this address tomorrow afternoon at two."

"Sure thing," I said, taking the paper from him. I ran quickly through my schedule for the next day in my head. An appointment at the hair salon would have to be rescheduled. Although politely worded and delivered with a smile, this wasn't a request. I glanced at the paper. All that was written on it was an address in Throckmorton. I thought I knew my way around Throckmorton; it's not a very big town. But the street wasn't one I recognized.

"Oh, and please inform Sandy. I believe his last class of the day is over by then."

The door opened and Mrs. Gilbert marched in. "Visiting hours are over, Dr. Holmes," she said sternly.

"Not a problem, Mrs. Gilbert. We were just leaving," I said, leaping to my feet. "Come on, Ernie." We bid Dr. Holmes a hasty goodbye and left him to deal with Mrs. Gilbert.

§

"Look, Ernie, you have to admit he has a point. We don't know what we're up against. " Ernie had done a remarkable job of keeping his opinions to himself while we were still at Holmes' house, but once we got in the car he let loose.

"I don't care!" he responded hotly. "What a bunch of cowards. Think what it would mean!"

"Don't be so stubborn! We're in over our heads. Didn't you hear Dr. Holmes say that Seth—or Briggs, or whatever his name is—couldn't possibly be acting on his own?" I pulled up at the curb in front of Ernie's house. "Anyway, at least something positive has come out of it. We get to go back to the science lab, and this time we don't have to spend the whole time watching over our shoulders...or jammed under a desk. This is a golden opportunity. We need to be figuring out how to make the best of it. "

He took a deep breath. "Ever the voice of reason. Sorry, didn't mean to go off on you." He got out. "Thanks for the ride."

"Hey, for what it's worth, I feel the same way you do. But I've had enough excitement to last me a while."

"You're right," he said before he closed the door. "See you tomorrow."

A Moving Experience

"We don't mind riding in the back, do we boy?" said Sandy as he opened my car door. Willis, groomed and pedicured anew, jumped in and curled up on the seat as though my car were his personal chauffeur-driven limousine.

"I'll just be happy when this is over," grumbled Ernie as the climbed into the passenger seat. "I've had enough surprises to last me for a while. What do you think it is this time, Margo?"

I shrugged. "Your guess is as good as mine." I typed the address Holmes had given me into the navigation app on my iPad and followed the directions of the electronic voice.

Near the edge of the campus, we turned onto a street lined with warehouses. The route guidance directed me to grim-looking three-story building. I parked at the curb.

"Are you sure this is the right address?" asked Ernie when we got out.

"Positive," I replied.

"Well, your GPS has been known to send us off on a wild goose chase on occasion," said Ernie as we got out of the car. "Or maybe somebody's playing a trick on us."

"Not Holmes' style. Anyway, we've been in scarier places than this, and in the middle of the night no less...relax!" I replied.

But I double-checked my doors to be sure they were locked, and we went up the cracked and buckling sidewalk. The only windows were frosted glass bricks that were almost opaque with grime. Metal front doors, once bright blue, were faded and mottled with rusty patches. Sandy jostled the door lever without success. "If I see even one rat, I'm *so* outta here." He pushed down hard on the lever and the door screeched open.

We couldn't have been less prepared for the sight that greeted us. The spacious lobby was furnished like something out of a magazine, with sleek, contemporary furniture. Vibrant abstract art adorned the walls, and in one corner was a ceiling-high metal sculpture. A uniformed security officer sat behind a long desk positioned unobtrusively to one side. We gathered our wits and headed toward him. He greeted us politely.

"We have an appointment to meet Dr. Ben Holmes here at 2:30," I said.

The guard flipped through some papers on a clipboard. "Yes, second floor and to the left—the elevator's right over there."

We headed in the direction that he pointed. Willis's toenails clicked on the polished concrete floor as he trotted along behind. Ernie punched the call button and we surveyed our surroundings while we waited.

"What do you think this place is?" asked Sandy.

"Offices for an architect, a video production studio, and a fashion designer," said Ernie.

"I thought you said you'd never been here before. How do you know that?" I asked.

"Because it says so right there." He pointed to a glass-enclosed directory on the wall.

"Maybe we're going to get some kind of award. Or a bonus!" mused Sandy.

"You just hold on to that thought," replied Ernie.

"We'll know soon enough," I said. We heard a ping as the elevator doors swished open. Inside, the elevator was all chrome and glass. When we reached the second floor, the door opened smoothly and revealed a long, carpeted hall lined with doors punctuating bare walls.

One door opened and Holmes appeared in his motorized wheelchair. "Welcome! Right this way, everyone. You, too, Willis."

We followed him into an enormous L-shaped room with brick walls. It was about the size of a high school gym and had a worn wood-plank floor. The ceiling consisted of exposed ductwork. Translucent frosted glass windows covered most of one wall, letting in the afternoon light. Willis checked the place out, sniffing in corners and occasionally wagging his stubby tail.

"So, what do you think?" asked Holmes. He was like a kid with a new toy. I don't remember ever seeing him so upbeat.

"It's very nice but what is it?" asked Ernie.

"What is it? My dear Ernie—this is your new lab."

Suddenly everyone was talking at once. "Dr. Holmes, what...?" "When can we move in?" "Who...?"

He held up a hand, laughing merrily. "After your recent....ah...adventures, our patron became understandably concerned for your safety. We did a bit of searching and found this facility, which we hope will be more than adequate for your needs. Come, let me show you around." We followed him around the room as he maneuvered the wheelchair deftly by its joystick.

In the short end of the L was a small kitchen equipped with a refrigerator bigger than the one in my house. "We've even ordered a new coffee maker," Holmes said. "It should be arriving any day now. It's one of those newfangled contraptions where you just drop in a little capsule." Sandy caught my eye and made an enthusiastic thumbs-up behind Ernie's back. "I saved the best for last," Holmes continued. "If you'll follow me." He maneuvered the wheelchair through a doorway, and we entered an empty room with a concrete floor. About the size of a typical bedroom, it was several degrees cooler than the outer room.

"This is your new equipment room," said Holmes, obviously relishing the look of delighted shock on Ernie's face. "It has a separate climate control and its own backup power supply independent of the rest of the building. It's also fireproof. I thought we might put a rack of servers in here so you could have your own local area network. That should leave plenty of room for storage for your other equipment. But best of all, it opens onto its own loading dock."

"You mean, I won't have to keep my equipment in my spare bedroom anymore?" asked Ernie. I had sudden visions of a tidy garage with room for a second car.

We followed Holmes and Ernie onto the dock outside. We were on the second floor, but the building was built on a slope so that this side was almost at ground level. There was a bay big enough for two cars to back into and a roomy platform at about bumper height. A short flight of steps to one side went to the ground level. Beyond it was a parking area big enough for a half-dozen cars or so.

Ernie was ecstatic. "This is great! Not only will I be able to reclaim my guest bedroom, but I won't have to kill myself lugging stuff back and forth to my car! And we'll be able to park right here!"

"I think you'll find it satisfactory, compared your current setup," answered Holmes. "I predict a noticeable improvement in internet access. And there's something else—very important: 24-hour security."

"Dr. Holmes, is there some way we can say 'thank you' to our...the person responsible for this?" I asked.

"Well, as you know, our benefactor prefers to remain strictly anonymous. But certainly, I'll convey your thanks."

"When do we move in?" asked Sandy.

"Whenever you want." Holmes smiled. "Here are your access cards."

§

In the days that followed, we may possibly have set a new world's record for getting everything packed. It seemed like a dream. Before I managed to get a grip on the fact that we really were moving out of the horticulture pavilion, we had everything packed and ready to go. Ernie, Sandy, and I got up bright and early one sunny morning and spent the day shuttling between the horticulture pavilion and the new space, our cars loaded with computers, gadgets, and boxes of odds and ends.

By early afternoon, my back and feet were aching but we had one last trip to the horticulture pavilion to make. I backed my car up to the back door of the lab. Ernie shoved the brick against the door. "That's good right there," he said, reaching for the handle to pop my hatchback open. He went inside and Sandy came out with a box and shoved it into the back.

"How much more is there?" I asked.

"Not much," said Sandy. "Just a couple of boxes and those old computers."

I followed him inside, where Ernie was wrestling with a garbage bag that had been stuffed to overflowing with trash, trying to tie it closed. "Need some help?" I asked.

371

"Nope, got it under control." Our voices echoed crazily in the now empty space. He pushed the bag aside and picked up the broom. "Just let me finish this and we're all done."

"We'll meet you outside, then," I said, hoisting a box labeled "Ernie—Personal."

I paused in the doorway to watch Ernie sweep up the last bits of debris. It felt strange to see the place empty like this. I had fond memories of this place, but I also remembered standing in this very spot with Seth's knife digging into my back. That memory was too fresh—I could hear his voice all too clearly, describing his plans to kill me and record it for Tim. I wondered if he really would have gone through with it. My gut instinct said that he would have, and that he would have enjoyed every minute of it.

"That about does it," said Ernie, tossing the garbage in a Dumpster.

"I guess we're ready, then. Um...I'll meet you there. There's something I have to do first." I took a deep breath and marched down the sidewalk and around the building toward the front, where the usual contingent of the unemployed, the sub-literate, and the easily amused were lurking in their usual spot. Sandy and Ernie, no doubt overcome by curiosity, were right behind me.

The shouting started as soon as they saw us, of course. In seconds the din was deafening. I held up my hands. The noise subsided but slightly. "You're all skeptics right? You believe that what we do is evil, misguided, silly, and just plain wrong...correct?" The noise level shot up then quickly started to subside. "My organization believes that ghosts are out there. Why don't you form an organization dedicated to proving they're not? There's about to be an empty space here that is already wired for all the high tech gear you could ever use. Challenge us. If we're full of bunk, prove it!"

I surveyed the crowd. Most of them appeared dumbfounded, but I detected a spark of interest in some eyes. A young man, one that I'd seen before, stepped forward.

"Will you share your evidence with us?"

I admit I hadn't actually thought this through very well, and was rather taken aback by his question. "I don't know..."

"We could look at your evidence from a different perspective...one that could be helpful," he said, "and even necessary from a scientific standpoint. It might be beneficial to both sides."

"Fair enough," I said. "Do any of you have any experience doing this kind of work? Find people who are qualified to be a part of this and write up some ideas. I'll bring it up to my boss."

The young man turned to his cohorts and they began chattering enthusiastically, but otherwise the crowd, like a slowly deflating balloon, began dwindling. There were a few half hearted high fives, but mostly they just walked away in small groups, buzzing quietly among themselves, trying to sort out this new development. I couldn't help myself. "When you write up the proposal..." I yelled after them. A few paused and turned around. "...use spell check!"

§

A surprise was waiting for us at the new place. I pushed the door open with my foot and peered over my boxes, expecting to find the new space in the same state of chaos as we'd left it an hour before. Instead, streamers and ghost-shaped balloons hung from the ductwork. On the wall, a large hand-lettered sign liberally decorated with glitter said "Congratulations from Mrs. Cartwright's Grade 5 Class." For the briefest of moments, I thought I had somehow stumbled into the wrong place, until I spotted Chester's pudgy face among the assembled crowd of 30 or so kids.

"Well, don't just stand there in the doorway, Margo," said Ernie irritably. "What the...?"

"Surprise!" yelled the fifth grade class in unison. That Mrs. Cartwright, Principal Golding, and Dr. Holmes, leaning on a cane, were there, smiling and laughing like kids themselves, eventually registered in my brain.

Within seconds we were surrounded as a dozen kids reached to take our burdens from us.

"Where do you want this, Ms. Monroe?" asked a little girl with blonde pigtails as she divested me of my box of Ernie's stuff.

"Put the computers on that table over there, and the rest of the stuff wherever you can find a place, I guess." In our absence, busy little elves had assembled computers, arranged furniture, and unpacked a few of the boxes that we had left piled in a heap in the middle of the room. Our new lab no longer looked like a warehouse.

Several tall lab tables had been draped with colorful plastic tablecloths. On one of them was a huge cake in the shape of a cartoon ghost. A bowl of dubious-looking foamy orange punch and an array of goodies of every description were arranged on another table.

Mrs. Cartwright's offered me a cookie shaped like —wait for it—a ghost. Her round cheeks were flushed and she had a sparkle in her eyes that I'd not seen before."Principal Golding contacted Dr. Holmes to find out if there was something the class could do to show their appreciation. We know you're busy ..."

"Not at all! This is a wonderful surprise and we could use a break. We've been working all day. Look at how much work you saved us. I might actually get to take a day off tomorrow," I said.

"Well, the kids just think you guys are the greatest. Theodore's story is part of the curriculum now. The class loves it. We're researching the other orphans' stories, and some students have even expressed an interest in doing volunteer work to help the needy. You have no idea how hard it is to get these kids interested in something besides video games. It's something of a miracle, really."

It was all a little bit overwhelming. All I could do by way of reply was to give her a big hug.

"Thank you," I managed finally. "I can't tell you how much that means to me."

I helped myself to some punch and surveyed the scene. The kids seemed to be having a great time. A group of little girls, among them the blonde with the pigtails, was crowded around Sandy. They gazed up at him adoringly as he entertained them with a story about Willis. Chester was dragging Ernie around from child to child, proudly introducing him to his classmates. Ernie went along with stoic good humor.

I was nibbling the cookie when I felt a tug at my sleeve. I looked down to find myself surrounded by a throng of fifth graders. A little girl in a Hello Kitty T-shirt and glittery pink high-top sneakers seemed to have been the appointed leader. "Can we have your autograph?" she asked in a breathless voice.

"Auto—? Uh, certainly." Childish hands thrust pieces of paper at me.

I was still scribbling signatures when I heard a delicate ping-ping-ping. "Quiet everyone! May I have your attention please!" Dr. Holmes was tapping the punch bowl with the cake knife. As if by magic, the room fell instantly silent. "I'd like to welcome our young scholars. We're thrilled that you could join us today on this most auspicious occasion. In a moment I'm going to ask Margo to do us the honor of cutting this delightful cake. But first, I believe there are some presentations to make. Mrs. Cartwright?"

"Thank you Dr. Holmes. Class?"

Chester and another little boy ducked under a table and produced a mysterious wrapped object that they held from view behind them as they joined their teacher and principal by the punch bowl. The parcel was clumsily wrapped in brightly colored paper (decorated rather incongruously with dancing pandas). Chester blushed and cleared his throat. "The whole class chipped in and had this made up for you." As soon as he handed me the parcel, I could tell that it was a framed picture. Carefully, I peeled off the tape and unwrapped it. An enterprising young Photoshop genius had scanned and enhanced the photo from the 1920 yearbook. As I studied the serious face staring gravely back at me from the gaudy frame, tears came to my eyes. I passed it to Ernie and Sandy.

I took a deep breath and cleared my throat. "Thank you so much, kids. I can't imagine a more appropriate housewarming gift."

"That's not all," said Chester. "Okay, Gina."

A little girl with chocolate skin and a head full of unruly dark curls marched importantly to the front, carrying a large piece of poster board, holding it with the back to us. She handed it to me and said in a shy, barely audible voice, "We all signed it." I held the poster up for everyone to see. The kids and Mrs. Cartwright had signed their names in markers of every color of the rainbow. Some of them had also drawn ghosts, and one budding young artist had managed a recognizable sketch of Theodore. Principal Golding's signature was also there, I noticed.

"Thanks, everyone. This is such a lovely surprise. I think I know the perfect place for this—right on that wall over there."

Ernie, looking a little misty-eyed and still clutching the portrait of Theodore to his chest, said, "This is the first time a client has ever given us presents or thrown us a party. Thanks, kids. We really appreciate it." Chester looked so proud of himself I thought he might float away.

"Before we dig into the cake, I'd like to make an announcement," said Principal Golding. "The school board has approved the money for a memorial plaque. It will be inscribed with the names of all the children who died at the orphanage. We're going to need help collecting the names, so we're looking for volunteers to do research."

Pandemonium abruptly ensued. Excited kids jumped up and down and shouted "Me! Me!" "Can I?" "I want to, Mrs. Golding!"

"All right, everybody calm down. Everyone who wants to is welcome—we're going to need all the help we can get."

The New Prof

We all put in extra hours over the next few days, arranging the new space to our satisfaction. Ernie seemed particularly contented to spend hours on end in the new server room. I was on my hands and knees one morning, helping Ernie string cable, when the door opened and in strolled Dr. Holmes, accompanied by Dean Cresswell and a petite, dark haired lady. She had a trim, athletic figure and a spring in her step that made her age difficult to guess, but I estimated her at around 50.

The lady wore an elegant pastel suit, and Dean Cresswell was formally dressed and dapper as always. I was suddenly acutely aware of the grubby jeans I'd thrown on this morning on the assumption I wasn't going to see anyone I knew. Ernie was likewise appropriately attired in a tattered Sid Vicious T-shirt and baggy shorts. We mumbled some self-conscious greetings.

"Good morning, Margo, Ernie," said Holmes. He was carrying something in a brown paper bag. "I hope we didn't catch you at a bad time, but we have a couple of items of business to share with you. First, Margo Monroe, Ernie Stapleton, allow me to present

Dr. Floriana Dominguez, our new professor of science."

"It's a pleasure to meet you. I've heard so much about you both," she said, shaking our hands warmly.

I ushered everyone to a sofa and some comfy chairs we'd arranged in a corner under the framed portrait of Theodore. Ernie had lobbied for a businesslike conference table and chairs, but Sandy and I outvoted him and he'd reluctantly agreed finally that the little sitting area imparted a cozy atmosphere.

"We won't take much of your time," said the dean, with an amused glance at Ernie's shirt. "I know you're busy trying to get everything finished. But I wanted to thank you personally for your work and we thought you'd like to know the school is establishing the Nigel Pritchett Charitable Trust. Each year, starting with the next academic year a handful of lucky students who show exceptional promise in the sciences will be awarded full scholarships. We thought it fitting for you to know about it before I make the general announcement at tomorrow's faculty meeting. You look relieved, Mr. Stapleton...surely didn't you think I had bad news for you this time?"

"Well, now that you mention it..."

"I'm not always the bearer of bad tidings," said Dean Cresswell. "However, there is something of some importance I need to discuss with both of you."

Ernie cast a sideways glance at me, looking like a guilty schoolboy. I noticed, however, that Dr. Holmes, seemed to be enjoying himself immensely.

"You're probably tired of hearing this, Ms. Monroe, but you put yourself in grave danger. Surely it occurred to you or Sandy that somebody would be interested to know about the impostor in our midst?"

"I'm sorry, Dr. Cresswell. I didn't want to bother anybody over the weekend," I replied.

"I know I don't have to point out that it could have been much, much worse," said Dr. Holmes. "Weekend or not, no one would have taken offense to a phone call for something of this magnitude. In the future, please don't be so cavalier."

We offered our apologies. Ernie straightened up in his chair, looking relieved.

"Well, now that we have that out of the way," said the dean, rubbing his hands together, "I thought this might be a good excuse to have a little celebration." He nodded at Holmes, who produced a bottle of champagne and some plastic glasses from the paper bag. Dr. Holmes peeled the foil from the top and twisted the cork deftly. It came out with a festive pop.

When everyone was holding a glass, Dean Cresswell said, "Welcome Dr. Dominguez. Here's to your success and the continued success of the science program."

We learned that Dr. Dominguez was a native of Puerto Rico who'd spent the past several years in Chicago. She and Ernie discovered their mutual interest in gadgetry, so they hit it off particularly well. She spoke with the slightest of accents and was vivacious and animated. A couple of times I caught Dr. Holmes casting frankly admiring glances at her.

The conversation turned—inevitably, I suppose—to my recent encounter. I couldn't resist telling Dr Holmes about my experience with Irmalene that day.

Dr. Holmes chuckled. "Nothing surprises me where Irmalene is concerned. You might be interested to know she's the one who threw the rock through the window. I got a call from campus security. They found it on the surveillance tape...not that I was particularly surprised," he added. "The rumor is that she's also the one who was keeping the protestors stirred up."

"I don't get it," said Ernie. "What did we ever do to her?"

"Nothing, really. But Irmalene seems to be in constant need of dragons to slay. If she weren't feuding with us, she would be feuding with someone," mused Holmes.

"She should be fired!" exclaimed Ernie.

"That's a bit harsh, Mr. Stapleton," said the dean. "She's an exemplary teacher that would be difficult to replace. She's had a chance to air her grievances, and I feel I can assure you nothing like that will happen again."

"Try not to judge her too harshly," added Holmes. "Her life hasn't been easy. The nephew you met is the only family she has. He came here as a teenager after his parents were random victims of street violence in Jamaica. His mother was her sister. I can't begin to imagine what it must be like, suddenly finding yourself the sole support of a child you barely know, and under such circumstances."

A half hour or so later, the champagne long gone, our guests were about to head for the door when Holmes paused and said, with a twinkle in his eye, "Before I forget, there is one more thing. You might want to find a better use for this." He pulled something out of the paper bag and handed it to Ernie. It was the web cam Ernie had set up in the science lab.

Ernie took it from him sheepishly with mumbled thanks.

Naturally they were no sooner out the door than Ernie and I were on the internet checking Dr. Dominguez out. It took less than half an hour to reach the conclusion that she's really who she says she is.

Thanks From the Other Side

Sandy handed Willis's leash to Ernie reluctantly. "I hold you solely responsible for anything that happens."

"Just take it easy. We'll have your homely little pal back safe and sound in no time," Ernie replied. The dog hopped into Ernie's car without so much as a backward glance at his owner. As we drove away, Sandy waved forlornly, looking as though he'd just lost his best friend.

When we got to the science lab, Willis sniffed daintily at the door, then sat down and looked up at us with imploring eyes, whining softly.

"Come on, boy. There's nothing to be afraid of." Ernie tugged gently at his leash. The dog glared at him balefully but gave in. "Do you have the key?"

I stuck a hand in the pocket where I'd stashed the key. "What the...?" Something was in that pocket besides the key, and I knew damn well I didn't put it there. "Did you put this in my pocket, Ernie?"

"Put what in your pocket?"

"That piece of plastic that came from Dr. Pritchett's office. The one that fell off the shelf when I went in there the first time."

He looked at me the way one might look at someone who's been searching frantically for their lost glasses, only to find them on top of their head. "Wasn't me. I didn't even know you still had it. Come on, unlock the door. We don't have all night. Scratch that —we do, actually."

But the door, as it had before, popped open at my touch. "Looks like we're expected," said Ernie. He propped the door open with a couple of equipment cases then unclipped Willis's leash. The dog sauntered into the lab, stopping on the way to sniff at the threshold. In front of the door to Professor Pritchett's office, he growled quietly, then began to whine.

Ernie gave him a quick scratch behind the ears. "Hold that thought, boy. First we have to test my invention." He busied himself putting various gadgets and meters in place while I set up the video camera. The dog watched us disinterestedly.

I turned the lights out and we gathered around the table. We waited while the computer model started to grow slowly from the bottom up. When it finished, Ernie said "Here goes. We'll try the temperature overlay first. Keep your fingers crossed."

Ernie exhaled in relief as glowing figures appeared roughly in the shape of humans, computers, and a dog. A stream of numbers flickered across the bottom. "It saves the readings in a database," said Ernie. "We'll be able to compare them with the base readings from the previous investigations."

"Brilliant," I remarked.

"Yes, it is, if I do say so myself. Now I'm switching to EMF mode. Watch!" Small glowing filaments appeared along the base of the walls, brighter in some areas, and around our computers. "The wiring in this building might charitably be described as vintage," said Ernie. "Those brighter areas are electrical outlets. The filaments you see here are the old wires giving off higher readings."

I pointed to the area of the screen that represented Professor Pritchett's office. Parts of it showed up unusually bright. "What's going on here?"

Ernie rotated the model so we could get a better look. "That's odd. Last time we were here we didn't get any unusual readings in there."

"Let's go have a look," I said. "Hey what's that?" Ernie was holding a gadget that he'd retrieved from a bag of assorted odds and ends. "Not that again." It was his spiffed-up speech synthesizer.

"Just humor me, will you please? You gotta admit the late Professor Pritchett seems to prefer communicating electronically. What could it hurt?"

Willis made a weird little noise that was neither a growl nor a bark. He was now standing at Ernie's feet, shaking all over. But when we opened the door to Professor's Pritchett's office, he bounded in ahead of us.

"After you," said Ernie.

The room seemed untouched since our previous visit. The chair was standing a few feet away from the desk under which we'd spent so many uncomfortable hours. Willis ran around the perimeter of the room, sticking his nose into every corner. He stopped near the chair, then sat down and stared intently at something.

I shone an infrared flashlight on Willis. "See anything?" I whispered.

"Nope."

Willis wagged his tail, delighted, at whatever it was that he saw that we couldn't. He sniffed the area around Professor Pritchett's desk, then curled up with his head on his paws, still thumping his tail from time to time.

Ernie placed the speech synthesizer on the edge of Professor Pritchett's desk and turned it on. "All right, here goes." The device began making a soft noise.

I went back to the outer lab and glanced at the 3-D model on the computer screen. The EMF levels in the office were off the chart and appeared to be getting stronger.

Willis now appeared to be asleep. Ernie stepped over him gingerly and placed his contraption on the edge of the desk. "Is there anybody in here with us? Professor Pritchett, if it's you, thank you for letting us in your office. We just want to talk to you and let you know everything's okay. We'd really like to hear from you. This device uses radio frequencies to generate a little extra energy. We're hoping you can use it to communicate with us..."

Suddenly, the device began to make noise, a stream of random, meaningless words. *"Rain, sleeping, car,"* squawked a harsh electronic voice that reminded me of a robot in a bad 1950s sci-fi movie.

"You see?" I said, "It doesn't make sense. Those are just random words..."

"Nice dog."

Ernie gulped so loud I could hear him. "I didn't program those words into it!"

Goose bumps broke out on my arms. "Professor Pritchett? Is that you? That's Sandy's dog. His name is Willis. You remember Sandy—he was in your class last semester."

"Good dog, nice dog." It repeated the phrase a few time then was silent. For a minute the only sound was the white noise being generated by Ernie's device.

"Ernie, this is just silly. Turn it off and let's…"

The box abruptly started up again, but this time it was a different voice. *"Danger, they must not…help —they must not…it's very dangerous. Man…fraud… he's a fraud…danger. He must not…"*

"Professor Pritchett," said Ernie. "There's nothing to worry about. Seth is in jail and he won't be going anywhere anytime soon except to prison. We're all safe. Ben is safe."

The voice from the box changed again. This time it was the voice I'd heard before—on my voicemail and in EVPs. *"At…peace…now. Margo, Ernie. Friends."*

Epilogue

The Rhonda Q. Mills Magnet School for the Gifted and Talented built a memorial garden in a neglected corner of the school playground. In attendance at the unveiling were a handful of school board members and minor city dignitaries and the entire team, including Elaine. She and Ernie stood together, discretely holding hands, and I wonder how long it would last this time.

A small, bubbling fountain and a couple of concrete benches had been hastily installed, and a brass plaque mounted on the outside wall of the school gymnasium. "In Memory of the Lost Orphans of Norton Township" stood out in sharp relief. Theodore's name and dates of birth and death were emblazoned prominently on it. The plaque was covered with the names of dozens of children, along with dates of birth and death, although sadly, many dates were missing. In spite of the best efforts of the kids and volunteers from the community, it proved impossible to track down all the information. On a few of the entries, only the child's name was known. I think it was this, rather than the unexpectedly large number of names on the plaque, that made me the saddest.

Or maybe it was the news that Holmes had delivered just before the ceremony started. Pulling us aside, he had asked, "Which do you want first? The good news or the bad news?" Our boss is not a man given to feeble attempts at humor, and indeed he wasn't joking. The mysterious philanthropist who funds our operation decided to surprise us by quietly arranging for a survey with ground-penetrating radar. Using the plat maps that Sandy found, the surveyors covered as large an area as they could. This turned out to be the modern-day playground, a sidewalk, and a narrow patch of lawn to the faculty parking lot. Many graves had been located and were now marked with tiny sapling trees. That was the good news. The bad news was that the number of names on the plaque outnumbered trees three to one. Ernie in particular was incensed when Holmes broke the news to us that well over half of the children's graves were likely lost forever under the foundations of the newer buildings, or even under the parking lot.

Unfortunately, there was no way to know who was buried in the small graves. A thorough search failed to turn up any records. Was Theodore's grave there, somewhere under the playground? I liked to think he was there, rather than under the sad little strip of grass on the other side of the fence, where spindly saplings now swayed in the breeze. Or, worse, under the teachers' parking lot.

A new group, cleverly calling themselves The Skeptics, had been awarded our old space in the horticulture pavilion. Irmalene, when we couldn't avoid her, started being incredibly friendly to us. That is, until she learned she wasn't going to take over our old lab space after all. Fortunately, we don't have to deal with her that often anymore. There is a happy postscript to her story, though. Our wealthy patron, whose identity we still don't know, decided to reward her nephew Rufus for his role in apprehending Digby Briggs. He used the money to invest in a fleet of cabs. Shiny new Dread Lion taxi cabs soon began appearing around town, and airport travelers were seen to argue over who got to ride in one.

The Indian Springs High School boys' basketball team made it to the state championship, but were eliminated in the first round.

Toby Garcia received an award and a promotion. I haven't noticed him hanging around much. Do you suppose he's over his crush on me?

I braced myself for the protestors to follow us to our new location, but so far none have materialized. Either they haven't found us yet, or my invitation for them to put their money where their mouths were scared them off.   Not that I'm complaining. I don't miss having to wade through throngs of people shouting and waving signs in our faces.

The team got bonuses, of course. I plan to use mine to take Tim on a romantic holiday in Paris. In the meantime, our caseload keeps us plenty busy. There's always an adventure around the corner. Thanks for reading.

The End

Apologies to Zeppo.

About the Author

Sue Latham is a native of Texas, where she now lives after living abroad for many years. Her travels have taken her to every continent except Antarctica and she has survived volcanos, earthquakes and floods. She has an opera-singing  parrot and has recently adopted a rabbit that is particularly fond of cookies.

Find her online at www.suelatham.net, on Facebook at www.facebook.com/SueLatham.novelist and Twitter @SueLathamTX.

Sue Latham

www.ingramcontent.com/pod-product-compliance
Lightning Source LLC
Chambersburg PA
CBHW020818180626
46814CB00001B/8